Editor: **Trevor Croft**
Front Cover Art: **Eve Ventrue**
Back Cover Art: **Owen Essen**

Special thanks to the following people for giving feedback on one or more of the stories in this collection: Cammie Adams, Elizabeth Abel, Tadeu Aratel, Chad A. Ballard, Jessica Baron, Amber Bates, Annie Bee, Adrienne Berg, Lisa Berkman, Anthony Blake, Brittany Blake, S. Bleu, Daniel Boddy, Paul Boyson, Killian Brauer, Stella Brians, Patricia Carey, Dorothy Darnell, Charlene Delfin, Rosie Amber Dibi, Emmeline Dodge, Neve Donovan, Jane Dugdale, Rosan Duran, Melissa Edwards, Jeff Essen, Zoe Flynn, Stanley Forbes, Michael Fretwell, Clive Gill, Gwendolen Gray, Chris Green, Paige Haswell, Robin Henry, Natasha Hensley, Stephen Huntley, ann james, Sly Jones, Theophil Kaufman, Kheka Ladouceur, Mike Lawrie, Lua Leggett, Amy Lerner-Maddox, Emma McNairy, Josh Lonsdale, Sherry Marie, Zimm Montage, Victoria Nesbitt, Amailia Nesingwary, Lee Owens, Alexia Peaston, Paft, Ryan Page, K.W. Rea, Shane Rose, Cam Ross, S. M. Savoy, Shelly Schulz, Ann Shaughnessy, Mike Sherer, Amy Sprague, Grannie Stein, Lynn Tack, Karl Tobar, Vermilion Wilde, Bett Wilson-Foley.

www.Animatico.com

The back cover art is based in part on a photo of Owen Essen by Bett Wilson-Foley.

Animatico Media
Chapel Hill, NC, USA
www.Animatico.com

Ordering Information:
Quantity sales. Special discounts are available on quantity purchases. For details, contact the publisher at the website above.

ISBN: 978-0-9982455-0-8

1st Edition, PGR: 02ISHB-2

Library of Congress Registration Number:
TXu001963382

www.OwenEssen.com

THREE EYED MAN

BY

OWEN ESSEN

PREFACE

It was a cool fall morning. The leaves danced like snowflakes to the ground and the air was as crisp as a fresh picked apple.

Everyone in my house was asleep, and would be for some time yet. But I had awakened early with a strong desire to walk in the woods.

I crossed the street and crawled through the brambles to get to the little trail that passes my house and leads, after some time, to a clearing with a little shack and, at other times of the year, a great expanse of milkweed flowers.

I had been walking for nearly thirty minutes when I saw smoke rising up through the barren branches ahead of me. Intrigued, and with no other destination in mind, I followed the smoke up the rocky hill 'till I found its source.

There at the top of the hill sat a lone man, draped in blankets, shivering by a tiny fire. Hearing me approach, he stood. As he turned to face me, I saw just how large he was. 6'6" easily. And built like a horse. His skin was the color of dried caramel, criss crossed by faded tattoos. His clothes were worn vintage and at the front of his big shaven head was a third eye, staring right at me just like the other two.

There was an aura about him that told me he was very wise but also very troubled, and potentially dangerous. For several seconds I intended to run. But there was something about him that made me unable to turn away.

His tattoos I found particularly intriguing: a kaleidoscope, a highway, balloons on fire. And so, rather than run, I decided to try and strike up a conversation with the man.

"The ship on your chest, is it The Essex?" I asked him. (I recognized it because of the whale.)

He nodded slowly.

I thought again of running.

"My name's Owen," I said with a smile.

"I know."

There was no running at that point.

"I'm sorry, have we met?"

He shook his head.

"Can I sit down? Do you mind?"

"You will sit down whichever way I say."

I sat down. Rather slowly.

Suddenly he stepped towards me, offering his hand for a good shake. Which I accepted, but not before noticing a rather unique tattoo on the palm of his left hand. A pyramid. Familiar looking. The one printed on the left side of every one dollar bill in the United States, I realized.

"You're from Chapel Hill," he said. "Born in Durham."

"That's right. Where are you from?"

"Waukegan."

I nodded. "Like Jack Benny."

"Who?" He looked confused for a moment, then cracked a smile. "I am playing with you, Owen Essen."

I laughed politely.

"I. See. All." he said slowly. "The present, the past, the future, for every living thing on the planet." He leaned forwards. "Because of my third eye."

"Oh, that's interesting. I just assumed it was a birth defect."

I watched the flickering of the fire for a moment.

"So, what they say about having a third eye, it really is true then?"

"I'm afraid so," he said somberly. "It's maddening."

"I'm sure."

He took a pot off the fire and poured me a cup of tea.

"Well, I'd invite you back to my place, but my dogs are a little funny about strangers."

"That's okay. I'm better off out here anyway."

We sipped our tea.

"You must have some incredible stories, at least. Seeing everything for all time and all."

"Yes, I have seen many great stories."

I hesitated for a moment, then remembered he already knew what I was going to ask.

"Say, I'm a writer, I wonder if you wouldn't mind,"

"Telling you a couple?"

"Right."

He looked distant for a moment.

"Only, if you don't mind, I mean."

"I will tell you."

I waited.

"You're going to write a book, you know," he said.

"Am I?"

"Yes, and you're going to call it Three Eyed Man."

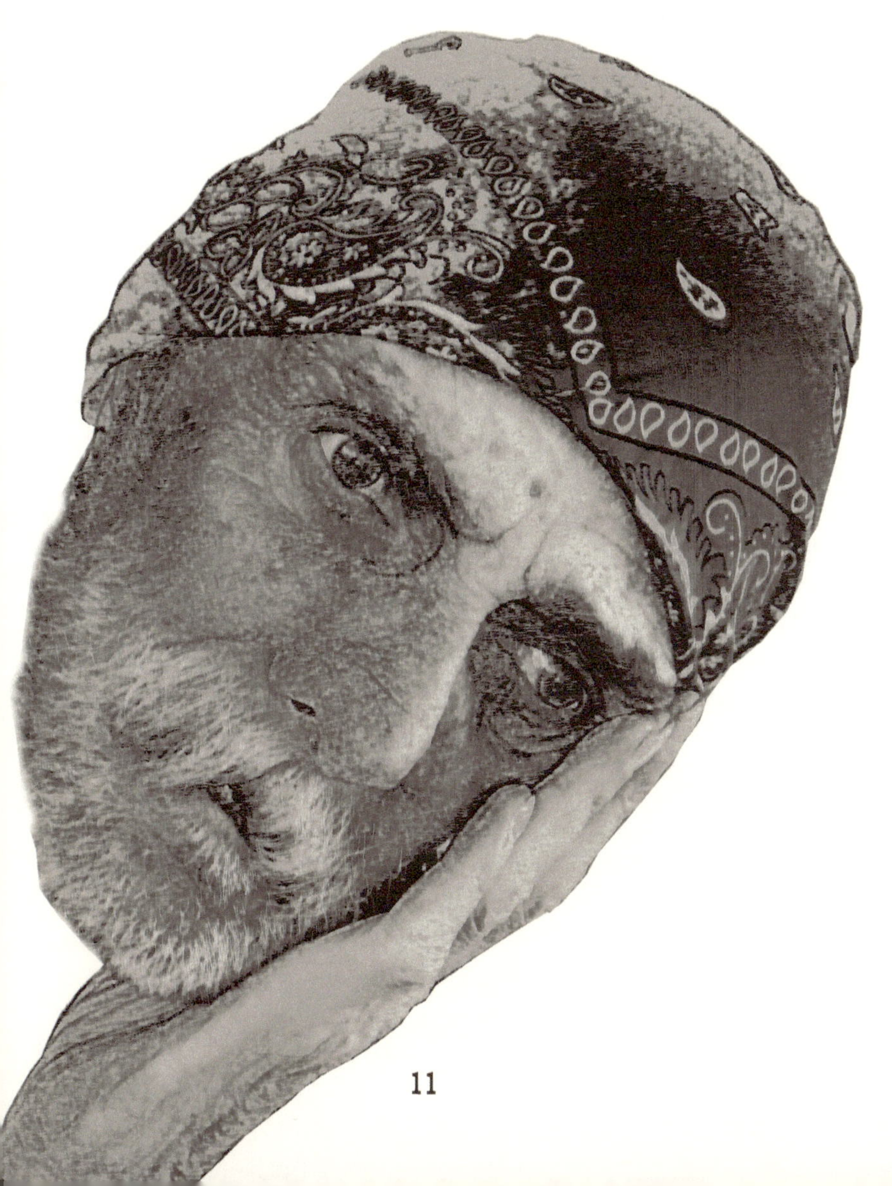

TABLE OF INNARDS

THE MAN ON THE FLOOR..............................14
THE LADY OF THE WATER..............................18
THE PINK WIG..............................20
CAVEMAN..............................22
SONG OF THE WEARY TRAVELER..............................23
THE TATTOO..............................24
THE ONE SIDED FRIENDSHIP..............................31
THE YOUNG MUSICIAN..............................32
WAITING FOR THE TIGER..............................34
ALL THEM CALLING..............................34
SAFFRON..............................35
KING OF THE EMPTY DESERT..............................37
THE CLIMB..............................69
WATCHING..............................71
LOCKER 99..............................83
FINAL TREE..............................152
THE TRUTH ABOUT THE WORLD..............................154
SUPERSTITION..............................155

The Man on the Floor

Frank Parishey had no false pretenses about the sweetness of retribution. He knew from the beginning that driving that little piece of lead through Sampson's head would bring him no sort of relief. It was more a matter of procedure, really. Sampson had killed Ella, and so Frank had a certain responsibility, a debt, to his wife and to his family as a whole. It was a matter of honor. Something that had to happen.

And so, Sampson lay there on the floor. Wriggling in the shadows, trying to slip from between the ropes that bound his hands and feet, his eyes blazing, scared of....

It was a grand living room, although not at all warm. Old world imperial furniture sat on an oriental carpet. The heavy red velvet curtains that once blocked out the light of day had long since been rendered ineffective by moths. The chandelier, like most things in the house, had not been polished in some years. Much of the detail of the room was lost in the dim lighting. A huge limestone fireplace gave what illumination there was in the room, enough to make out the two figures.

Parishey just sat there. He was tired. Physically, emotionally.

"Do you know why you're here?" Frank rested his head against the back of the chair.

It was a rhetorical question, of course. The man had three old socks in his mouth. He couldn't answer.

"I'm Parishey. As in Ella Parishey. Perhaps you remember her?"

The man on the floor tensed at the name and began to struggle even more violently.

Parishey slid the clip out of his gun and checked it. Full. He was stalling. He could tell it was full from the weight.

Sampson did his best to squirm away, squealing like an injured animal. Frank took several steps closer. *Better to get it over with*, he thought.

He wasn't angry at Sampson. Not really. He loved Ella, to be sure, but he... he was just too tired to be angry. Perhaps that was it. So much had happened in the past few months.

Parishey clicked off the safety.

Perhaps he should take the socks out. Give the man a chance for last words.

No, that wouldn't do. He couldn't have the fellow making noise when he....

Frank studied the man for a moment. There was no one around. And he could always put the old things back in when it was time for the end.

He carefully pulled out the socks. Sampson gasped, shaking his head violently as though to throw off something dirty. He looked up at Parishey like a chicken on the block, breathing in and out with his whole body. Frank noticed for the first time how sweaty both of them were.

What would my father say? he thought to himself.

"Never show weakness to your enemies," the old man used to tell him. "They'll stab you in the back when you least expect it." Frank shuddered.

"Is there anything you want me to tell your family?" Parishey wouldn't look him in the eye.

It sounded silly after he said it. Of course he couldn't tell the family. But perhaps he could send a letter. He pondered the question, his mind wandering.

"You're going to kill me?"

"Yes."

"Then why..." Sampson spoke hesitantly. "Why haven't you killed me yet?"

Parishey tensed his shoulders.

"I don't know." His father's words rang in his ears. "I can now, if you like." He raised his gun and Sampson flinched.

"Is there anything you want me to do? You know, after..." Frank looked him in the eye for the first time, but turned away immediately.

"Why should I tell you?"

Frank considered for a moment, watching the dim firelight dance on the walls, and overhead.

"No," he admitted finally. "No, I suppose you shouldn't."

He bent down and started to put the socks back in the man's mouth. "I can't let you scream," Frank told him apologetically.

"If anyone could hear me, I'd be screaming now."

"Yes." Parishey lowered his hand. "Yes, I suppose that's true." He let the socks fall to the floor.

Standing up, he pushed the safety off again and pointed the gun at the man's head. He paused, looking into Sampson's terrified eyes.

"It's just that I'm not really angry at you." Frank shrugged, almost apologetically.

"You're not?" Sampson studied him trying to see if this were some sort of mental trap. He raised himself up a little. "Don't kill me, then! Let me go!

I can give you money, and the house. Whatever you want!"

"Why did you kill her?"

Perhaps hearing him say it would give him the anger that was necessary to—

"I didn't realize she was your wife. Honestly. I wouldn't have if I'd known."

The Sampsons and Parisheys had a long-standing rivalry. Frank didn't think his wife would've gotten any special treatment. It was just talk.

"I asked why you killed her."

"It was an accident. I mistook her for someone else." He looked away as he said it. Frank could tell it wasn't the truth.

"That's a lie! You knew exactly who it was you were killing. Was it because of the feud? Is that why?"

"No!"

"Then why? Tell me now or I'll—"

"You won't believe me!"

"What?"

Sampson looked up at him. He was shaking.

"I said you won't believe me."

It was quiet for a moment. Just the sound of Sampson's breathing, fast and shallow there on the floor.

"Did you love her?" Sampson asked.

"Of course I did."

"I don't think you did. That's why you're not angry at me. Why you haven't killed me yet."

Frank considered this for a moment before realizing how insolent it was. He kicked Sampson several times in the back of the head, causing him to bleed a little from the nose. He started to raise his gun, but something made him stop once more.

"What made you say that? About me not…"

"You didn't treat her well. Did you?"

"Sure I did. I gave her everything she ever wanted."

"You bought her everything she ever wanted you to buy," Sampson corrected. "But you didn't love her. And you didn't treat her well."

Frank opened his mouth to respond, but he knew not what to say. How was he letting this happen? Letting this tied hog on the floor insult him? Him with a gun in his hand? A Parishey, no less!

"How often did you hit her?" Sampson asked.

"What?"

"She said you hit her a lot." He struggled to prop himself up.

"You knew her?"

"Yes. Of course I did. You think I killed a complete stranger?"

"You said it was an accident. That you didn't know who she was."

"No, it was an accident. But I did know who she was."

"How did you know her?"

Sampson had begun to calm his shaking, and now spoke boldly, with a seeming absence of fear. "I met her at one of your parties. Several of us came to watch you. But I ended up watching her instead. I figured she was a maid. I didn't find out she was your wife until after she died."

"A maid?"

"She came back to my apartment with me and—"

"Back to your apartment?" Parishey growled.

"Yes. We got to know each other fairly well after that. She said she loved me and I—"

"So you killed her."

"I told her not to do something and—"

"Who are you to tell my wife what to do, you son—"

"I told her! I told her not to do something. And I had a gun. I didn't mean to shoot her, but I was upset and—"

"You threatened my wife with a gun?" He said it softly enough, but as soon as he had out with it Frank felt the anger finally take him. The idea of this piece of shit telling his wife what not to do! Of him threatening her with a gun! Of him killing her!

He too began to shake. Began to feel the acceleration of the anger, the sense of power that comes with fury. That driving, terrify rage that overtakes all men. This time when the safety came off, he did not hold back. He pumped the whole magazine into Sampson's gut. Yelling nonsense as the red flashes drove into the man, Sampson screaming, writhing there on the floor. His body coming apart. Blood seeping down into the cracks in the floorboard.

And the clip was empty. And Parishey had to stop. He just stood there. Watching Sampson moan, somewhere between this world and the next.

The poor dying man reached down, clutching his own innards, and looked up at Parishey one last time.

"She wanted to kill her husband. I told her not to. That's why she's…"

The Lady of the Water

I used to sit on the beach when the moon was full. The nights when the very clouds had gone to sleep, and nothing but the moon, the sand, and the water were left in this world to keep me company. On those nights, I would watch the somber light of the moon sink down upon the crashing waves, and wait for my one love to visit me. The Lady of the Water. The one whose curls were the foamy crashing waves, and whose skin was the soft sandy floor that kissed drowned men's bodies. Looking into her eyes was looking into the horizon. Incomprehensible depth led me through generation upon generation of seafaring peoples.

She would come to me, walking slowly over the dim waves. I don't believe I ever heard her speak, but I could always hear her voice in my mind. Whispering to me. Telling me she loved me and no one else. I would run down into the surf to meet her. And there, in the salty shallows where once great waves die, we would hold each other.

Soon the pink light of the outside world would knock upon our door, but for now there was only the rising and falling of the water, the heartbeat of her world.

Everything felt so perfect at times like that. But in the back of my mind, I never forgot that it would end and that I would be pulled away from this world 'till the moon again grew full and high overhead.

"We could never be together," I felt her say. And it was true.

She could never come with me back to my world, and I was bound to the land.

"Come away with me," she whispered, or perhaps it was the wind.

"I love you," I could feel her calling. "I love you."

Sometimes we walked along the surf together. Watching the patterns of the water and the sand. Waiting always for that pink light.

"I love you," she called. "I love you."

Soon the man in the old black shoes would pull upon the chain that bound me to the land. Soon I would be taken back into the world of dust and dry skin. But for now the man in the black shoes was sleeping. He was in a different world a million miles from mine.

There was only the moon, and the sand and the sea. Just me and The Lady of the Water.

We would sit for hours sometimes, staring into the darkness, trying to spot the subtle glint of passing porpoises. I have often wondered if they were real or imagined. She always said they were real.

"Come see for yourself!" She would think. And she would walk out past the breakers.

"I can't go with you," I told her. But she didn't listen.

"Come with me," she called. "I love you. I love you."

I sat there on the beach. Watching her walk away.

"Come with me," she called again. "I love you. I love you."

In that minute, time seemed to stop. She was still as I stepped out into the cold, dark water. I felt the soft sand sink beneath my feet.

I expected the chains to catch me. To hold me back to the world I knew. But I went deeper and deeper, and nothing stopped me.

The swells became bigger and farther apart, and the sand beneath my feet grew harder.

Soon the water kissed my neck and splashed on occasion to my sweaty hair.

She was there with me, holding out her hand sometimes as we walked.

"I love you," she whispered. "I love you."

Soon I could no longer touch the surface of the water. I found I could no longer breathe. That my lungs burned and my extremities became numb. But I kept walking along the bottom.

My muscles grew weak with deprivation, and by and by I could walk no longer. I collapsed upon the soft sand retching as my stomach burned. I reached up towards the surface, twinkling star-like overhead. But I couldn't reach it.

She was still there beside me. Smiling at me sorrowfully. Her hair dancing in the drifting waves.

"I love you," she whispered. "I love you."

I reached one final time for the glistening surface. And then I opened my mouth, and let her stream into me, to fill me. The dust on my soul was washed away and I became forever a part of the world I had sought. Forever a pore on her skin.

The Pink Wig

Her hips swayed enticingly as she crossed the harsh expanse of the dimly lit parking lot. She was very thin, and her hot pink swimsuit matched both the color of her hair and that of her stiletto heels. They looked hard to walk in, I thought, but she was managing. She saw me, standing off in the shadows, beside my car, and started walking a little faster towards me.

It was fake, of course. The hair, I mean. And the persona. She was probably a Harvard business student, or a secretary at some big law firm during the day. All week long she'd work her ass off, fall asleep on the couch, a frozen dinner sitting on the coffee table between her and the evening news. All week long she wore pantsuits, and called her boss 'sir' and made bad coffee.

Then, Friday night, she'd want to make up for it. She'd put on the fake eyelashes, and the heels, and pretend she was badass. Maybe she was. Who am I to say?

All I really knew about her was that I'd never met her before, but she was about to let me fuck her in the back seat of my beater Volvo station wagon. Really, I didn't think much about her. No more than the passing thought as I watched her walk casually across the asphalt. Then she was there, and I touched her back and kissed her, and she climbed inside the car, and then I didn't think any more about her, other than who she was that very moment on top of me.

We didn't think much about anything in those days. Not while we were at the raves and the bars and the parties. And the rest of the time we were too tired to think about it, so we didn't. We just felt it.

We felt the bass drops, the sweaty bodies pressed together on the dark dance floors, jumping up and down as one mass, the EDM. You felt that, rather than hearing it most of the time. The liquor that said who you were, or at least how much money you made. The drugs.

The critics said it was shallow. Maybe it was. But I've always thought they misunderstood it. The people in it were no philosophers by any stretch of the imagination. They were too busy living it to spend any time thinking about what it meant.

I've always thought it was as much nihilistic as it was shallow. They didn't think about it because they didn't want to. It was too awful. And so they just stayed in the moment and felt it.

I didn't think about who the girl in the pink wig was. I just felt her.

Felt her breasts pressed against my chest. Felt my own orange swimsuit sliding off. Felt myself slipping inside of her.

I didn't think about the next day. How by morning she'd be gone, and I'd be hungover. I'd probably wake up hungry, and I'd want to go to McDonald's and get an egg sandwich or a parfait or something like that. And I'd pull out my wallet and maybe I'd have a hundred dollar bill or maybe I'd be shit broke again, because I was never good at managing money. But I didn't think about that until it happened. I just felt her kiss me as she pulled away. Watched as she produced a condom from Bassnectar knows were. Felt her slide it on.

That proved it. It was just a persona. The whole pink wig, white girl twerking thing. She'd probably had a boyfriend a week ago. She'd probably wanted to marry him. Wanted the whole white picket fence, 2.5 kids thing. And he probably said he wasn't ready to commit, didn't want to settle down yet. And they'd had a fight. And "broke up." And she'd decided to let a new guy have her every night 'till Joe-whoever got wise to "what he was missing" and came back with a ring.

That's what she wanted really. Not me plowing her in the shadows of a dark parking lot. That was fun for a little while, but she'd trade it in a heartbeat for Mr. Right, nice house, and good kids. In truth, I would have too, were I in her shoes. And damn they looked to be some uncomfortable shoes.

CAVEMAN

Please know, I spoke not in spite,
You truly do look like a troglodyte,
With matted hair, long, and nit filled,
And your clothes all covered in the mammoth you killed.
Your knuckles you bare at me as a weapon,
Do I look like some prey that ought to be leapt on?
Oh, there you go, knocked me to the grass!
(I'll bet this is how he tries to get ass....)
What is that stick you raise in the air?
You'll live the stereotype if you don't take care.
I just have three more things to say,
If you keep wearing skirts like that peo—

Song of the Weary Traveler

On my face falls soft warm sand,
Released gently from an old man's hand,
I have walked a hundred miles,
Wondered foggy mountains and luscious isles,
Now this inn, this bed becomes my home,
Until tomorrow when again I shall roam.

The Tattoo

Greg Larson was at least two sheets to the wind when he stumbled into the old tattoo parlor on 13th Street, smelling of cheap beer and cheaper cologne. His hair was messed, as though by wind, and his clothes were as stained as the shag carpeting that covered the parlor floor. It was an odd sort of place. He wasn't quite sure what it was. Perhaps the yellowed lighting, or the low din of the air conditioning. It definitely had an unfamiliar feel about it.

There were no other customers present when he entered, which made sense, considering the lateness of the hour. The only other person in the room was a tattoo artist, whose shiny head served as somewhat of a contrast to Greg's three day stubble. Tattoos mingled across the artist's face and arms, and his eyelids sagged in a way that gave him a tired, removed look.

He put down his copy of Slaughterhouse-Five when Greg entered and looked at him in a bored sort of way, waiting to see what the customer wanted.

Grinning, Greg shuffled up and handed over a crumpled magazine photo of a scantily-clad Playboy Miss October, wearing nothing but a fur coat.

"I'd like her," Greg said, still grinning, "right here on my arm." He rolled up his sleeve and sat down in the old tattoo chair. It had holes in it, and the ripped synthetic stuffing was coming out. After a moment, the bald fellow assembled his tools and began to work.

Greg laid his head back, studying the yellowed drop-ceiling and the rough-brushed mock-plaster walls. He tried not to think about the needles, but presently his head began to swirl, his vision to shake, and perhaps for the beer or the needles, Greg passed out.

He came to several hours later, lying against the outside wall of the tattoo parlor. It was painfully bright when he opened his eyes, but his pupils adjusted shortly. His head ached from the drink, his arm ached from the tattoo, and his whole body was sore from sleeping on concrete and bricks. He rolled up his sleeve to have a look at Miss October, but instead he saw an odd sort of animal. Greg studied it for a few moments, and then decided it was probably a dragon of the Western kind. It had beady eyes and a huge mouth, wide open to show tremendous teeth. But the tattoo had a stylized Eastern feel about it, very two-dimensional, rendered in all black ink.

Greg pulled himself to his feet to go cuss out the bald fellow for giving him the wrong tattoo, but he found that where the parlor had been was nothing but a solid brick wall. He sat back down on the curb, his head throbbing. He must've walked after getting the tattoo. The parlor must be somewhere behind him.

He thought of trying to find it, but he decided he was too hung over. For now, he just wanted to go home.

Greg couldn't remember where he'd left the car, and was in no state to drive it, even if he did. Patting his shirt pockets, he found several quarters and walked over to a pay phone.

"Hello," answered Carla on the fourth ring. She sounded irritable, like she was in a hurry, and clearly resented the distraction.

He didn't say anything at first. He listened to her voice for a moment as he put his thoughts together.

"Hello?" she said again, now with a slight air of curiosity.

"How've you been, Carla?"

"Greg? Is that you?"

He considered for a moment. "I think so…."

She didn't answer.

"So, how've you been?" He tried to get the conversation going again.

"The same as I was when you stood me up last night." She sounded mad now.

"That's the reason for the—" Greg stopped himself. "I stood you up last night?"

"Yes…."

Greg needed to choose his words carefully or she'd hang up.

"Um… do you know why?"

"Forget you, Greg!" She was talking very fast and loud, which exacerbated his headache and made him cringe, but he dared not protest. "You treat me like a newspaper. Something you can throw away one day, and pick up again the next. But no! I won't let you treat me like that."

She hung up.

Greg sat back down on the curb.

In the end he just walked home. It wasn't far, but it was far enough to give him sore legs and a loss of breath.

"Fuck you, Carla," he muttered as he finally pushed the door open. She couldn't even give her own boyfriend a ride home. But he'd stood her up. Greg fell back onto the torn-up musty sofa that dominated his living room. His head still hurt. What had gone wrong? Something about a newspaper….

I'll figure it out after the headache passes, was his last thought as his eyes drifted shut.

He dreamed that a black cat sat on his chest, licking his arm. As the cat continued licking, his arm became irritated. He wanted the cat to stop, but he couldn't move, and the cat just kept licking. Flakes of his skin began to come off on the cat's tongue, but he couldn't move, couldn't push the cat off.

By the time he woke up the sky had turned inky. His arm still ached.

That wasn't unusual after a tattoo, but somehow this feeling was different. In addition to the burning sensation, there was also a distinct crawling, an awful, spine-tingling feeling, like cockroaches burrowing beneath his skin, moving around, hopping from nerve to nerve.

Greg pulled up his sleeve to see if perhaps the creature was becoming infected. He stopped when he saw it, though. The dragon's mouth was closed.

He was almost sure it had been open before… but he'd been hung over.

Perhaps it had been closed all along.… But Greg remembered the teeth.

He had a very clear memory of the dragon's exposed teeth.…

He went in the kitchen and splashed some water on his face, and looked again. He studied the great detail the bald man had put into it. It was unlike any tattoo he had ever seen. It had a certain air about it. Different from… Greg looked at it carefully. Different even from how it had looked earlier.

He couldn't quite figure what it was. Perhaps it was the eyes. They looked different somehow. Perhaps more of an emerald tint than Greg remembered, but maybe that was just his imagination getting a hold of him.

The animal seemed to be staring at him, and Greg stared right back, studying, each daring the other to.…

The left toe twitched. Greg could've sworn it. His eyes widened but he wouldn't allow himself to blink. He kept a fixed stare, waiting for.…

Nothing happened. Perhaps nothing had happened before. Maybe the effects of the previous night were still holding on a bit. Or maybe it was the light.

His apartment was dim. He'd been thinking how he needed more lights. It was probably the.…

The mouth opened. Suddenly. The dragon breathed fast for several moments, as though it had been holding its breath.

Greg pulled the sleeve down over the beast, horrified by its movement, but as soon as he did, he discovered that the idea of the thing beneath his clothes, out of sight, terrified him still more. A moment later his sleeve was up, and he was staring at the dragon again.

It was still now, and Greg began to wonder if perhaps he had imagined the whole thing. But as he looked at it very closely, he realized that it was, ever so slightly, breathing after all.

Greg was frozen. His hand twitched a little. There was no room left for doubt, no remaining hope of a mistake. All that was left in him was a sense of un-graspable dread, the realization of someone who is faced with an incomprehensible threat. He could not even begin to think of what to do, but he tried to.

He had to keep it a secret, Greg knew that much. If word got out people would be scared of him, indeed he was scared of himself. He would lose his friends and become estranged from his family, and have no one left but—Carla. He had to tell Carla. She was the only person he really trusted, and he had to show someone, to find out if it were real, or if he were losing himself.

Greg leapt upon the phone, pulling it off the hook and quickly typing in the number. No. He had to talk to her in person, or she'd just hang up on him again.

A short while later he found himself standing in front of Carla's door, staring at the sixes below the peep hole. They reminded him of dragon scales. Doing his best to keep his hand away from them, he knocked.

He heard movement behind the door, and finally it swung open. Her face fell when she saw him.

"Oh, it's you."

"Carla," he said, trying to smile, "I've come to apologize. I wasn't acting right."

"I know," she said sarcastically. "That's why I left you."

"You left me?" Greg asked, temporarily distracted. Had it been that bad?

She looked confused, on the edge of tears even, but she didn't answer.

He held up his arm, finally, exposing the dragon to her.

"You got another tattoo, Greg. That's great." She looked at the floor.

"I did, but it…."

"Greg, I want to finish talking about us," She wouldn't look at him. "Not the stupid stuff you do when you're drunk."

"Listen, it—"

But he stopped himself this time, or rather the dragon did.
He could feel it again, the cockroaches beneath his skin, his nerves and pores twitching, wavelike. The dragon was moving.

Carla saw it too, and looked as he must have: ghostlike, mouth open, eyes wide, and skin the color of plaque.

"It moves," he said softly.

Without saying anything, she led him inside. Three cats scattered off the couch as they sat down. He stared at her, she still looked pale.

"I don't understand it." She frowned with all her spirit. "Why does it move?"

"I don't know."

They sat in silence for a moment, both trying to process what was happening.

"It wasn't just my imagination was it?" Carla sat completely still, studying the small clouded window showing little but the grey sky above.

"I don't think both of us would have imagined it independently."

In the distance a buzzard sank down to the ground, the heat pockets inevitably disappearing from beneath his wings.

"I'm sorry." She looked away, towards her hands. "I should've been standing by you through this.... I guess I just thought...."

Greg gave her a moment to finish, but when she did not, he hugged her.

"Have you told anyone else yet?" she asked.

He told her he hadn't, that they wouldn't believe him.

"So show them!"

"But it doesn't move all the time."

She thought for a moment, and then walked over to a closet in the side of the room.

She pulled a dusty old super-8 camera from the shadows. "We have to document it," she said softly.

It had become late by that point, and they began to tire. As one of them nodded off, the other would shake them back awake, and so on in hopes of documenting some flicker of movement. But all the dragon did was breathe slightly, too imperceptibly for the old camera to pick up. Finally they both fell asleep.

Greg dreamed that the black cat stood on his arm, its claws out, painfully digging into his skin, touching the cockroaches that crawled beneath. He was frozen again, and watched helplessly as the cat lifted its front paw and slowly put it down on his upper arm. The awful crawling sensation followed. The cat was walking up his body. And the horrid bugs were following the cat's claws.

He awoke with a start, choking. He couldn't breathe. It felt as though someone had him around the neck, but when he felt for a blanket or bit of loose clothing, his hands found nothing. Desperately he fell over towards a nearby mirror, and saw in his dark reflection the unmistakable outline of the dragon, sprawled out over his neck, clinching itself, constricting his bluing skin.

Carla awoke beside him and saw the beast about his neck. She gave a little scream of shock, and then came at it. She hit the dragon with her hand, tried to scratch it off, but it was no use. Greg was dying in front of her, and there was nothing she could do.

His eyes became dimmer, his touch weaker, and he sank back against the wall.

"Please," she cried to the dragon, "Please, don't kill him."

The animal kept its form clenched across his neck.

"Please," she begged again. "If not for me then for you... If he dies then his flesh will rot away, and you with it.... Do you want that, dragon? To be consumed by mold and dust away into the dirt?"

It un-tensed its muscles slightly, as though it were considering. Then, after a few long seconds, it released its grip completely. Greg coughed and sputtered for several moments, but then regained his breath. Carla stood there, watching him breathe deeply on the floor. *It could be over any moment,* she thought to herself. *Any time it could just kill him, and there's nothing we can do about it.*

Helplessly she went to the kitchen and made tea. It would feel good on a sore throat, she thought. When she came back into the living room, Greg was sitting soberly on the couch, rubbing his knees slightly, the tattoo still on his neck.

She handed him the cup and then a bit of newspaper gesturing meanwhile for him to be quiet. He took a sip from the cup and set it down on the table. His attention now turned to the piece of news print. Holding it out of the tattoo's view, Greg studied it. It was an advertisement for a new service being offered at the hospital: a certain technology that used lasers to remove tattoos.

He looked up at her smiling, a sudden sense of hope coming over him.

On the ad she had circled the time 8:30 AM.

And so it was that the next morning they made their way to the hospital in Carla's well-worn Volvo. They spoke very little, fearing that if either of them did, the tattoo might discover the nature of the trip. Carla drove, and Greg sat in the passenger's seat, idly staring out the window.

It was when they were at a stop light that Carla looked casually over at Greg, and saw the tattoo moving up his neck. She nearly screamed again, but she held it in this time. Instead she simply watched in horror as the creature moved slowly onto Greg's chin, then onto his upper lip, and then into his mouth. It slipped in and disappeared into the darkness within the man.

Greg scratched his head, and looked perhaps a little bothered by something, but didn't seem to realize what had happened. For a moment, Carla nearly yelled at him, almost told him that the tattoo was within him, but she realized, painfully, that it would do no good.

Looking over at her he noticed that she looked pale.

"The light's green," he said. "Is something the matter?"

"No," she uttered after a moment. "It's just, the tattoo— it's gone."

"Gone!" He checked his neck in the rear view mirror excitedly. "It is gone!" He looked beneath his shirt to be sure.

"It just disappeared," Carla said uncomfortably.

"Disappeared!" Greg was beaming. "That's great!" He laughed with joy and relief.

Carla forced a laugh as well.

At Greg's insistence they bought a nice bottle of wine to celebrate.

The two of them sat in Carla's living room, drinking, one far merrier than the other, until his stomach ache hit. It was sudden, like a blow to the abdomen, and caused him to drop his glass and grip himself. He collapsed upon the couch, a distant look in his eyes, and a terrible pain within him. It felt as though the cockroaches were eating his innards now, tearing him up from within.

Carla quietly led him to her bed, and let him grip her hand as the convulsions started. She got him the waste bin when he began to cough up his dinner, and when he began to cough up blood, she knew it was the end.

"Please keep holding my hand," he said once, lifting his sweaty reddened face towards her weakly between vomits.

"I will," she said, and she gripped his hand tighter.

Everything slowed around five, and by first light he was dead. Finally she released his hand and fell upon him.

"I love you, Greg," she sobbed. "I love you." She paused for a moment. She felt an odd tingly sensation in her right hand, the one Greg had been holding when he....

A look of terror came over her as she finally lifted her palm into the thin ray of light now coming through the window. On it was a dragon, smiling at her with the familiar big black teeth. At its feet lay a single human body.

The One Sided Friendship

When I ask, you ignore,
I don't know what for,
When I speak, you do not reply,
Yet I will not break down and cry,
When I flirt,
Your reply is, at best, curt,
I admire your looks, your sense of style,
But for all I know, you could be a pedophile,
I wish you'd speak, wish you'd say my name,
But you're just a picture, in a window frame.

The Young Musician

There was once a young man who wanted more than anything to be the greatest musician of all time. Every night he would sit for hours outside the local bar, plucking the strings of his sitar. In that time he would neither hunger nor tire, nor be afflicted by thirst. He would play steadily as the moon set, and the city lights faded, and the grizzly old drunkards finally shuffled off to find a place to lay their heads. Finally, the barkeep would close his business and tell the musician in a friendly, paternal way to go home and sleep, and the musician would. But the next night he would be back in front of the bar, playing again.

The young man became the best musician in the province, and men and women came from all over to hear him play. But the man wanted more, he wanted to be the best in the world.

One night he decided to pour his soul into the music, and the young man's song burned and glimmered with every depth of the human soul. Experts and noblemen alike came to marvel at the beauty and the pain of his music, but the young man slowly realized he had poured his very being into the music. Everything he had, everything he had ever thought or felt, every loving memory, every deeply set scar flowed into the music. His very soul was in the song, and the moment he stopped playing, he would cease to be anything but an empty shell.

As the days began to pass, hundreds of people came and camped around him, to listen to his music. But the young man began to feel the aches of exhaustion. He forced himself to keep playing, though, knowing full well that when the song stopped, so would he.

More and more people came to listen as the musician played on. Each day he became more and more tired. Several times he tried to tell the people what was happening, to get advice, or at least comfort, but they just looked at him and smiled, nodding in a friendly way. They couldn't hear him over the music.

As the days wore on he became more and more desperate, but also more and more tired. Finally, on the morning of the fifth day, the musician, seeing his own shaking hands and his pale paper skin, knew the song was nearly over. His very life flashed before his eyes. He saw his childhood, and he put it in the song. He saw his mother's face, and put her eyes, her touch, her wrinkles, her every flake of skin into the song. He saw the moment he fell in love with the woman he would never get the chance to marry. He saw her long, dark hair, blowing in the evening breeze, her smile. The smile that told him she loved him back. He remembered what that felt like and he squeezed every last drop of it into his song. There was no last note to the song, yet on the morning of the fifth day, the village fell silent for the first time since the song had begun.

The people stopped their talking and dancing, and looked at the young musician. His eyes fell shut, and his once steady hands fell limp off the sitar.

The man never awoke. He was just a shell after that. The morning the music stopped, his soul flew out into the universe. In the early dawn of morning, a person who listens very carefully can still hear the reverberations of the young musician's song, echoing softly over the mountains and lakes and seas of the world.

Those who have heard it will tell you he was a success. The young man truly was the greatest musician of all time and space.

There is a tiger in my room,
No one else seems to see,
He will kill me, I assume,
But everyone just lets him be,
At times I have thought to run,
But he is much faster than I,
So I sit and wait 'till I am done,
A tear drops from his eye.

All Them Calling

All them calling,
All them writing,
All them wanting, looking, waiting,
All them asking, "helping," suggesting,
All them here, in my face,
I've kept going, like a race,
But I'm tired, tired, tired,
And I think I'll take a rest.

Saffron

In the Easternmost part of the world there once lived a young man who loved to sit by the old river in the forest. He would meditate there for days on end, beneath one of the old trees that grew in that part of the world. The animals of the forest stopped noticing him, and grazed and burrowed around him, but he took no notice of them, for his focus was on his thoughts. He concentrated unceasingly on the ways of the world, and of himself. He thought of a great many things and came to a great many realizations. From these realizations, he gained wisdom and ability.

He realized that it would be possible to walk on hot ashes by moving quickly, so as not to give the heat time to burn him. On a different day, he came to the conclusion that it would be possible to lay on a bed of nails, due to the distribution of weight. One day he decided to imagine a single flower. He thought of it for hours, which ran into days, and then into several months. He focused for weeks on each petal, imagining in vivid detail each speck of color. He could visualize each piece of pollen. He could feel every pore and vessel. Then one day, he opened his eyes and floating before him was the very flower he had imagined. He had concentrated on it so meticulously that it had come into being.

For many more years the man practiced this new found art of materialization. He became faster and faster, until he could create an object in only a few minutes. The man would walk for hours in the forest creating things around him, and every time he created something the process became easier for him.

One day he returned to the village of his birth, a homely place of mud huts and thatched roofs. A famine had befallen them in his absence. So upon his return he created bowls of saffron rice for them. And they loved and respected him, and called him Saffron endearingly.

The man loved to take long walks alone in the forest, and on these walks he found his increasing speed gave him new abilities. He imagined stones appearing in the river bed as he walked across. And when he was tired, he imagined himself a place to rest. He found he could fling himself from a tall tree, and on his way down imagine a large fern to catch him.

There was a young boy from the village that saw the man in this act, and tried to imitate it himself. Naturally the fern did not appear, and the boy's arm was broken. The man found, though, that he could imagine the boy's arm healed and it would be so.

Faster and more able he became, still. Flowers and song birds followed him everywhere he went, for his ability was now such that even a casual thought would be realized. The village was prosperous and healthy, for the man of the forest filled their stomachs and healed their wounds.

Several other village boys tried to imitate the previous, thinking that perhaps the fern would appear for them, like it did for Saffron. One in particular was not so lucky. This boy fell upon a smaller tree which pierced his chest and the boy bled to death before Saffron could heal him.

He was brought before Saffron, the wise man from the forest, in hopes that he could imagine the boy alive once more; after all the man became more able every day. Unfortunately, before the wise man could imagine the boy alive, he imagined for one split second himself, and everyone in the village dead like the boy. And so it was.

KING
OF THE
EMPTY DESERT

Chapter I

I walked alone through the night, across the never ending sand dunes, with the infinite shimmering abyss of space above me. It had been many days since I'd seen another human and my thoughts had ceased to exist only in my head. It puts great pressure on a man's head and a man's heart to be alone as long as I was.

In all that darkness and sand the only thing that really scared me was that indefinite, unsurpassable isolation, and yet I had come to realize in recent months that I could not survive without it.

I had been married recently. It seemed like such a long time ago, like a dream almost. But she'd been real. Beautiful, too. Long dark hair with ripples that matched the sand. She had the sweetest smile I have ever seen, but this is not a love story. At least not one about a woman.

Do you know what it is to fear death? Not in the far off hypothetical way that idle people, and perhaps great thinkers, do. But to look the bastard in the face, to smell the sweet pungent smell of the rotting and to be jittery in the same instance both for terror and ecstasy. Do you know what it is to spend every hour dreading the next hour because you know you'll spend it dreading the next hour after that?

Do you know what it is to be surrounded by people with whom you are familiar, with whom you smile and laugh and talk with frivolity, knowing the whole time that one or both of you holds behind your covered back long sharp gleaming knives that could at any moment be plunged deep into another unsuspecting back?

I have known these things, and somewhere along the way they bred in me a great restlessness, a sense of fear and despair that swelled up in me for reasons I do not understand whenever I was close too long to one of my own species.

That is why this is not a love story. I am not made for love stories.

Chapter 2

I preferred walking at night to walking in the day time. In the daytime the sand was too hot on my feet, the bright sun scalded my skin and obscured my vision, and the great expanse that surrounded me, and was visible in the light of day, made me uneasy.

At night there was a certain calm about things in the desert. Night was the safe time. I walked at night.

You have to be religious if you spend a lot of time in the desert. Or at least some kind of spiritual. There's too much emptiness to not believe in anything.

So I talked to God when I got really lonely and got tired of talking to the sand and the wind. He was a good friend, because he already knew me so well and I didn't feel like I had to hide anything.

It wasn't bad, really, until the water ran out. I don't know how long it had been at that point. I hadn't been keeping track. I'd left in the middle of the night, all of a sudden. Emily had been asleep and I didn't wake her up. And ever since then it'd just been 'keep moving' and 'keep moving' and I hadn't put much thought as to where I was actually going or what I needed to bring with me along the way.

Chapter 3

I knew things were bad when I stopped sweating. That's a very bad sign when you're in the desert. 'Keep moving' I kept telling myself and 'keep moving.' When you stopped moving, you were dead.

But damn I was tired. It was funny how your mouth being dry could make you feel so damn tired.

Pretty soon my skin started feeling like paper. My lips were like leather and I waited for my vision to go because I knew that would really be the end.

It was going to come, I realized. Pretty soon I was going to lay down out there and I wouldn't be able to see anything anymore, or hear anything anymore, and, well, I'd lay there for the rest of time. No one would know where I'd gone. And even if they had, it would be too late.

Might as well enjoy the last little bit I thought, and I lay down on one of the sand dunes. My eyes still worked and I decided that the last thing I wanted to see was the sky, so I lay on my back and looked up at the greatest expanse man has ever seen. The deep black ocean of the night sky, with a million shimmering lights winking at me telling me I would soon be one of them.

You have to be at least a little bit religious if you spend a lot of time in the desert.

Keep your eyes open, I told myself. *Keep your eyes open wide so that you can look as long as possible.*

You could see everything in that sky if you looked long enough. I saw my mother, how much she had loved me, how hard she had fought. I saw my home, the land of the dates where I had grown up. Emily, whom I'd once thought I loved. Perhaps I had.

I thought of being young. Of becoming a man. Everyone must think of those things when they are about to die. The fantasy of boyhood, treasure, honor, glory, love and so forth. Treasure turned out to be ephemeral. Love even more so. Honor and glory, who could say. But I was preparing to die as alone as anyone could be, so none of that mattered now.

I was back to the date palms when morning first peered over the horizon. It was a soft orangey light I had not thought I would see again. It shone smooth and decorative as though someone had spread gold and copper leaf across the dunes in the night.

It was obstructed only once by a small figure moving gracefully towards me.

Chapter 4

The desert showed me, through the sandy haze, the most beautiful creature I had ever seen. She seemed to float just above the sand, to glide rather than to walk, and I could not tell for the sorry life of me where her hair, if that is what it was, ended and the gold of the sunlight began.

"Who are you to die in my desert?"

Then she was there, directly in front of me.

"I apologize," I said. "I meant nothing by it." I hadn't realized I could still speak.

"Well, see that you don't."

I hadn't seen anyone in some time, and never anyone like her. I suppose I may have been gawking a little. Still I was wary of her, due to circumstance. I knew not if she were an angel or a demon.

"Are you distrustful of women," she asked, sensing my uneasiness.

"I'm distrustful of everyone."

"Hmm," she said, somewhat disdainfully. "And why is that?"

I considered for a moment.

"Do you know what it is to fear death?" I asked her. "Do you know what it is to plunge a dagger deep into a man's heart?"

"Have you done it?" she asked with a kind smile.

"Sure I have." I crossed my arms defensively.

"That's very brave of you, I suppose." She was wearing a cross about her neck. Perhaps she was an angel, then. Still, I mustn't jump to conclusions.

"I wonder," I said, thoughtfully, "if you could lead me to freshwater. So that I may not die in your desert."

"I could," she said, raising her chin slightly. "I can bring anything into this desert."

Chapter 5

And she could. She brought me a grand oasis with water and birds and lush vegetation and even date palms that made me think of home. It was a Garden of Eden; it was life.

"How long can I stay?" I asked the creature when I had drunk and eaten.

"For the rest of time, if you like."

"That's very kind of you," I said, "but really, I'll most likely stay only until I get my health back."

"That is up to you," she said "but just know that you can take nothing with you when you go."

"No water or food?"

"You can take nothing with you when you go. It will turn to sand as soon as you step outside this garden."

I considered for a moment.

"When I came here, I came with as much water and food as I could carry. I have no idea where the next city is. If I leave here and take nothing with me, I'll die in the desert for sure!"

"Perhaps so." There was something cold and far away about how she spoke.

"Then I can never leave."

"You can leave if you like."

"But I'll die if I leave!"

"That choice is up to you."

Chapter 6

With one conversation that heaven turned to, well, I wasn't completely sure. There was still something peaceful about it, at least on the surface. I was content to sit for hours watching the fish swim in the brook and the birds singing and flying from branch to branch in the trees.

Still there was an uneasiness about me. The thought of being trapped for eternity terrified me. I was supposed to 'keep moving' and 'keep moving.' Staying put was death. I knew myself; I would get restless and uneasy and—

The creature was there sometimes. And goodness she was beautiful.

The way the water sparkled when she was around. The way the birds all looked towards her.

Sometimes I found myself mesmerized by her, hypnotized by the sway of her body and the way her hair blew in the wind (it was her wind) and I found myself thinking, deep inside, that maybe I would like spending all of time with someone like that.

Mostly she didn't speak to me, though.

"You're like another animal for my garden," she said one day. "So innocent, like a child."

What did she mean by that, I wondered. "I'm not that innocent."

"I don't understand you at all."

"I don't understand you at all, either. Perhaps that's what I like about you."

She didn't say anything and I felt uneasy because of the innocence thing.

"Do you know what it is to fear death?" I asked her. "Do you know what it is to plunge a dagger straight through a man's hearts?"

"Have you done it?" she asked with a kind smile.

"Yes."

"No you haven't. I asked your friend God and he told me you hadn't."

"I have!" I crossed my arms defensively.

"Why, you've never stabbed a man at all! Much less in the heart. You're innocent as my other pets."

"Fine, what if I haven't done it? But it doesn't mean I couldn't if I wanted to."

"Oh?" She was teasing me. She was making fun of me! I wasn't so sure I wanted to spend eternity with her after all! Or maybe—maybe it was just how beautiful she was, and I was embarrassed.

"You said you could bring anything to the desert, didn't you?" I asked her.

"I did."

"Good. Then bring me a man to kill. Then I'll prove I can do it."

"All right." She frowned slightly. "You do it and I'll be yours and only yours. You'll be my King. But if you can't do it. Then you'll be mine forever and always and I'll be your queen."

She spat on her hand and extended it to me. I held back for a moment. It sounded like a risky deal. But then, it was forever and always for me either way. This was my only hope for escape, and I was a man. So we shook on it.

Chapter 7

The sun and the moon circled our little garden many time. With every passing iteration of day and night a quiet peacefulness grew stronger and stronger deep inside my soul. Where once I would've been restless, I found myself sitting for hours watching the fish and the birds and the leaves blowing in the wind. I found myself sitting for hours. And then I found myself sitting for days.

It was a strange place, and time didn't seem to work the same way.

Sometimes I felt as though I were becoming an observer to the world, rather than an active participant in it. That should've terrified me, and on some level it did. But I still sat for hours and then days because the roots of that strange plant they call sangfroid had already set its roots deep inside me.

I had nearly forgotten about my bargain with the strange she-creature when I came across the man that she had brought for me. I was walking in our little garden, checking to see that everything was in order, when I saw a shape on the edge of the water, drinking desperately with gasps from our little spring.

He was an old man, with a grey beard and ragged clothes, and as soon as he turned to face me, I knew who he was. I have never been so sorry to see anyone in my life, and in that instance that strange plant they call sangfroid ripped from me and in its place was a terrible, sickening uneasiness. Because the man that kneeled before me was none other than Emily's grandfather.

Chapter 8

"My boy!" he said. "I'm so very glad I found you! I have been searching for you for many days now."

I fingered my knife uneasily. It was still on my belt. "Looking for me?"

"My favorite granddaughter was distraught when you left. Wouldn't eat, wouldn't leave her room at all."

"I didn't know she loved me like that."

"She married you, didn't she?"

I kept silent, so the old man continued with his story.

"I promised her I would go into the desert to find you. Everyone else said you were a lost cause, that she was better off without you anyway. But I stood up for you! Because I knew how much you meant to her. And I promised her I would go into the desert and find you and bring you home!"

"We can't go home."

"What do you mean?"

Where was that wiley she beast? Was she watching me now? Waiting to see if I would fail?

"There's enough food and water here to feed an army!" The old man exclaimed with a grin. "We're saved!"

I fingered my knife uneasily. It was still on my belt.

"Come," the grey bearded man said. "Let us make camp. We shall stay here 'till our strength is restored, then strike out for home."

I took my fingers from my knife. I would wait. I would wait until the ideal time. He was weak now and it would not impress the she beast much if I killed him when he was like this. I would wait 'till his strength was renewed. 'Till he was ready to set out for home. And I would cut out his heart then when he was strong and alive again. That would impress the she beast, I thought to myself. That will impress her very much.

Chapter 9

I let the knife at my belt slip to the back of my mind and worked side by side with the man to build shelter, fire and traps. We became somewhat close, he and I. We were both the sort of men that would go along without talking much. And we understood each other in the way that people like us can, sometimes.

We built a nice little world for ourselves in that desert. A shelter to keep us protected from the sun. A pit to protect our fire from the wind so that we could be warm on those cold desert nights. Traps so that we could catch whatever we liked.

The woman with the golden hair was not around in those days I shared with the old man, and it was only he and I in the little oasis.

I tried not to think about how it would end up. For now, we were friends. In that moment, I truly did see him as a friend. And I tried not to think about how it would all end up.

Chapter 10

There are beautiful sunsets in the desert. And the old man and I used to sit every evening and watch them.

We were usually silent when the sun was setting, out of respect. But one night the old man spoke.

"We have stayed here together many nights now," he said. "We have grown strong and healthy again, in our bodies and our spirits. And tomorrow, we must set out again for the place where we were boys."

"We must set out again," he said. And I remembered about the knife at my belt and my deal with the strange woman. What was this 'we'? Why had I let there be a 'we'?

"Perhaps a few more days," I said in desperation. "That we may ensure our strength is at its full capacity."

"A man will never be at his full capacity 'till he is home," the old man said with sad smile and a slight nod.

"Nonsense!" I exclaimed. "I've never felt so well at home! I don't feel my strength is at its full capacity yet! I need a few more days!"

The old man seemed surprised by my outburst. I had never spoken to him like that before.

"Fine," he said, seeming a little confused. "If you need a few more days, then so be it."

Chapter 11

Several more days passed. I spent much time fingering the knife at my belt. Checking how tightly I could hold it. How easily it could slide from my belt when the time came.

"Think how impressed she will be," I told myself. "When you kill him, then you will finally be a real man."

And finally the day came, and the old man told me "Now! Now, my boy! The time has come for us to go back out into the empty desert!"

His eyes glimmered with excitement, his skin was full of color, his arms were rugged and strong....

I drew my knife. Took it from my belt and raised it stepping closer to the old man so I could get a good hit. Could take him quickly, with as little pain as possible.

Was I crying? Perhaps I was crying. I could not tell.

The knife did not feel as tight in my hand as I'd hoped. (He was staring at me with those big, healthy eyes. He was gaping. Asking me what I was about to do to him.) The knife did not come from my belt as easily as I had hoped. (And I stepped closer and closer to the old man.) Think how impressed she will be! (He let out a little cry. "What're you doing, my boy? What is this knife you come at me with?") Think how it will feel to be a man!

Think how it will feel to plunge my knife deep into his chest. (She will be so impressed! You will be her king!) How it will feel to drive it with my palm through his shirt, through the first layer of skin, between the bones of the rib cage. (She will love you for it! She will love you and you will take her.) How it will feel when the thick, gooey blood splashes on my face and my arms and…. (Step closer, step closer! You must always 'keep moving' and 'keep moving.' I can almost reach him!) How it will feel to cut down Emily's grandfather, when he came here to save me.

I dropped the knife.

Was it on purpose, or was it an accident?

The old man stared at me, hurt in his eyes.

"You are a troubled man," he said softly. "Perhaps it is best if you do not return with me."

He turned, lifted his pack and walked out into the great expanse of sand.

Chapter 12

I sat alone by the spring. Waiting for her to come. I had failed, so I knew that she would come now. After that I did not know.

I waited for some time. The birds were there and the fish and the leaves blowing in the wind. But I did not see those things anymore. I only looked down. Looked down, and waited.

She came finally with the setting sun, just as she had the first time I saw her. Her golden hair mixed with the last rays of sunlight and then she was right up close, standing over me, whispering and yelling in my ear.

"Do you know what it is to kill a man?" She asked wickedly.

"I do not," I said. I tried not to look at her.

"Then you are mine and I am your queen."

Chapter 13

In the morning she was my queen, but she was no longer beautiful and angelic. Her soft skin sank in the night and turned the color of cobwebs and mold. Her hair, once golden, became the same color and became coarse and thin. Her nose grew and her eyes shrank and there in the bright sun of morning stood before me a hag, but she was my queen.

She stripped me of my clothes and rode me far out into the desert. The sun was hotter than I had ever felt it and it burned my bare skin. I had not had a drink since the old man left and my mouth was as dry as the sand. But whenever I slowed the slightest bit, the old hag lashed at me viciously with her whip.

"Run fast!" she cried. "Run faster for your queen!"

Then when we were several hours from the oasis, she pulled on my hair for me to stop.

"This is the place." She climbed off me. "This is the place, now dig, slave!"

"I have no shovel, my queen."

"Nor do I. Perhaps a few lashes of the old whip would help?"

The sand was hot and burnt the skin of my hands as I tried to dig. I went for what seemed like hours and yet I barely made a dent upon the surface.

I felt so weak, the world swam around me. I would not have been able to stand.

"I'm dying," I whispered. "I'm dying and then I'll be of no use to you." That was the silver lining of it, I thought for a moment. I won't be her slave any more if I die.

"You won't die!" she screeched. "Not for long, anyway. I have a spell to make sure of that!"

She kicked me hard in the gut. "Now, get back to digging."

Chapter 14

I dug all day. My skin looked like raw meat from the sun and the whippings. My very bones ached.

When the sun finally began to set, she filled in my hole, climbed onto me and lashed at me as I tried to run the several hours back to the oasis.

"There was no reason for the digging," I wheezed when we were back in the oasis. "You had me do it just to torture me."

"There was a reason for the digging, only you failed." She splashed water on her face to clear the sand. "Now come into the shelter with me."

"Lay down." It was dark inside the shelter. I could see her a little in the moonlight that seeped through the cracks in the walls.

I lay down.

She ran her hand along my body, feeling me. Her hand was cold. I think I would've rather it been a knife.

"Put this in your mouth." She handed me a strange object. I did not know what it was, but I put it in my mouth.

Most of that night I don't remember. Thankfully. Only flashes. She finally fell asleep at some point. I was thankful of that, though I never got to sleep myself. At some moment, just before sunrise, when she was still asleep, she was beautiful again, like she was when I first saw her.

But when morning came, she was again a hag.

Chapter 15

"Why have patches of your skin turned black?" she asked me.

"From the sun, my queen."

"I don't like the way it looks. Cover it with mud."

Chapter 16

She again road me far out into the desert.

"Dig faster this time!" she shrieked. "You must make it the whole way in a single day!"

I tried to dig faster, in hopes I could complete whatever the task was and go back to the oasis and the shade. But my fingers were numb and weak and the sand slipped through them, slowing my progress.

"Perhaps if I had a shovel, my queen, then I could dig faster."

"Perhaps. If I had a shovel to give." It was a flash of something else in that moment there. Something other than hate. Then it was gone.

"Don't talk back, slave!" And she lashed out at me again, knocking my bare body to the scalding sand.

Chapter 17

I don't know how long it went on like that. It all blurred together. Digging, digging, digging. Then back to the shelter and "lay on your back" and "stay still" and sometimes other things that I tried to forget.

My skin began peeling off in big pieces, from the sun, I suppose.

Just digging, digging, digging. Whipping, sometimes. Less often now, because I knew what she wanted. But then at the end of every day she would fill in the hole again. And it would be starting over again the next day.

Was it always in the same spot? I didn't know. It all looked the same. Sand, sand, everywhere. The great emptiness of the desert. Once it had seemed like freedom, but now none of that.

Chapter 18

"Everyday you fail! Couldn't you dig faster?" she asked. "Before, I mean. Before I was your queen?"

"I am weak, my queen," I said. "From the sun and the work and not drinking enough."

She was quiet for a moment. She could tell I was not lying.

"Then tomorrow you shall rest."

Chapter 19

The oasis was still. The birds were gone, the fish were as still as they could be. It was only me and my queen, sitting by the spring.

"Drink, my slave," she whispered sweetly. "Drink so that you may grow strong."

I drank.

"Use mud, my slave," she whispered sweetly. "Use mud on your skin so that it may heal."

I rubbed the cool, soft mud across everywhere on my body.

"Now rest, my slave," she whispered sweetly. "Rest, so that tomorrow you can dig deeper than ever before."

Chapter 20

The sun was setting, like the first time I saw her. We were still sitting by the spring. Quiet. Everything still.

"My queen." Was that me? Was I speaking to her?

"Yes, slave?"

"May, I ask you something, my queen?"

"Yes, slave. You may ask, then we shall see if I will answer."

"What do I dig for?"

"Not what," she said. "But who."

"Who?" I said. "A man? Was he your lover?"

"Sshh," she whispered, softly as the night breeze. "We must go to the shelter now."

Chapter 21

As soon as I awoke, I knew that something was wrong. It was in the air, in the ground, in the bed beside me. Was not her. She was gone.

I rose slowly, and to the— There, by the spring, in the mist of the morning, stood the old man, Emily's grandfather. A shovel thrown casually over his shoulder.

And there she was, standing beside him. Beautiful and thin and golden again. And as bare as I was. I had never seen her that way before. She was entrancing. Only, I could tell the old man could not see her, so I tried not to get—

"I sent for a shovel," she said. "I sent for a shovel to make your digging easier. I didn't know that he would bring it!"

She was clothed again. He still could not see her. Could not hear her.

There was a pulsing in the air.

"You've come back," I said.

"For Emily's sake, I returned," he said. "Perhaps it was the desert that made you mad. Please, God, let it be the desert. That I return you home you shall love and care for my granddaughter and not betray her in the night as I fear you shall."

I wanted a way out. Oh, I wanted a way out so desperately! I did not want to kill this old man before me.

"Then bring him with you," she said. "To help dig. If you succeed, I shall let you both live."

There! There was the way out. There was at least a chance of a way out.

"Please, God," he said. "Let it be the desert that drove you mad."

"Not the desert," said I. "But a beautiful demon."

"A demon, you say."

"That is correct, I'm afraid."

"I should have known that no oasis would occur of natural forces in this part of the desert. We're too high."

"I should have known too." I looked at my feet. "But when you are desperate for water, you are desperate for water."

"That is the truth. We are a long way out. The perfect hiding place for a young and troubled demon. Do you remain under her control?"

"I'm afraid so. She wants something from me. Something, thus far, that I have been unable to provide."

"What?"

"Her lover is buried in the sand, some ways out from this oasis. She forces me to dig for him."

"And if you find him?"

"Then she promises to let us both live."

"I see. Can she be trusted?"

"I don't know."

"Tell him I can be," she said.

"She can be."

"Then, my boy, let us dig!"

Chapter 22

She led us to the spot. The old man brought his shovel. And when we were there, we began to dig. It was the hottest and driest it had ever been, but the digging went much faster with two of us, and with one of us having a shovel. We dug deep into the sand and earth, 'till when we stood in the bottom of our hole we could barely see the light of day. When we reached about this point, we began to hear strange noises. At first very faint; we thought perhaps a desert cat had come to torment us. But the deeper we sunk into the Earth, the louder it came, the more we realized the noise came from beneath us and it was no cat.

After we had dug all day and the sun had sunk low in the sky the demon woman appeared at the bottom of our little hole, floating just above us. It was narrow and dark by that point. With barely enough room for the old man and I to stand side by side, and dark 'till she came with her fiery golden hair floating above us.

"No more shovel," she said. "You're close. But from here you must continue by hand."

The old man was having his turn with the shovel and I took it and set it down at the edge of the hole.

"You must finish before sunset," she said solemnly. "At sunset Anarak will check the desert for holes. If he finds any, I will be in trouble and so will you if you're still here."

Anarak. Who was this Anarak?

We dug a little more vigorously, but only with our hands now, so the going was slow.

Sand, sand, sand, sand. So much sand. Above us, below us and on every side. Sand, sand, sand, sand. And then something else. The old man saw it first. Something not sand. Something flesh. A small hunk of warm soft flesh protruding from the sand where the old man dug. The flesh was crying. And a few moments later we saw that it was a babe!

A small, soft and handsome looking babe! Not more than eight months old.

She heard it too and no longer than we had the thing from the sand all three of us plus the shovel were again up on the surface.

"My baby! Oh, my darling baby!" She reached to take it from the old man but I snached it first.

"First, set us free! As you promised."

"I promised to let you both live." I couldn't tell if she was smiling or frowning. "I made no guarantee towards either of your conditions of servitude."

I set the baby on the sand and, taking up the shovel, aimed it at it's head. The baby burst into tears.

She screeched. "You horrible monster! Let me have my baby!"

"Let me have my freedom, woman!"

"Give him to me! Oh, please! Let me have him!"

The last bit of the glowing sun sank behind the distant sand dunes. It was night, and the night whispered in our ears.

"Who is screeching in my darkness? Who murders the calm of my night?"

The baby fell silent. The woman still whimpered a little.

And then there was another with us. Standing among us.

Long, dark, matte hair. Skin the color of talcum powder, but with a rich milky quality to it, eyes like the stars, clothes like the dunes. He was as solid as you or I, but there was an ephemeral quality to his presence with us.

"Anarak," the demon woman whispered.

He studied us with his glowing, beady eyes.

"What do you intend to do to my child?" he asked me calmly.

"Your child?"

"We're taking him!" My demon woman cut in.

"But Soles, it's my turn with him." There was a terrible calm about him. An ironic calm that made everyone else feel uneasy.

"You don't treat him right!" she blurted. Her whole person quivered. "You keep him buried deep in the sand all day long!"

"I think he likes it down there."

"How could he possibly like it down there?" She was frantic. "Please let me have him! He needs his mother!"

It was quiet for a time. She waited for what he would say. We all waited for what he would say. And finally: "Summi Artificis declared what would be the rotation of the day and the night, and you have violated that agreement and now I shall go with our son far away and you shall not see him again."

She screamed in despair. Collapsed to the sand. Anarak smiled a cruel, terrible smile. And then stepped forward toward the baby. I had been so mesmerized by the spectacle before me that I'd nearly forgotten that the baby still lay on the sand beneath my shovel. But seeing the creamy devil step toward me, I strengthened my grip on the shovel.

I did not like to be in this situation, but I knew it may be the only thing protecting the old man and me from eternal servitude.

"Release the child, boy," Anarak said to me. "You know not from which deck you draw your card."

"No one ever knows which card he shall get, but with a bad hand, you must draw all the same."

"And if the new card should make your hand worse?"

"Then you shall think how another card could have just as easily made it better. And you shall not regret your choice, for you knew it had to be done."

"Unless you gambled stupidly."

"Yes," I admitted. "Unless you gambled stupidly."

Anarak looked deep into my soul. "You, child, are gambling stupidly."

Then a flash of light and I was on my back, writhing like a roach, sores rising and popping on my now burning skin.

The woman sobbed in despair.

And the old man stood quietly as Anarak held the baby in his arms and disappeared into the night.

Chapter 23

I never thought I would wish to continue digging, but I did after that. The entirety of our master's existence had faded. She sank into a deep depression, but not the quiet kind. An angry and violent depression.

She would transform the old man and I into all manner of vile shapes. Mostly she would make us appear as Anarak, then beat us to death with some heinous weapon. We would die, blood seeping from our mouths, our eyes swollen shut, our limbs and fingers hacked completely off. We would die there, our blood flowing freely through the ripples of the sand.

But we would not die for long. As long as we were her slaves, we would never die for long.

The oasis died in the way free things do. The vegetation rotted away and the animals that once lived there ventured off into the desert as a last vie for survival.

Some nights, after she had finished with me and had finally fallen asleep, the old man and I would try to escape. We would run as fast as we could across the sand. We ran 'till our weak bodies gave out, and then dragged ourselves.

"Are you still breathing," I'd ask him weakly.

"I wish I wasn't," he'd said.

"Me too." I'd drag myself a little faster. "If only we could die in the desert like honest men."

The old man would retch, throwing up from exhaustion and sickness.

"Anything?" I'd ask.

"No, my boy. I haven't had anything in me for weeks."

We always asked the same questions. Said the same things. It was comforting somehow.

"Perhaps if we bury ourselves in the sand, she won't be able to find us in the morning." He suggested one night.

"It's worth a try."

We stayed under the sand for a long time. Hours passed. I thought we may suffocate. Hoped even. But we did not. We waited. It is quiet and still in the desert. Quiet and still and hot.

I thought back to the time before I met the demon woman. When I was young. When I felt young, that is. When life was "keep moving" and "keep moving." And now here I was, buried beneath the sand, trying to be as still as I possibly could.

We were not buried so deep that we could not hear the sound of her coming towards us across the dunes. Stormy along with the eerie desert wind. That was the most terrifying noise I have ever heard. It would haunt me 'till the day I died.

Then, there she was. Standing over us. She knew where we were of course. Of course she did. 'Twas only our madness that made us think she wouldn't.

The sand was hot. The sand was hot, hot, hot. ...laying on top of it. Her over us. She had a maul. She had a maul. She stood over us and we laid on the sand that was hot, hot, hot. And she stood over us, her awful paper legs there in front of me. And her with her maul. And she was telling us how it was going to be the worst ever. And she meant it. With her big thick rusty maul. And us laying on the hot, hot sand. And her—

I could not. I could not. I could not. Not, not face another day of dying. A man's heart is not made for that torture. Though our vessels were regrown, our minds and souls died a little every time. And I could not, not, not.
So then there was me grabbing her legs, her awful, rough paper legs. And her being surprised and shocked because I'd never done something like that before. And her being surprised and shocked so that she didn't fight back right away and I pulled her to the hot, hot sand and she hit it with an awful screech and dropped her thick, rusty maul which I grabbed immediately.

There she was. The old hag. Laying on the hot, hot sand. And me with my thick, rusty maul. It was not an opportunity I'd have again. I knew that. If I failed, the maul would be for me. Again and again, the maul would be for me.

"What're you going to do, slave boy?" She whispered in my ear. She was laying on her back on the hot, hot sand and I was standing over her with my maul. But somehow she whispered it in my ear. "What're you going to do, slave boy? You can't possibly kill me. No matter how hard you swing."

I swung, swung with everything I had left. Right at her head, only it hit sand instead. And she was behind me and standing on her own two feet again and cackling and saying "You can't possibly kill me!" with wild witch eyes and wild witch hands, and I knew that she was right. I couldn't possibly kill her.

The old man knew it too. He never got up. Just kept laying there on the hot, hot sand. Waiting to see what would become of us.

I couldn't possibly kill her and we all knew it. And yet, if I gave in and gave her back her rusty, old maul, it would be for me. Again and again, it would be for me. I couldn't do it another day. Somehow I couldn't do it another day. A man's heart is not made for that torture.

And the witch-hag kept moving and moving so that I could not get a clean hit and finally, in desperation, I brought the big heavy maul down on the old man's head. His skull cracked under it's weight. I felt it crunching in my hand. And that which once gave him thoughts spewed forth green and yellow upon the sand. And his eyes, they were the most terrible part. The way they got so distant and far away. With a kind of pain in them lasting long after his heart stopped beating. His eyes made me believe in Hell.

You have to be at least a little spiritual if you spend much time in the desert.

Chapter 24

"They'll be no reviving him this time," I told her.

"No?"

"I'm your king now," I told her. "We had a deal, with no stated time constraints. And I killed the man you brought me to kill and now I am your king and you are mine and only mine."

She looked away from me. She was old and wind swept and she looked out into the distance with a great, profound sorrow.

"I could revive him, if you commanded," she said quietly.

"And then I would not really have killed him and I would no longer be your king."

She didn't answer.

"Let the old man stay dead!" I declared. "Now, then, speaking of old. Why do you look so pale and wrinkled and saggy? Why don't you look young and beautiful like when I first met you?"

"I looked young and beautiful because I was free and happy." She was very quiet about it.

"And now you belong to me so you'll look this way and worse for the rest of our eternity together?"

She nodded slowly.

"Damn! What do I want with an old hag?" I spat in the sand, and she turned away. Perhaps there was a tear. I don't know.

Chapter 25

"Now then," I began. I'd just made her re-build the oasis and I was feeling much better about things. "You said you can bring whatever you want into the desert, correct?"

"That's right." She wouldn't look me in the eye.

"Or should I say whatever I want!"

"What do you want?"

"Well to start with I need a woman I can stand to see naked! Bring me Emily!"

In the morning Emily was there. Very lost and —"I came looking for my grandfather, have you — oh my! It's you! Oh, I thought you were dead!"

"I have been, off and on."

"We should go home. Mother will be so worried. Have you seen my grandfather?"

"He died, I'm afraid. Old age struck him in the night. And why should we go back? Here I am a king!"

"A king of the empty desert?"

"It's not completely empty. We have this nice oasis. And I have this wretched hag to do my bidding."

"Oh, you speak of her so viciously! Your time in the desert has changed you," Emily said. "Perhaps you've gone quite mad."

"Quite mad indeed, but what does that matter? In any case, I figured you could stay here and be my plaything."

"Your plaything? I don't think I like the sound of that!"

"I don't think you have much choice in the matter. This is an enchanted oasis. You can't leave. Not in practice."

"What about mother?" She looked scared, and for some strange reason that made me happy. Perhaps my time in the desert had driven me quite insane.

"I'll bring her to live with us! Maybe she can be my plaything as well."

Chapter 26

I brought them all. All of it. I was the King of the Empty Desert and I built it up and made it great. Brought the date palms and the beautiful women and the soldiers and I controlled the demon woman who controlled the life and so I controlled everything in my vicious, mad way.

Had I always been vicious and mad?

I didn't think I had. I thought I remembered a time when I was quite the opposite. But it didn't make much difference.

Chapter 27

"Guards, who have I not ravished? I want another virgin tonight!"

"You've had them all, my lord. There are none left." He was a thick, strong Berber man that always wore a turban about his head.

"What about you, have I ravished you yet?"

Chapter 28

"Guards, that blade of grass needs trimming. No, not that one! Three over. That one on your right."

Chapter 29

The sword hung above my head. Ever present. Ever precarious.

Power does strange things to a man's temperament. You would think it would make him calm and secure. Because what does he have to fear when he is the most powerful for many days walks? And yet, in my experience, power breeds instead a great uneasiness. A sickness, almost. And with all that power, what is one supposed to struggle against? It is in man's nature to struggle against something. But when you are as powerful as I was, the only thing you have to struggle against is yourself.

"You can kill and love and none of the others have any say in it."

"Then I am no longer human?"

"Were you ever?"

"I was once."

"That's not what my friend God told me."

"Do you know him, too?"

"Intermittently."

Chapter 30

Who was this boy who stood before me? I did not recognize him and he is one I would have known. And how did he dare to speak to me as he did?

"I'm here about a murder," he said finally.

"And whose murder would that be?"

"Yours," he said coldly.

I laughed.

"You are a child and I am a king."

I had my Berber man lash him to a palm tree somewhere on the other side of my oasis.

Chapter 31

I liked to gamble. Especially when I knew I would win.

My favorite sport was finding lost travelers out in the open desert. The closer to death the better. And then going after them, and making the old hag make me appear all god like and saintly and pretending like I was going to save them and all and bring them to my oasis and letting them drink my water and eat my food.

I liked to gamble with them. And I always knew I would win. It was best when they really thought they could win but then of course, none of them actually ever did.

Chapter 32

I got bored a lot. Being all powerful tended to have that effect.

Sometimes I would pick different ones of my citizens and make them fight.

"Kill him! Kill him like I killed Emily's grandfather!" I would shout. There were no secrets about that anymore. What did it matter? They all hated me. I knew they all hated me and that just made me all the more awful.

Because if I said for them to pretend to love me or to pretend to be my friend or what have you, they would have to do it, because what could they do? It was my oasis, and my water, and my food.

And I kept them alive, even when they died, but they still hated me. But if I said for them to pretend to love me or to pretend to— like the Berber man. He was one of my best mates. That's what I liked to say.

"Berber man, you are one of my best mates."

But of course he didn't feel that way about me. I made him kill his brothers all the time. I loved how big and muscley he was and how he could break their arms with one hand.

"Berber man, you are one of my best mates." And he would smile and thank me and address me as his lord, because if I said for them to pretend to....

Chapter 33

"Guards! Whom have I not ravished? I want another virgin this morning."

"You've had them all, my lord. There are none left." He was a thick, strong Berber man who always wore a chain about his ankle.

"Are there no new travelers for me to molest?"

"No, my lord. I'm afraid not."

"What about the boy from the other day? The saucy one. Said he was here about a murder."

"What of him, my lord?"

"You lashed him to a tree as I did bid thee do?"

"I did, my lord."
"Well, let me have at him!"
"I would be careful with that one, my lord."
"I can handle him. What's his name?"
"Anarakson."
"Funny name," I said. "I'll call him Peter."

Chapter 34

There was something alluring about the boy. Something about the way his skin matched the sand, the way his hair matched the sun and the way his eyes matched the stars. He seemed to float rather than stand, even as he was lashed to the tree.

I thought for a moment that perhaps I was in love with him, but of course that was silly. I was probably not even human anymore.

And yet, there was something alluring about that boy.

"Hello, Peter," I said.

"My name is Anarakson."

"Not a very pretty name."

"Anarakson. Son of Anarak. I believe you know my mother."

"I have known a lot of people's mothers." I grinned at him.

"Release me and my mother now and we will go quietly into the night and you will never see us again."

"Why ever would I want that?"

"It's that or I kill you."

"You're really not very intimidating when you're tied to a tree. Not that you particularly were before."

I was tired of this silly talking, so I had my way with him and then went to look for the Berber man so I could make him kill something.

Chapter 35

Anarakson was still tied to the date palm, helpless and alone. That monster hadn't even bothered to restore his clothes from his ankles. He watched the sun setting around him in this strange place and realized what a horrific new world he'd walked into. Perhaps he'd been naive about this man's power. But no, his mother was here. He was here for her sake and that's all that mattered.

All those long nights of endless wandering with his Father. "Keep moving," his father would say, even when his son's feet hurt and his eyelids sagged. And Anarakson kept walking all those endless lights, looking out into the darkness and wondering about his mother.

But would he ever actually see her? Or would it be endless days of this monster toying with him? This perverted monster pretending he—

"The dagger between his legs is his worst." A girl stood before him. He hadn't seen her approach. "I should know."

He was mesmerized by her, in a way he had never been by anyone before. She had long dark hair with ripples that matched the sand, and the sweetest most sympathetic smile he had ever seen, with more than her fair serving of sadness.

"I'm Emily."

"I'm Anarakson."

She paused for a moment, studying him. "How did he trick you into coming here? Was there a wager?"

"No," he said. "I came willingly."

"You're the first I've heard say that."

Chapter 36

I selected an old man called Misertus. I liked him because he reminded me of Emily's grandfather.

"Kill him with that rusty maul I gave you," I shouted to the Berber fellow.

Chapter 37

Anarakson watched the birds playing at the edge of the water. He was still tied to the date palm. He had never stayed in one place this long in his life and it made him restless.

Two figures appeared from behind him.

Two women— Emily and another. An old woman with grey hair and paper skin. She stared at him with a cautious smile, nervous eyes— his eyes.

"Mother?"

"Inlustris? My son?"

"Your son, yes— Anarakson."

"Of course he would tell you that was your name."

"Is it not?"

"Let me look at you, my son. Oh, my son, you're now a man! You were but a babe the last time I saw you. What has your life been?"

"Many endless nights, walking, hiding, fighting, but I have seen much of the world."

"And you're happy?"

"Never completely 'till I have found my mother. But now, perhaps. What is this place in which you reside?"

"Hell."

"Then why do you stay?"

"Why does a fish stay in his pond? All the time knowing he will swim in circles for the rest of his days."

Everyone was silent.

"But you're stronger than he. You're a different sort of being. Why not strike him down and end his sorry life?" the boy asked.

"I am bound by a wager from many years ago. I must do whatever he says."

"And if I kill him?"

"I must revive him if he orders me to do so."

"Must you? Then how am I to free you all? And myself for that matter?"

Chapter 38

Then it was just him and Emily. Alone together. Standing near each other. The water and the stars shining as one pattern.

"I've never met anyone like you," he told her. "You helped me when all you knew of me was my name."

"There's not enough kindness in this place."

"There's not enough kindness in most places."

She let the sand run through her fingers, let the cool night breeze dance in her hair.

"What will you do when you're free?" he asked her.

"I don't know." She looked out into the darkness. "My whole world is here now. My whole world has been brought here, all the people, all the—brought here and destroyed. Chewed up and spat out by the one who rules this place."

"He will be dead soon. I will find a way."

"Then I suppose I will find a way to put a chewed up world back together again."

A lone bird darted across the sky.

"What will you do when this is done?" she asked him.

"Wander, I suppose. It's all I know."

"Have you ever tried staying in one place? Sending down roots? Building a life for yourself?"

"No. My father is the only one I have ever known for any extended length of time. We never stay in one place more than a week or two. 'Till I came here to see about a murder."

"A rescue."

"What?"

"It's all in how you phrase the thing."

The moon sank low in the sky.

"You know, if you ever did feel like settling down, you could consider doing it.. with my village."

"And with you?"

"Perhaps. You seem like a nice boy."

"Nice, yes; a boy, I'm not sure."

She smiled curiously. "Are you a demon, then?"

"I don't like labels."

"How else is one supposed to know what they're eating?"

"By the taste."

"Alright then, I'll let you know what you are once I get to know you better."

"Sounds fair."

She shook his hand and disappeared into the night.

Chapter 39

"Guards, whom have I not ravished? I want another virgin before breakfast."

"There is no one else, my lord. You have had them all."

"Every old woman, every babe in its crib, every cripple and every soldier?"

"Yes, my lord. All of them."

"Then prepare the boy. The saucy one from the other day. I should like to have him again!"

"Very good, my lord. How should I prepare him?"

"On his knees. And bring me my favorite maul."

"Yes, my lord."

"Oh, and Berber man?"

"Sir?"

"Round up the whole village. I'm in the mood for a little voyeurism."

Chapter 40

Emily was already there when the Berber man came to bind Anarakson's hands.

"He wants you on your knees," the man said, almost apologetically.

"Can you tie my hands loosely?"

"I'm afraid not, boy. If these knots fail, he will torture me for days."

"He will not have the chance."

Emily stepped forward. "Please Izem, give him a fighting chance. For all of our sakes."

The Berber man studied her.

"Do you love this man, Emily?"

(quietly) "I do."

"Then perhaps it is best if you do not stay around to see what our lord is going to do to him."

Chapter 41

This is how a king walks, I thought to myself as I stepped towards Peter. That beautiful boy, tied up and kneeling. Legs beneath his body. Face leaning forward.

I was in love with him. I was pretty sure of that now. He was not a man like me. He was weak and soft and androgynous, and that was what I liked about him. He could be a boy when I wanted him to be, and a girl when I wanted him to be. I liked him even better than Emily.

She was there watching, standing near my Peter. And my Berber man was there too, holding my lovely rusty maul out to me which I took and held up triumphantly to the village. The whole village was there! It was a grand, spectacular occasion! All of them sharing in my pleasure. I must be the best King in the world!

"I am the best King in the world!" I shouted. I knew better than to phrase it as a question, they were too stupid to answer questions. But I loved them anyway. Especially Peter. I loved Peter especially.

I'd already had the Berber man strip him, and I admired how soft and clean he looked and how thin and weak. Almost birdlike. Especially when he was tied up like that.

"Undress me, Emily," I commanded. And she did. And I stood there in the sunlight, naked before my whole kingdom. *They must admire how good I look,* I thought to myself. *I am the best King in the world!*

And now all I wanted to do was take Peter, that thin, wiry, pale skinned boy.

I stepped closer to him, till I was just inches from his face. He wouldn't look at me. He just stared down at the sand.

I slid my maul gently over his hair. "I love you, Peter." He didn't look up. "Look at me, Peter. Oh, please look at me. Look at me now!" He looked up. I smiled at him. I wanted him to know I really did love him. I wasn't just pretending. I really did love him. And oh, how terrible it was that none of them would ever genuinely love me back….

"Now, open your mouth, Peter!"

The demon woman was watching us. I winked at her. Everyone was watching us.

I must be the best King in the world.

"Oh, Peter, I really do love you. Your mouth is so soft and wet…."

Then suddenly, pain shot up through my body. I looked down and I could see blood dripping out of Peter's mouth.

"Peter! What are you doing?"

But he only bit down harder.

I clobbered him with my maul. Oh, it hurt so bad! I beat him harder and harder in the head. Blood was dripping down the side of his head. Awh, fuck, it hurt! I swung to hit him again, but this time he grabbed the handle of the maul with his hand. How had the knot come undone?

I tried to step back but he still had me in his mouth, biting down harder and harder. I let go of the maul in agony and grabbed his hair, pulled on his hair as hard as I could.

"Please, Peter, stop this, I really do love you!"

The villagers all just stood there. I was the best king in the world! Why didn't they come to help me? After all I had done for them! Those stupid bastards.

I couldn't even see Peter's face anymore, it was so covered in thick globs of blood. His blood, my blood all mixed together. Harder and harder he bit, 'till with a horrible, agonizing rip I was free… or at least most of me was.

Peter stood now, the rusty maul still in his hand.

The villagers stepped back, and it was just Peter and I both standing naked and blood-soaked in the sunlight, clear and crisp in the eyes of God.

"You're a monster," Peter said. "You've done terrible things to these people!"

"I am a man!" I shouted. "And a king! And I have done naught but what a man and a king is allowed and expected to do!"

He ran at me and swung at my right leg. I could feel the bone snap and I fell to the ground and grabbed handfuls of sand to keep from screaming. It didn't work and I screamed anyway.

He brought the maul down on me again, breaking my other leg.

It was over now. I knew it was over now. I was no longer a man. No longer a human. They were right about me. I was a monster.

"Oh, but I couldn't help it!" I shouted in desperation. "You think I wanted to be the way I am?"

Peter struck me in the chest and I fell back upon the sand. I could see the sky over head. You could see anything in the sky if you looked long enough. I saw my mother. How much she had loved and believed in me. I saw Emily. Before the trouble. When she'd first told me her name. When she'd first gotten me to settle down. And that was all I had time for, because after that I saw that old rusty maul coming down towards my face, gleaming in the desert sun, and that short sharp sound of crushing bone.

Chapter 42

Anarakson was a hero after that. He was David and he had slain Goliath. Quickly. Before the monster could command the woman to save him. Why had he not ordered her to intervene? Anarkson did not know.

There was not rowdy celebrating, for they had all been through far too much together for that, but they all sat for a long time by the water and watched the sun set dancing in the ripples.

Then in the morning they set about building a new world for themselves. They buried the body and the weapons and everything that made them think of their late leader. And made arrangements for how their new society would be structured.

Through it all, Anarakson felt a growing uneasiness. He had known his place in this little village when he'd had a purpose, but now that the purpose was fulfilled, he knew not what to do with himself.

He was with his mother for the first time. And that was good. And of course there was Emily. One day, she said she would marry him if he asked her, and she was the most kind and beautiful girl he had ever met, so of course he did.

And they were married by the water and his mother was there, and very happy about it, and Emily really was such a great girl.

They never talked about all the bad stuff that had happened, but of course they all thought about it. Anarakson still tasted the blood in his mouth. Still felt the crunching of bone in his hands.

"Do you think God will remember what I did when my time comes at the Pearly Gates?" he asked her once.

"I think God looked the other way when all of that happened. He saw nothing. It's as though you never killed anyone."

But of course he did. The man was evil and wicked, so why did it matter? Yet, still, he knew what it was to kill a man.

Mostly they didn't talk about it though.

And the sex? Well, they had both seen how wicked a thing that was to do to someone, so they avoided it as much as possible.

Mostly he just liked sitting under a date palm with Emily and sipping tea together as the sun set. That was a nice time. When they sat together like that. That was when he knew he loved her.

But the other times he got restless. He had never stayed in one place this long before and it made him nervous. "Keep moving" and "keep moving" his Father had always told him. "Staying still is death." The worst part was the nights. When Emily slept so soundly, and he was alone in the darkness with the crunching of bone and tearing of flesh and the soft, warm sound of the monster breathing in his ear as the foul creature took him.

"Aren't these people a rotten bunch," he'd think to himself. And he'd start to wonder if he'd be better off without them.

He'd go for walks when he really couldn't sleep. Every time he'd go a little further from the oasis. From the familiar date palms and familiar faces. Every time he'd go a little further. And one night, he realized he'd been walking for several days and never looked back.

It was too late to go back now, and in truth he didn't really want to. He looked around— he'd been so damn unaware 'till now— and he looked around to take it all in. This old familiar world he belonged in.

In all that darkness and sand, the only thing that really scared him was that indefinite, unsurpassable isolation, and yet he had come to realize in recent months that he could not survive without it.

A man could turn into anything when he was alone in the empty desert.

The Climb

I've dreamt of a great emerald palace.
S'pose I drank the kool-aid from a golden chalice,
Touched the stars in the pavement,
Seen the cars pass with the blank tint.

"You will fall" whispers the man beneath the ladder,
Yet I climb on, madly, like a hatter.
"You will be lost in the dark" I hear him call,
But the view is sublime, I am in awe.

Watching

There was once a time when men killed men with sticks and stones. Then came swords and spears and they made it faster, so you didn't have to hit the other man quite so many times. After that, mankind invented guns, so that he could distance himself still further from the blood and the furious passion that is death.

War is a grisly business. Sometimes there is glory, and sometimes there is necessity, but there is always death and there are always those that must inflict it upon others.

In the great progress of society, we have, in the year of our Lord 2015, devised ways of killing each other oceans and continents away. With missiles and with the infamous *drone*.

And the naive masses of civilian society assumed, innocently enough, that with such a glorious new invention our men and women of the armed forces could now lead "normal" lives. No danger, no professional heartache, no seeing the people you kill.

Why, these damn drone pilots are barely even soldiers!

Yet in late 2011, the US Air Force capped the number of Unmanned Aerial Vehicles ("drones") in order to investigate 'elevated stress levels' and even PTSD-like symptoms showing up in many of the craft's pilots.

Addie Riley did not read that report.

She was a pretty, young, dark haired Sensor Op that'd recently started working at a semi-secret control center somewhere in the Eastern United States. By day, she was a soldier in Pakistan, by night, a mother and a wife.

She spent her days submerged in a dark little room, surrounded by glowing screens and control panels. Watching. Always watching.

Niel Linden sat beside her in his wheelchair. Big boned and greying, he'd been a "real pilot" once upon a time, but a nasty crash had changed all that. And now he lived vicariously through the Predators he flew halfway around the world.

The lights flashed on in the little room.

"Looks like the main power's back on," Niel said dryly. He was the driest damn person Addie had ever met.

"Just a drill." Sam Smith, their commanding officer, came over the intercom. "Everything's back to normal."

Niel and Addie stared intently at their screens. Watching.

"It's so bright," Addie observed.

"Yeah," Niel agreed. "Let's turn them off again."

They were watching a compound somewhere in Pakistan. Who knew why, exactly? But that'd been their job for months now. Just to watch that compound. Watch everyone that came, went, lived, played, worked, cried and married in that walled oasis.

"Aamirah's watching her again," Addie pointed out. Aamirah was the little boy that lived in the compound.

"He definitely likes her."

"You might be right.... How old do you think he is?"

"I dunno. Seven or eight?"

"And has a crush already?"

"Oh, didn't you ever like anyone when you were seven?"

"I guess I did."

They sat in silence, watching the boy watch the girl.

A faded old truck pulled up to the compound.

"Who is that?" Addie asked. They knew all of the regular comers and goers.

"I don't recognize the truck. I'd better tell Smith."

Sam Smith was a tough old soldier. Been in the Air Force since he graduated high school and had made officer's status with impressive speed. He was in his office when he got the message from Niel, cross referenced it to the other feeds he'd gotten that day, and made a call to his superior.

"Hello? Yeah, Smith. Listen, we just got intel on a weapons shipment to compound 13. Yes, sir. We think it's preparing for something. Some operation, or maybe a visitor. Yes, sir, we'll keep you posted. Yes, I'll send over the pictures right away."

*****

WATCHING

The sun shone bright overhead as Addie's burnt red PT Cruiser whipped into the parking lot. She was late once again to her son Adam's soccer game.

Her husband Joe was there, as always, standing dutifully by the edge of the field.

He is a simple man, Addie thought to herself. *But he is a good father.* She watched him for a moment, standing a little ways off before he saw her.

"Hey, there you are." He saw her. She was caught, so she went to stand beside him, walking fast as though to cover up for not being there sooner.

"Took your time getting here," he said, more as an observation than an accusation.

"I needed time to unwind," Addie snapped back. She crossed her arms defensively.

Joe didn't notice.

"They're behind," he said, gesturing vaguely to the field.

"They'll catch up," Addie said harshly.

"Eh, I dunno about that." He didn't seem to notice how his words made her skin crawl.

They watched the game. Adam was no David Beckham, Addie noted.

"Hey, you see that girl over there?" He pointed.

"The one with the dark hair?"

"I think Adam likes her."

"Oh, really? She's cute. What's her name?"

"I dunno, Sara, I think? Harry's daughter."

"Oh, okay." She nodded.

Adam went for a kick and missed the ball entirely.

"So how was work today?" Joe asked.

"Fine. Just, well, you know."

"You can't talk about it, I know."

"Right.. Did you have a good day?"

"It was pretty good." He smiled impishly. "This one lady came in. She asked to buy bread, right. Bread, in a hardware store. The lady was a foreigner, it turns out. Hardly spoke any English. She was just going all over town, trying to find somebody to sell her bread. I told her we sell boards and nails, not bread. It was the funniest thing. Jacob and I laughed our asses off."

Adam tripped and fell.

"Oop, he's down." Addie leaned forward trying to see.

*****

Addie and her son sat around their small, round dinner table. Joe served them mashed potatoes and crispy fried chicken.

"Well, it was a good game, son," the father said with an amiable smile.

"But, we lost.."

"But you played well. Eat some mashed potatoes."

Joe finished serving and joined them.

Addie was distracted. Adam was still thinking about the game.

"Okay," Joe interrupted their silence. "What barks, can balance a ball on its nose, and lives in Washington?"

"The president's dog," Adam ventured a guess.

"No, the Presidential Seal."

Adam laughed.

"What do you call a snake who works for the government?" Joe grinned. "Come on honey, you should get this," he teased his young wife.

"What, a TSA officer?"

"No, no. A snake that works for the government. A civil serpent."

"Huh." Addie was still distracted.

"Okay, last one. What did the stop light say to the traffic camera?"

"What?" Adam had left the game behind him.

"Don't look, I'm changing!"

Adam chuckled.

Addie rolled her eyes playfully.

Adam laughed for real.

Pretty soon none of them could stop.

*****

The control room was silent except for the harsh, low hum of a half dozen computers and monitors glowing in the darkness. Addie and Niel sat before them, like moths hopelessly and eternally obsessed with the light in front of them, seeing nothing else, looking nowhere else.

Though their bodies were left behind, their souls were not in that little dark room, but thousands of miles away in a compound in Pakistan where a group of kids played happily in the sunset.

"They got presents for the kids," mumbled Niel.

"What'd they get?"

Niel glanced at his notes. "Junaid got a kite. Abu, three CDs. Ali, a new top. Aamirah a soccer ball. And a crystal for Abraham."

"Aamirah got a soccer ball?"

"Yeah. Look, he's playing with it now."

Sure enough, there in the lower right hand corner of one of Addie's monitors was an eight year old boy passing a new-ish soccer ball back and forth to himself.

"He reminds me of Adam, sometimes," said Addie absent mindedly.

"Don't say that."

"Why not? I just mean, well, they're about the same age. Both soccer, both—"

"I know what you meant, but don't say that."

Addie stared at him, a bit confused by his harsh response.

"When you're on a bomber, you're killing specs a hundred miles below," said Niel. "And that messes with your head. But this, you see their faces. You watch 'em for a month before. You watch 'em when you push the button. And they're right there in crystal clear HD the whole time they're dying. Bombers fly away before that, but they like us to stick around and watch. Count the bodies. Make sure we got 'em all."

"God Niel." Addie shuttered. "We're just watching them right now."

"Right, now we're watching them. Yeah. But all I'm saying is, when the time comes to push the button, do you wanna watch your son get burnt away, or some faceless terrorist?"

*****

Addie's burnt red colored PT Cruiser rolled along the back roads headed home. She liked to take her time, and frequently forewent the highway for a more scenic route.

"Everyone agrees, in the years since 9/11," an NPR reporter said across the radio "everything has changed. I mean, we have—"

Addie's hand darted to the center dial and she flipped the channel to some upbeat pop music.

*****

They stood in the dimly lit kitchen, the three Rileys. They stood very still. Completely mesmerized by what they saw on the floor.

A roach. Large and shiney. His antenna dancing frantically in the cool, stagnant air.

"Why are we watching it?" Adam asked, without taking his eyes off the thing.

"I dunno." Addie didn't so much as blink, either.

They stared at it. Studying it. Becoming it.

"Let's just kill it," Joe said finally. He wasn't as entranced by it as the other two.

Nobody moved. They just kept—

Then, as though breaking free from it's spell, Joe lurched forward and finished the thing.

The other two remained still a moment longer, watching the place on the floor where the bug had been.

Adam was the first to leave.

"We should re-caulk the outside walls," said Addie as she too left the room.

"Where you going?" asked her husband.

"I gotta go sit down. Kind of a stressful day."

"Oh, yeah?" He stood close to her, conveying what he imagined was intimacy. "Me too. We had so many customers today. Which is good, you know? But my feet are killin' me."

Addie stared at him, struggling with the growing divide between them.

"Let's take it easy tonight. Huh?" Joe said after a moment. "Maybe watch a movie or something."

Addie nodded, her mind back in Pakistan.

*****

Joe never woke up when Addie left in the mornings. She rose, showered and dressed alone. Then climbed into her old car and went to work, never speaking to another human 'till she was in the dark little control room around which her life revolved.

Watching. That desert sun rising over the little compound. Children playing. Women stringing up laundry. Men coming and going. It had long since ceased to have context in the larger picture. It was only the compound. The place where Addie spent her days. Watching.

It was another hot day. The desert sun burning like fire on the golden sand. Addie could tell by the way it reflected the light (as well as the temperature readouts on a screen in front of her).

The children played in the shade of a date palm. The women hung up laundry that would no doubt dry very fast today. And that strange black pickup came once more to the little compound.

It seemed out of place, somehow. Shiny and black in a world of ancient earth tones.

There was another man this time, besides the driver. The new man was much taller than the other, with a long dark beard, and a confident, almost prophetic way of walking.

The other men of the compound all came out to greet him. Practically bowing as they shook his hand. Then they ushered him inside.

The exterior of the compound became quiet and still. But the UAV kept watching.

*****

"Addie?"

She snapped away from the screen, realizing she had been alone 'till just then when Niel had re-entered, carrying a stack of papers.

"Addie?" he said again.

"Huh? What?"

"They got an ID on the new guy. Hafiz Zakir. A known Taliban leader." He looked at her for a moment, staring, studying her. Thinking about what he had to say. "They ordered a kill."

She didn't say anything. They simply studied each other. Trying to remember to breath. Postponing.

"Come on," Niel said finally. He wheeled himself back over to the controls and prepared for what had to be done.

"Connection confirmed?" Smith's voice crackled through their headphones.

"Roger, connection confirmed," Addie said almost inaudibly.

"Roger, connection confirmed."

"Possible target just outside building. Designate new target, target six."

"Pilot copies."

"Sensor copies."

The checklists dragged on like a horrible countdown, haunting Addie's mind, pumping adrenaline through her veins like some unmanageable drug that in one instance made her both want to run out of the building screaming and also blow the compound away with an awful laugh. Like the whole business was some sick joke.

"Target six re-entering building. Confirm target in building."

"Roger, sensor confirms."

Then she'd catch herself, her mind would again retake control of her body, and she would be self-conscious for the terrible thoughts she had. She was going to kill these people. Including Aamirah, the little boy that—

"Building has priority."

"Sensor, lock up target six with tail 201."

"Roger."

"Pilot, centennial requests weapons rundown."

Niel went through the list.

Then it was time for the pre-launch checklist.

"PRF code?"

"Entered."

"AEA power?"

"Entered."

"AEA bit?"

"In progress… passed."

"Weapon power?

"On."

"Weapon bit?"

"Passed."

It was rhythmic, like the beat of a war drum.

"Pre-launch checklist complete."

"Pilot, sentinel, you are cleared to engage the compound at your discretion."

Addie's heart was in her throat. Her wrists throbbed. Her stomach felt like it was constricting.

"Pilot cleared to engage the target. Launch checklist. MTS auto track?"

"Established."

"Laser?"

"Laser selected."

She thought she might black out. She hoped she might black out.

"Arm your lasers."

"Lasers armed."

"Master arm is hot. Fire your laser now."

She could barely hear them. She was far away. She was watching, a small dark haired woman sitting in a small dark room. Watching.

"Lasing," the woman said.

Niel leaned forward in his chair. He was a wolf, foaming at the mouth, staring intently at his prey. A predator's blood pumping in his veins.

"We're within range." There was no one in the world but him and his prey. "Three, two, one, rifle."

There was a ringing noise. Or maybe it was only in Addie's head. Everything was silent. She didn't dare move. She couldn't move. Niel licked his lips, leaning forward in his chair, watching.

He was softly, almost imperceptibly speaking numbers. "Three, two, one, impact."

With his final word, the entire compound disappeared into a cloud of fire and dust, dissolving away into a field of rubble. They watched as a few blackened corpses still squirmed in the blackened sand. Then, one by one, fell still forever. One held on to what appeared to be a ball.

They began to count.

*****

It was night when Addie finally stepped back into her family's home, with sweet, silly Joe popping his head around the doorway. "There you are honey!"

Adam appearing from behind him. Holding his soccer ball.

"Mom!" he ran and hugged her.

Addie saw his soccer ball and shuddered.

"Not right now, sweetie." She pulled away and started up the stairs towards her bedroom.

*****

She sat in the dark, not even bothering to take her shoes off.

Joe opened the door and slipped inside. "What was that about?" Then he saw her. "Are you okay, honey?"

She struggled to keep her composure. "I had a rough day at work."

"Oh, okay." He didn't really understand, but he sat down beside her sympathetically. "Do you wanna talk about it?" He was unsure of what else to say.

She didn't answer, so he hugged her.

"It's okay, honey. I have hard days sometimes, too."

"You work at a hardware store," she said harshly.

"Yes, I know that. And you fly drones."

"UAVs."

"What?"

"They're called UAVs. No one really calls them drones. That's a media word. They're UAVs."

He didn't say anything. Just sat, watching her.

"Listen, honey, I killed people today. A lot of people. Even children. I killed them."

Again he hugged her, just held her this time, and for the first time she started to sob.

Suddenly she tore away and stood screaming "I killed people today! I killed children at work today!"

Just outside her closed bedroom door stood Adam, listening to something he would never admit to hearing.

By and by, the soldier cried herself to sleep there at the foot of her bed. She dreamed strange dreams of walking through a golden wheat field. Of two boys, an American and a Pakistani, that held hands as friends. She smiled at them, feeling free and calm for the first time in a long while. 'Till that familiar buzzing noise returned, polarizing the air.

"I know what that is," said Aamirah, turning away from them.

Then her alarm went off. She got up, got ready for work. And it was time to do it all again.

LOCKER 99

Prologue

James hadn't left the house in almost a week. The days and nights ran together, lost of anything unique to define and separate them. He paced a lot. Slept, ate, though not much. He checked his newsfeed sometimes. Read dumb statuses by people he hadn't talked to since the spring. He'd get bored, and close the window. But then he'd pull it up again a half hour later. Hardly any of it was new by then, just the same old statuses that were dumb the first time. But he read them again anyway. Just trying to touch those people who had once been a part of his life.

It had been nearly three months since the racket collapsed. Rob had long since disappeared, and none of the rest of them spoke anymore. It was just too complicated.

Everything that'd happened that year spun through James' head like a kaleidoscope, making him want to throw up all the time.

Book I: James Grey

Chapter 1

You were never ready when the car stopped. It always seemed like you ought to have another half hour. Quarter at least, but there was nowhere else to go. The car came to a choking final stop, and the man or woman in the drab pantsuit would turn around and look at you, with their forced puppy eyes, and ask if you were ready. And of course you weren't, but you never said that. You just nodded, and waited as long as you could to clip off the safety belt, and then as long as you could after that to push open the door, and step outside, never knowing what lay ahead of you.

Pantsuit would always put their hand on your shoulder, like they knew you, and walk you up to the door. And the new couple would come out and gawk at you, like a strange animal that they were terribly excited to look at, to touch and prod. But they never really got it. For them, this was a happy moment.

Felicity wasn't there when I first met Burason. She'd ended up in the hospital after our time in Centennial went sour. Nothing too serious, but enough that'd she'd be a few days late coming.

Rob was such a mystery to me, to all of us really. I don't think I realized it fully until after he left, that summer after senior year, laying on the floor of the tiny bedroom I'd lived in as far back as my memory went, the wet warm air pressing down on my skin, and the weight of adulthood positioning itself on my shoulders. Yet my mind never seemed to go to the future in those months. I always found it behind me. With Lesa, Abi, Tommy, and Rob. Especially Rob. I've never been able to forget him. He may slip into the shadows of my memory, at times, like some long past dream. But he's always there listening, watching. Touching, slightly, my daily actions.

Even now I pass groups of boys on the street, lost souls in dark clothes, their hair wiped before their eyes as though to protect them from the world that had become so distant from them. I see wrinkled old women cross the street so as not to pass too close to them, but I just stare, because it was Rob, and me, and the others.

Rob was everywhere for me, for a time, yet also nowhere. Everywhere, in that he colored the way I saw the world after that, and nowhere, in that I never saw him again. Never knew where he went, or even if he was alive.

Some days I'd drive by Burason's house, where he lived when I knew him. Just to see the place again, or I'd pull out the old letters and read them again. Most of what I knew about him came from those crumpled sheets of paper. He never talked much about himself, his past or his future, except in the letters that he'd written to Anne, back when things were going well.

He'd steal printer paper from the teachers' lounge, and scribble out great truths in his cryptic handwriting, as wavy and mixed up as his dark hair. He'd fold the paper twice, and slip it up into Anne's locker. She'd read them, and write back from what I could tell, and save his letters in an empty cookie tin beneath her bed.

I took them just after Rob left. She was pretty shaken up, and Abi and Lesa were worried her parents would end up with them. It wouldn't do anyone any good for it to get out what happened that year. It was over, by that point. So I ended up with the letters. To read and re-read. To be haunted by.

You were never ready when the car stopped.

That was how Rob first came to Incipien.

Chapter 2

I didn't think much of Rob one way or the other when he first came to Silva High. None of us did. I had a few classes with him. He dressed in dark clothes and sat near the back. He never talked in the beginning. Just stared off into the distance in such a way that no one could tell if he was listening to nothing, or to everything.

He never volunteered in class, but I had a sense his grades were good.

Decent at least.

He neither smiled nor frowned in particular. It was as though he were in another world, and only on occasion was dragged back into this cold, grey place in which he was, at that time, of little more consequence than a shadow.

I remember the first time I knew this planet was lucky enough to have someone like you in it, Anne. It was my first day here. Silva seemed at first such a drab and morose place to me. Mr. Bartlett's room smelled of old paint and sea spray from a can. He had long tables, and students' art pinned haphazardly to the wall. On one wall, a student had painted 'Draw Something Beautiful' in great loopy letters. (They always write "inspirational" things like that on the walls, don't they?)

I looked back over my shoulder at the long cinder block walls, just outside the classroom. They stretched out, deep into the school, plastered with posters warning of rape and drug use. I looked at the other kids who approached behind me, their faces sunken and pale, their clothes messed and practical, their frames just a touch large from too long spent typing essays. There was a little plant, sitting on one edge of the room, and I went and sat by it, a weak vestige struggling to hang on in this dim new world.

"Draw Something Beautiful," the sign said, and I wondered to myself what I could possibly draw in this place.

That's when you walked in.

Immediately, you were different from the rest of them. Where they shuffled reluctantly, regretfully, you walked tall and proud, as though you were going to your very own party. Your hair was dark and slightly curly, and you had it fixed perfectly for the first day of school. You smiled at your friends as you entered, completely above this grey place I had sunken into. And why wouldn't you? No room in that school was dark and dull when you were there.

Chapter 3

Rob always wrote like that. He didn't come across that way in person, but in the letters… they were meant only for Anne, so I try not to judge him for them.

The letters about the first few weeks were such a contrast to what this place became to him. It was his oyster, I think. But at first he saw only the crusty shell, caked with algae and rough sand. He found the pearl quickly, though, and by the end he didn't want to leave.

That last night, when he finally said goodbye to me, I thought I could see a tear on his cheek, but it was too dark for me to know for sure.

Chapter 4

You didn't sit near me, at first. And I didn't dare move to sit near you. 'Draw something beautiful' Mr. Bartlett said. I drew the plant.

I was so very lost in those days. The bell would ring, and streams of students flowed from the school, so anxious to go wherever they were headed. But I knew not where to go. The school was soon empty, and I didn't want the attention and probing questions I worried would come if I stayed too late. I never wanted to go home, though. Not then. Not until Felicity came some time later.

I would just find a park bench, and look at the trees, and wait.

I never met Burason. Not properly. From what I gathered, Burason was his last name, though I never heard Rob give the man a prefix. I pieced him together a bit from the letters, and the one time I saw his face, near the end. A tubby fellow, receding hairline. I believe he did IT work of some kind. Made enough to live comfortably but not extravagantly.

He'd had a pretty fucked-up childhood, apparently, though the letters never gave specifics. Only that he used to tell Rob "Fish eat fish, boy. They only come in two categories, and that's dependent on who's got the faster jaw."

Burason didn't say much to Rob, besides little catchphrases like that, and the occasional chore he wanted done. He didn't really want Rob, though Rob himself didn't understand that until later.

Chapter 5

I shuffled into school a few minutes or so before the bell rang. Usually people went straight up to their homerooms, ready to put their backpacks down after the walk inside, but on that gray August morning, the great foyer of the school was filled with neater-than-usual teenagers greeting their friends and lovers after the break.

Lesa appeared to my left.

"You look tired," she announced correctly. The two of us and Abi had been at my house the afternoon before. She'd had to go home to finish her Brown app (she was applying early decision).

"You smell funny," she next asserted, observant as usual.

Thankfully the bell rang before she had a chance to prod further.

The senior homerooms were fairly small, in order to provide more teacher-to-student support for college apps. Lesa was in a different homeroom that year, as were Abi and Tommy. So I took a corner seat near the back. They always had you play games on the first day. Ice breakers. Little activities that were intended to make you connect with people, but usually just ended up being awkward.

Mr. Johanson, who'd taught in small charter schools like ours since he was twenty five, didn't tend to force that kind of thing, unless people weren't talking on their own. There were a few tight circles that I dared not penetrate. One boy sat near the back, like me. He didn't speak to anyone, just stared, watching everything. I'd never seen him before, so I went to introduce myself.

"Hey, you're new, right?"

"Yeah." He studied me for a moment. "I'm Robert. Rob."

"I'm James."

I just stood there for a moment, looking elsewhere as awkward high school boys do.

"So what was your last school?"

"I just moved here from Centennial. Kurtz High."

I nodded.

"You like it here?" he asked me.

I nodded, with an equivocal grimace. "Yeah, it's pretty good." You wouldn't let yourself be too enthusiastic at that age. Certainly not about school. "Good water fountains."

Truth is there's been times since then when I thought Silva High was the best thing that ever happened to me. Perhaps the worst too, there at the end.

Chapter 6

Felicity came to Burason's a week and a half after I did. She was still pale, and didn't walk with the strength she once had. Burason put her in a room by herself, and wouldn't allow me to visit her. He locked her away, and put the key in his wallet.

He said it was for her sake. She needed to rest, to not be bothered by me. But of course it was nonsense. And I missed her terribly. She was one of those chosen people with an infectious mood. When she smiled you couldn't help following suit, but when she cried it broke your heart. She was one of the few people that truly understood me, I think. If anyone did. Things had once been wonderful for us, I used to tell her. She doesn't remember back that far.

Sometimes we would sit for hours talking about what things had been like.

Chapter 7

I didn't think I'd been particularly friendly with Rob at first. Not overtly so. But more so than anyone else, evidently, because when the latter half of lunch came, he appeared beside me. Not forcefully. Just standing there, a little way off.

After a moment, he walked over uncomfortably.

"Do you mind?" he asked carefully, as though he were asking to borrow some large sum of money.

"You want to sit down?" inquired Lesa, with a smile, before I had a chance to answer.

He eased his weight onto the dense plastic bench. He wasn't carrying any lunch.

"So you're the new kid, huh?"

Rob nodded.

"From Centennial," I added.

"That's cool." Lesa forced her pita into a little tub of hummus.

There were four of us there, besides Rob: myself, and Lesa, who I was dating at the time. Tommy, a sweet, quiet kid, with a good sense of humor. Been born in New York, just West of Allen Street. And Abi. Her and Lesa had been friends since childhood. Abi was the rebel of the two. Lesa was the sweetheart. Or so we used to say.

"So what's Centennial like?" Abi always had her lunch divided neatly into little Tupperware containers.

"Dry, open. Sometimes hot, sometimes cold.... Beautiful when you're willing to see it." Rob studied her.

"Sounds lovely." Abi laughed a little. She did that a lot.

"How'd you end up here?" asked Lesa.

He looked away for a moment. "I never stay anywhere very long."

Lesa watched him for a moment, trying to discern some meaning behind his words.

"Hey, you hear back from Brown today, right Lesa?"

It took her a moment to break away from that murky boy before her, but when she did face her old friend it was with an anxious smile, saying instantly that, yes, BROWN was written on her calendar in big bold letters, and, yes, she'd been unable to think of anything else all day, but, no, she had no idea whether or not she'd like what she heard.

"Yeah, I'm supposed to."

Abi grinned at her.

"You know what you're doing next year, Tommy?" Lesa finished off her pita bread and opened a bag of pretzels.

"No, I don't know."

"Are you going to college?"

"I have applied to a few, but I have not heard back yet." Tommy had a strange accent. It didn't sound like New York.

"Do you know what you wanna do… what was your name again?"

"Robert Johnson Tenebris. Rob."

"Good to meet you Rob," said Lesa with mock formality and a handshake. "I'm Lesa." She grinned. "So do you know what you want to do with yourself?"

"I don't know either."

"You gonna be rich?"

Rob shrugged. "Might be nice."

Lesa made a face.

"Stop, Lesa, you're gonna freak him out." Abi giggled again.

"What're you talking about, Abi?" She held the face, lips pointed down, fishlike, eyes bulging. "I look seductive. Right, James?"

"Sexy beast."

"Straight up Dr. Chua." We all cracked up.

"Who's Dr. Chua?" Rob asked curiously.

"The principal," I said. Lesa and I exchanged looks.

"He's got a bit of a reputation," she explained. "With his secretary."

Then the bell rang, and we all went to class.

Chapter 8

Do you remember the second Tuesday of art class? That was the first time I ever spoke to you, in person. We all drew numbers out of a hat, and you became my partner. We were doing portrait drawing, and we took turns modeling. I don't think my drawings ever did you justice.

You told me about your family, about growing up in Jernigan. How you liked art, brightly colored birds and funny television shows. How you couldn't swallow pills, and didn't much like going to the doctor as a result. I remember us laughing together. You were good about that. And you danced when you felt like it, even if there was no music.

I'm rambling, I'm afraid. I just wanted to write and say how very glad I am about today. You're a wonderful person, Anne. A star in a too dark sky.

Thanks for everything,
Rob

Chapter 9

"Do you want a rice cake, Lesa?"

She didn't answer. She had her head down on her arms which were folded on top of the cafeteria table.

It was a big room, with tall windows that were filled completely by the image of the pine forests that surrounded Silva High. Long thin plastic tables were spaced evenly throughout the room, and a stage with thick velvet curtains loomed at one end opposite the lunch counter.

"Okay, fine." Abi rolled her eyes, and took a bite of the rice cake herself.

Lesa had called me the previous night, sobbing. She'd gotten the letter from Brown, as promised. A thin letter.

Rob was sitting with us again. He didn't talk, though. He looked uncomfortable and out of place, like a beggar in a rich man's home. Grateful to be there, but scared that at any moment he would be cast out, back into the emptiness between the tables.

"So what're you gonna do? What's your plan B?" I didn't like seeing her down.

"Be a hobo," she mumbled without picking her head up.

"It's a pretty fucked-up system," she snarled suddenly, picking her head up. We weren't used to hearing her talk like that. Not at that time.

She was the girl who got straight As, who always raised her hand in class, who was enthusiastic about….

We all stopped eating.

"It's a pretty fucked up system. You put your whole self in. One hundred percent. And it spits you out, and says you're not good enough. I have fucking straight As! I'm taking AP classes! I haven't spent a Friday night doing anything but homework since the 8th grade. For what? For some fucking college to say no?"

"It's Ivy League," said Abi, smiling sympathetically.

"Who the fuck cares? I'm going to Devonroke like half the other people in this school. I could've been getting high with Duncan this whole time and it wouldn't 've made any difference."

She put her head down again.

"Maybe you should." Abi shrugged, taking a bite out of her carrot stick. "Seriously. I mean, it's senior year. Live while you can, you know?"

Lesa picked her head up wearing a fairly neutral, slightly thoughtful expression.

"What're you going to do instead? Go home and cry?"

"Sounds like a reasonable possibility." She took one of Abi's carrot sticks. "Do you have any?"

"I'll talk to Duncan. Okay, everybody meet by… your car," Abi nodded at Lesa, "after school."

"What're we going to do?" asked Tommy, looking confused.

"Have fun for once!" Abi exclaimed smiling.

Everyone else was stony faced.

Chapter 10

You didn't admit you'd never been fucked up before. That was one of the unspoken rules of high school, at least among the guys. It was like saying you were a virgin. A sure fire way to lose friends and party invitations. So if you didn't want to end up finding friends in the Anime club, or in a drug program, if you were on the other end of the spectrum, it was best to give only vague and cryptic answers when asked "do you smoke?" For that reason, most of us went into senior year not really sure who did and who didn't. Some people were obvious, like Duncan, who'd been the school dealer for years. Most people you weren't really sure about.

But as I got older, I began to find out that more and more people that I would not have suspected smoked weed on a regular basis. Silva had an increasingly lively party scene, which had led to a divide in our grade. And I'm sorry to say our group of friends was on the less glamorous side of it.

If you had asked us then, we would've, for the most part, said that we did drink, and we did smoke, and that'd we'd slept with plenty of girls, but that we simply didn't like the parties that some of the less pleasant people in our graduating class were famous for throwing.

I knew, however, that I had not been high before that year. That I'd never had enough beer to be drunk. And that the furthest I'd ever gone with Lesa was second base. These secret facts placed in me a subtle insecurity that haunted me whenever the subjects were brought up.

I had never made a conscious choice to be lame. It was more a matter of circumstance. Duncan and his friends had discovered the joys of reefer and partying, and mine hadn't yet, except of course Abi. And perhaps Rob. I never knew for sure.

There was a certain allure about their world. Duncan seemed forever calm, forever smooth. He was respected. When he smiled at a girl, she smiled back. And his group of friends was as close to each other as they come, bonded, I suppose, over long nights of throwing up together.

All of us saw it, except perhaps Tommy. And that's why all of us showed up at Lesa's car after school, though if they were anything like me there was a knot in their stomachs that made the walk quite difficult.

Rob even came over, apparently unsure if we'd meant for him to come or not. Lesa, as usual, made him feel comfortable, though. And we all quietly piled into Lesa's car, and were off.

Chapter 11

The first time I ever went to Barney's, you were there. Sitting at the counter, sipping a strawberry milkshake. You wore a flower print sun dress, and looked rather like one of the 50s Coca-Cola girls that were immortalized on various posters around the old soda shop. Yet, even in my memory of that day, you are not faded as they are, but vivid and very much alive.

You seemed angelic, sitting in that sweet, happy place. Children scampered around their mothers, ice cream cones in hand. The man behind the counter wore a white paper hat, and scooped ice cream as his wife, a short blonde woman, late 50s, with a wide smile, prepared toppings.

That was the day the business started, or at least the foundations were laid. But for that moment, for that hour, or however so long it actually was, the world seemed a sunny and good place. Because there was no Escobar yet, no Burason. There was just you, and the sweet things, and the children laughing, and the old man behind the counter, with his paper hat, smiling at the customers he'd known all their lives.

Chapter 12

"Barney's? That's where you go to get your weed?" I took my sunglasses off and rubbed at a big smudge that obscured my vision. It didn't come off.

"Abi says Duncan's meeting us here in forty five minutes." Lesa parked her newish sedan in front of the old soda shop. "You guys want some ice cream?"

Tommy wanted some, so we all went in.

There were a handful of other people from Silva. Anne Dawson sat at the counter with a few of her friends. A couple of girls from the soccer team sat near the back giggling.

We got some orders of French fries and waited. Thirty minutes. Forty five minutes. An hour.

"Duncan's unreliable as fuck," exclaimed Lesa at one point, shaking her hands dramatically as she said it.

"Why do you buy from him then?" Rob had his hands placed thoughtfully on the table in front of him. It was the first thing he'd said since we'd gone inside.

"He's the only one at our school dealing," Lesa said after a moment.

"There's Escobar," Abi said factually. She had curly blonde hair. When she smiled, she did it with her whole face. Her laugh was loud and frequent, and she seemed to always say what was on her mind.

"I'm not buying from Escobar!"

"Who's Escobar?" asked Rob, eating a french fry. "Pablo Escobar?"

"No, it's not a person" I told him. "At least not in the local vernacular use of the word. Escobar's a group, has the market pretty much locked up here in Incipien. Wiped out all of the competition seven or eight years ago. Except for a couple high school kids. They just ignore guys like Duncan as long as they stick to their niche."

"Why not buy from Escobar?" Rob nodded to an old Corvette clock hanging above our table.

"Cuz' I don't wanna get my brains blown out." Lesa stood up. "I'm gonna go take a piss."

Rob looked at me inquiringly.

"Duncan's a nice guy. He smokes a lot." I gestured at the clock as Rob had done. "But he's chill. Gets along with everyone. I doubt he owns a gun." I ate the last of the french fries. "With Escobar, things get messy sometimes. Not a one of them that doesn't have a gun. You need it for the initiation." I smiled sinisterly.

I was being dramatic, and I knew it, but Rob just nodded and looked away, as though distracted by something.

"This is good ice cream," Tommy said.

"Gonna make me fat," Abi mumbled to herself.

I followed Rob's eye. He was staring at the group of girls at the counter.

"Hey Rob, you wanna go to the front and get me a spoon, so I can help Tommy with his Sundae?" I said, with a smile. "I don't wanna make Abi get up."

"Oh, I don't—"

I stopped her.

Rob looked at me questioningly. He didn't get it.

"On the far side of the counter," I prompted.

He stood up slowly, turned, and walked towards the counter. Anne was swiveling slightly on her stool, talking to a thin brunette I recognized but did not know by name.

Anne had shiny black hair that was usually arranged carefully. She was small, in height and scale. Her skin was a soft smooth pink, almost glowing when she was in a good mood. She moved in a springy yet graceful way, portraying her mood across her whole body. She smiled more often than not, which contributed to her nice, gentle look that, from everything I had heard, matched her disposition.

You could understand why Rob was taken with her. Even from halfway across the room, I could tell he was watching her. I suppose she must've been able to tell as well.

I was glad to see she smiled at him, as he walked past, and based on his body language, I think he smiled back. He didn't stop walking, but for a moment though, then, without saying anything, he got my spoon and sat back down.

"Do you know Anne?"

"Who?"

"Anne Dawson. The girl at the counter?"

"Oh, yeah. We have art together."

I nodded. Lesa came back from the bathroom.

By the time Duncan finally came, the horizon burned red and orange with the falling sun, and long shadows grew from the objects that had been well lit at the time of our arrival.

"We're closing," the man in the paper hat said apologetically.

And there, before we had a chance to get up, was Duncan, appearing like an apparition just on the other side of the front window. Lesa and Tommy went over to the counter to pay the bill, while the rest of us went outside to meet him.

Duncan apologized to us, but he still seemed a little lost somehow. His eyes darted around, he stumbled over his words, and I thought I could see his hands shaking slightly. He lacked his usual calm. He handed us a paper bag, Abi passed over the money we'd collected, and Duncan nodded and was on his way. Lesa and Tommy emerged from the old ice cream store, and we all piled back into Lesa's car.

Chapter 13

The last rays of the old sun sank behind the Western pines just as Lesa parked her car on the shoulder of some old windey road. Her headlights flicked off, and we were alone together in the dark.

There was a little dirt path that wove through the tall pines, and we followed it back deeper and deeper into the darkness.

"Not much farther," Abi whispered, as though speaking too loudly would alert some wily beast to our presence.

The canopy was short and thick, and I could make out very little in the shadows that enveloped us. After a while, a bit of light appeared ahead, and soon Abi led our little tribe into a clearing with mowed grass, and a rough dirt road that seemed to be part of some government park. On one end of the clearing, a metal structure rose up above the trees. It had once been red and white, I suppose, but the paint was now heavily chipped, and the ladder seemed only loosely attached.

"What is that?" asked Tommy.

"The old fire tower." Lesa stared at it, intrigued.

"Come on!" Abi grabbed the first rung of the ladder.

"That doesn't look very strong, Abi." Lesa looked at the latter skeptically.

"It'll be fine," Abi said.

And soon we had all climbed the thin little ladder, and sat cross legged on the hard metal floor of the pavilion at the top of the tower. Chest-high walls had been added to keep fire personnel from going over the edge, back before the tower had fallen out of use. It was lovely, though. You could see over the trees, all the way to downtown Incipien, glowing slightly in the distance.

The moon had come out by that time, and had cast us all in a dim, surreal light.

Abi opened Duncan's paper bag.

She rolled first, and the rest of us watched carefully, to save ourselves the embarrassment of admitting we didn't know how.

The fire tower seemed to burn that night, as smoke wafted up from beneath the painted metal roof.

"You can see forever," said Rob. "I am with you lot and you can see forever."

That was how it felt, too. For that night, for those hours of that night, the rest of the world was distant and strange, and all that mattered was the shimmering stars, the soft light of the moon, and the people you were with.

I banged on the hollow metal floor, and Tommy and the girls danced around giddily. I think Abi took her shirt off at one point. That was how free we felt.

We sat for a long time. Just sat.

Rob stared off into the darkness, mostly. He'd look back at us sometimes: Lesa waving her arms above her head, Abi unclipping her bra, and he'd smile in a distant, sort of almost paternal way. Not condescending, but as though he were in a different world that only intersected momentarily with that of the rest of us.

When our high sank down with the moon we cleaned ourselves up as best we could, tried to mask the smell with Abi's aerosol spray, and began the walk back towards Lesa's car.

Chapter 14

The next day Mr. Bartlett's class finished up the portrait project and Rob and Anne went back to different sides of the classroom, Anne to her group of friends: the thin brunette with ringlets, from the soda shop (I'd heard her name was Judy), a pretty red head, a friendly dark haired girl who often sketched dresses, and Rob to the, well, the "quieter" side of the room, where he tried to look busy rather than lonely.

That was a hard time for him. A new school, and new town. And the one thing that had remained steady in his life, Felicity, had been all but taken from him.

"I never see her," he told me once. We were at Abi's getting drunk. The others had gone outside to chase cars. That was one of the few times he ever talked even semi-openly with me. "Burason keeps her locked away all the time. She eats in there, sleeps. Fuck, she could be dead for all I know." He finished his drink.

"Did you ever ask him about it?"

"He says to me, that she, she's doing well, you know? Getting better. But still not well enough to see me. What kind of fucking bullshit is that? You know? I know Felicity, an— maybe he has killed her, and doesn't want me to know. You know? The little fucker."

He stared at the wall for a while, and I looked away, so as not to make him uncomfortable.

"He never talks to me, you know? Except, do this Robert. Sweep this out before dinner. Then he'll go off and eat in his room, and I clean up.... It's not even that he works me so hard. It isn't worse than Centennial in that respect. It's just, there's nothing else. It's like he pretends I'm not there."

Rob told some joke after that, and wouldn't speak any more about himself.

Chapter 15

Dear Anne,

I hope you don't mind me writing you this letter. Mr. Bartlett hung up all the portraits today, including the one you did of me, and I realized I never told you how good it was. You have a talent, and a lovely style.

I enjoyed meeting you, and I hope you have a wonderful rest of the year.

-Rob Tenebris
Locker 99

He dropped that on the table one day as he was leaving English class. I don't think he meant to send it, but I slipped it in Anne's locker when no one else was around.

Chapter 16

Pandora's box was opened, and none of us were going back anytime soon. We got fucked up when we had the chance. Lived, you know, like we were dying tomorrow. Except Tommy. He never smoked. He'd come along, but he'd just smile and joke around, the only sober one in a crowd of fools.

Looking back on it all, Tommy was more of a man than I was. When I didn't smoke, I felt like a pussy, and I'd lie and say I was something other than what I really was. Tommy never had airs like that. We all knew who he was. He was honest, about his abilities and also his inadequacies.

He ran a risk, doing what he did. People that don't go along with what their friends do tend to get left behind.

As for the rest of us, Lesa finished up her apps to several state schools, which didn't seem bad at all, once she had a chance to get used to them. Rob, meanwhile, kept watching Anne. Never followed her or anything. I doubt anyone noticed but me. But he was… tuned in to her.

She'd taken to holding Duncan's hand in the halls. Apparently they'd become a couple, which was a surprise to everyone, and most painful for Rob. Anne had tended to date the nice, even slightly nerdy guys, but Duncan was charming, and most girls like her reached a place, I suppose, where they liked, for a short while, to imagine themselves badass.

Of course that status was always relative to what had come before it, and in Anne's case, she seemed to deem the relationship status in and of itself sufficient. She didn't party with Duncan, didn't drink, didn't smoke from what I heard. I'd have been surprised if they even slept together.

But guys like Duncan could afford to be patient, since there were always three or four other girls on the side.

Chapter 17

Dear Anne,

I was so happy you wrote back! I didn't fully expect to send the previous letter, but I'm glad now that I did!

That's interesting about your art teacher when you were young. That does sound like a good way to learn it. And one impressive cat! Have you ever tried oil painting, since then?

Kindest regards,
Rob Tenebris

PS- Are you going to Kelby's party Saturday?

Chapter 18

"What'd you think, Rob?"

He looked at me confused. He hadn't been listening, and I knew it.

"Yes, or no?"

He smiled uncomfortably.

"Just say yes." I winked at Lesa.

"Yes?"

"There, he said it."

Lesa raised an eyebrow. "James and Abi think we should go to Kelby's party tomorrow night."

"You don't wanna go?"

"Hell no. It's gonna be a bunch uh slutty girls throwing up all over themselves, while the guys act like idiots. Are you into that kind of thing, Rob? Do you wanna go?"

"Oh, come on, Rob!" Lesa and I'd been teasing each other about it all morning. "Come with us!"

"Maybe.... I'll think about it."

"Okay." I took a sip of chocolate milk. "Think about getting pussy," I whispered loud enough for Lesa to hear. If I went she'd have to go, and she knew it.

Chapter 19

Dear Anne,

I totally get what you mean about the parties. I think I'm more of a "hot-chocolate-by-the-fire" kind of a guy myself.

And yes, the fumes are killer. Literally, I've heard, on occasion.

But that sounds like a wonderful place to paint. Do you think you'll ever go back someday? I'm sitting in my cold, dark house imagining being there beneath a palm tree, white sand beneath my toes, dabbing here and there on a painting. Sounds like a dream life.

Do you want to travel on your own someday?

Kindest wishes,
Rob Tenebris

Chapter 20

The thick wheels of my SUV finally slowed to a stop on their usual mark. I breathed a sigh of relief.

Lesa and Abi climbed out. We were very tired, our eyes bloodshot, and all we wanted to do was lie down and sleep.

Without saying anything I pulled the key from my pocket.

"There's someone on your front porch." Abi didn't seem entirely sure of it.

"Psh. My parents aren't back 'till Monday night."

"You sure?"

My head hurt.

"Stay here." I walked over to see who it was.

"James?"

"Rob? What the fuck are you doing here?"

His eyes were redder than ours, though in a different way. His clothes were ruffled and sweaty, and there was blood on his forehead.

"I'm sorry. I didn't know where…." He trailed off weakly.

"It's fine, man. I just— what's going on?"

Rob had decided not to go to the party, as had Tommy, expectedly. He now eased himself back into the wicker rocking chair he'd been in before, as though he now lacked the strength to stand.

Lesa and Abi, hearing Rob's name came from around the side of the house.

"Rob!" they both exclaimed, before they really saw him.

"Rob, what happened?"

Lesa turned to me. "You should unlock the door."

"James, I need your help with something." Rob looked up at me with a slight frown. In a single moment he seemed both a scared child and a grown man. He'd swallowed life whole, seen some rough shit in his day and kept walking anyway, but it was not with the vigor that young men do. "I need you to help me do something."

"What is it, Rob? You should probably come inside."

"I'm scared there isn't time."

"Time for what, Rob? What's going on?"

"Felicity. I saw Felicity tonight. I went to visit her. Only, she's not herself. I only saw her for a moment, from across the room. But she was not herself, James. She was not herself. I think Burason's been drugging her. I don't know why. But she was not herself."

I was confused. "So, what'd you wanna do, Rob?"

"I wanna fucking kill the son of a bitch!"

"What?"

"You heard me." His stern face melted away and he turned from the hardened warrior back into the lost child. "I've got to, James. I've just got to. Felicity might die if she stays in there. I've gotta save her."

We were all frozen, just looking at him. I was tired. Too tired to think. I couldn't deal with this now.

"Where can I get a gun?" He said it so softly, I thought I hadn't heard it at all, except that I could see the shine of his eyes in the dim orange glow of the street light. He looked up at me, expectantly, as though all the world lay on my irresponsible shoulders.

I studied him slowly.

"You said she was sick, didn't you?"

I stared at him.

"Yes. From what happened in Centennial."

"I don't have any idea where to get guns. Not without a permit."

His face sank.

"Rob, Felicity needs you here, not in prison." I stopped for a moment, trying to measure his expression in the dim light. "You will go to prison."

"And Felicity'll go to th' Pearly Gates, if she stays in there." He was on the verge of tears.

"What makes you so sure it's Burason? You said yourself she was sick. Maybe he's doing all he can, and it just isn't enough."

He didn't say anything.

"My parents are gone. We don't have any guns. You can stay here this weekend, if you want. And then figure out what to do next when we're all in a clearer state of mind."

"Okay," he said weakly. The talking had worn him out. He barely had the strength to make it up stairs, much less kill anyone.

We all went to sleep, laid our heavy, full heads on my parents' pillows and dreamed of places near and far.

Chapter 21

We rested that weekend. I knew Rob was worried about Felicity, but he knew he needed to get his strength back, and to clear his head. Rash action could as easily make things worse as better.

I watched TV some, which he glanced at with curiosity, but not much sustained interest. One night we watched *Scarface*, the old Al Pacino movie. He seemed to like that. It was the only time he sat for more than twenty minutes.

He stayed upstairs a lot of the time. Wrote lots of letters to Anne. Some long, some short. I never read them, then. But I'd see him writing.

He asked to borrow my camera one day, and walked outside for a long time. I didn't know at the time what he was taking pictures of. He deleted them all before returning my camera to me.

Lesa and Abi came over often, and sometimes Tommy. Abi made protein shakes that looked pretty but tasted disgusting. Lesa would drink them and comment on how *healthy* they tasted. Tommy brought his own food by that point.

We went for long wandering walks. And sat on the front porch telling stories. We'd walk down to the soda shop and get ice cream or French fries, or both.

Sometimes Rob went with us. Sometimes he did not.

Occasionally I heard him crying at night, but he was too proud to ever do it in front of anyone.

Monday, my parents came back, and we all returned to school. I don't know where Rob slept at that time. I suspect beneath a bridge or in some other public place. It was too late for him to return to Burason's, and I think he would've preferred the bridge anyway.

"Does Burason know you saw Felicity?" I asked him once.

"Yes."

"What did he say."

"He was very angry."

"Did he say anything?"

"I don't remember."

He had a big scar on his forehead after that. If the teachers said anything, Rob would've lied. He didn't like people meddling. There'd been enough of that already. He didn't trust them.

"The systems broke," he told me often. But he would never give specifics in regards to which system he meant, or in what respect it was broken.

Monday, we heard the news that Duncan had been arrested. Someone had given photos to the police, apparently, that showed him clearly in several transactions. If the more extreme rumors were to be believed, there were also photos of Duncan making love to the thin brunette from the soda shop, included for good measure.

Chapter 22

You never let them see you sitting alone. Rob had been lucky in that he'd found a place with Lesa, and Abi, and Tommy and me early on and was saved the discomfort of the lost wanderers.

Those that sat by themselves fell into two categories. The bulk where the asocial, the lowest caste of the school. Their clothes were haphazard and often dirty, and their hair was tossed and unkempt. Many had learning disabilities or mental illness, or had been ruined socially by some trauma in their past.

Occasionally, you saw people sitting by themselves that didn't seem to belong with those that did not belong. In some cases they were quite popular (the ones that didn't have to worry about being thought asocial). They were pretty, and funny, and kind, but they were sad. They sat by themselves because they felt alone, and no longer wished to pretend otherwise.

Anne had nowhere to sit after the photos were released. She sat on the end of an end table, and pretended to do homework as she ate. The entire school, after all, was talking, at that time, about how she'd been blindsided by her best friend. Duncan wasn't coming back to Silva, it turned out. Even if he got off, he'd been expelled. And to make matters worse, her parents had heard about it.

That was Rob's in. Under normal circumstances, he could only expect courtesy from her, for she was more popular than us, and particularly him. But now she needed someone she could trust, needed someone period. So, when Rob went over to talk to her and invited her to sit with us, she, reluctantly, agreed.

She was courteous.

Chapter 23

"Where the fuck're we gonna get shit from, now that Duncan's gone?" Lesa was working on her math homework. Rob, Abi, Tommy, and I sat around her living room. Her parents were still at work, and Anne only hung out with us during lunch, and even then she seemed distracted.

"Who do you think turned him in?" Abi was painting her toenails, which made the place smell like brain damage.

I had a pretty strong suspicion who turned Duncan in, but I didn't say anything.

It was quiet for a bit. Lesa kept doing her math, Abi kept painting her nails, and Tommy looked at the old photos Lesa's mom had placed here and there along the shelves.

"I think Burason might be an addict." Rob didn't fidget like the rest of us.

"On what?" I was eating leftovers from the fridge.

"Pills, I think. Either that or he's fucked up in the head, you know? He's always coming in with these little paper bags with orange bottles. The kind pills come in. I found a huge pile of 'em in one of the closets. Hundreds. No labels, though."

"Damn." I added more salt to the food.

"You keep telling us about that guy…." Abi's nails were now blood red.

"Sorry.. I was just making—"

"Oh, I'm kidding!" She smiled at him. "But, do you guys—"

"Abi, let him finish." Lesa lay on her stomach, thick math book in front of her.

Abi turned to Rob. "More?"

Rob shook his head.

"Bitch!" Lesa faked a cough.

"Excuse me, what did you say?"

"Nothing…."

"Well, anyway, I was thinking we should go do something fun!"

"Like?..."

"Like, I don't know. Just something. Anyone have ideas?"

We all stared ahead blankly.

"No Duncan."

"Lesa, you're just sitting there doing your freakin' math homework."

"Like I said, no Duncan."

"How much you figure a guy like Duncan made?" Rob cut in. "Say, in a month?"

"I dunno." Lesa kept her eyes on her paper. "Decent money for a high school kid. Even enough to get a small apartment when his parents threw him out."

"He got an apartment?"

"Yeah, a decently nice one, actually."

"Anyone else in the school deal?" Rob leaned forward in his seat, subtly.

"No. Not on a major scale anyway. That's how Duncan made as much as he did."

"Sounds appealing," I joked. Rob didn't laugh, though. He was focused on something. Completely. With the entirety of his body.

"Where did he get his supply?"

Chapter 24

Dear Anne,

She sounds like a lovely girl. Do you miss her now that she's away at college?

I have one sister, Felicity, who I love very much. It's just the two of us.

We live with a man named Burason. He is not particularly pleasant. But the courts have made him our "father". I sleep elsewhere, as often as I can, but Burason still has Felicity, and that's why I cannot leave him completely.

Someday I would love to get an apartment just for the two of us, and the people we love. No Burason, no pale faced women in pants suits.

As it stands, he keeps her in a room, and will not let me visit her, because he says she is tired and ill and needs to rest. I have known her all her life, and if she is sick, I should be the one to care for her! I snuck in last night. It was the first time I have spoken with her in months. I am afraid she is very sick. Her skin used to shine like silk, when we lived in Centennial, but now it is as dry and pale as this page before you. Her eyes have become dull and distant, and she does not stay with me more than ten or fifteen minutes before she falls back into the world behind her eyelids.

I am afraid she is dying, but I know not what to do. I have no money, nor do I have power over Burason. I feel as weak as I ever have.

I hope you do not mind me saying so very much to you. I realize that we do not know each other well, and normally I don't complain as I do now. But there is something about you. When we spoke in art class, everything about you seemed somehow good. Even your flaws, which you yourself admitted, seemed to me inextricable pieces of a wonderfully perfect whole.

Even in writing this excuse, I have no doubt said too much. If I have, I apologize. But please know that I mean them with the most sincere honesty and respect.

Kindest Wishes,
Rob Tenebris

PS- When you were dating Duncan, did he ever discuss business with you?

Chapter 25

Robert,

Don't apologize for your letter. It's been a lonely time for me, and you've been very kind. Please tell me if there's any way I can help you and your sister. It sounds like a terrible situation you're in.

I miss my sister very much, but at least I know she's safe and happy where she is. And that we will be together again soon.

If your sister is as sick as you say she is, she needs to be seen by a doctor. Even if that means going to the Police. I know you will do everything you can to save her.

Duncan did not talk business with me. I saw that side of him only once, when one of his suppliers had a meltdown while we were having dinner, and I went with him to help the man.

Sincerely,
Anne Dawson

Chapter 26

"I know where Duncan got his shit from." Rob sat down at our lunch table dramatically.

Anne and Tommy were off meeting with some club. Student Council, or Prom Committee, or Astronomy, or whatever it was they were a member of.

"Where?" Abi arched her back a little.

"Some mountain man type. Lives in the woods just on the other side of the highway. Apparently he's got some field back there that nobody but him ever goes to, and he sold to Duncan."

"That makes sense" Abi sat her sandwich down.

"Yeah." Lesa frowned. "Escobar would have all the big importers around here tied up."

"So can we buy directly from the mountain man?" Abi looked at Rob. She did that a lot.

"I think so. I'm just worried we won't be able to buy enough."

"Enough for what?" There was anxious curiosity in Lesa's voice.

"Enough to supply the whole school."

It got quiet for a moment.

Rob squinted, trying to feel them out.

"I need money," he said slowly. "They want Mary Jane." He looked around the lunchroom: all the people, all the groups. "And old beards n' overalls sure as hell can't walk in here to start handing it out."

It was quiet.

"We could make good money." I looked at Lesa. She seemed concerned.

"Twelve years."

"What?" I asked her.

"Twelve years we've been doing this. Getting up, going to school. Stay up late doing homework. Twelve years.... We get caught. Fuck, we get caught one time. It screws all that up. Screws up your whole future."

It was quiet a little longer. Rob seemed to look at something far off in the distance.

"You're right," he said finally. "You shouldn't throw all that away."

"And you're not going to do it either, right?"

He didn't say anything at first.

"Right?" She leaned forward in her seat, staring at him.

"You've got a future, Lesa. You're nice, you're smart, you're pretty. You'll get a respectable job, and find a nice husband, and raise good kids. But that's not me." Rob said this as cold as I think I'd heard him say anything to that point. "You think Burason's gonna pay for me and Felicity to go to college? You think Uncle Sam is? Fuck, I don't even know if I'd know how to be normal after.... Look, what I can do is take care of Felicity. Maybe if I make enough, she can even go to college and live some normal suburban lifestyle. At the very least, we'd have the chance to be free."

Lesa didn't say anything. She was quiet for the rest of lunch. She did not acknowledge what he said, because she didn't want to believe it, but she did not dispute it, because deep down she knew it was true.

Chapter 27

Rob got our first big wholesale buy through on a Thursday evening. Just in time for the biggest selling day of the week.

You never knew how many people smoked until you started dealing. Some kids were pretty obvious, proud even, and did it as often as their wallets could support. Far more of them, however, in head count if not spending, were good apparently "straight" kids. People like Lesa, and though I wouldn't have admitted at the time, me. People that were scared of being remembered as nerds, of having no stories to tell their children and grandchildren, and of being the damp sock in their circle of friends.

At the same time they wanted discretion. They had reputations worth keeping clean.

We made almost two hundred dollars the first day, and spoke with many more who promised to buy in the future. Soon I had more money than I'd had in my entire young life. I felt like a king, as though I could buy anything, do anything, be anything. Yesterday I had been a schoolboy, weak and undeserving of respect. Today I stood among Don Corleone and Tony Montana. Today I was a man. Today I had a reputation.

It was strange how people treated you differently once they found out. Some people that I'd known since kindergarten now would not look at me. (But I dismissed it telling myself it was them not me.) And there were others, lots of others, that viewed me as I'd come to view myself: a man deserving respect.

They held doors for me, deferred to me when we worked together in class, gestured for me to go ahead of them when we stood in line. They were little things, to be sure, but they made me feel very big.

Lesa and Tommy stayed out of it for the most part. Unlike Rob they had a future, unlike Abi they weren't badass, and unlike me they didn't wish they were badass. I suppose Lesa kept me grounded through it all, as much as she could anyway.

"You guys don't seem like drug dealers," she said at one point.

It was true. We dressed more like Ivy League boys than thugs, our grades were decent, and we acted generally as we had before.

"I'm sorry, but you don't." She smiled sympathetically.

"That's exactly why we'll be good at it," Rob said without even looking up.

He kept a level head through it all. I respect him for that. It's what we needed, though I began to see in him a certain aloofness that I both envied and despised. He was never really with us. I think he wanted to be, but he was not. For the same reason he could not live the suburban dream like Tommy and Lesa, and eventually me, he could not be truly with us. He was in the horizon. Staring off into the clouds, or the darkness, or something far away of which the rest of us would never know.

But access to that special place came at a cost. In his years of forced wandering, he'd lost the ability to connect with us. What he and Felicity went through had shaped him to be a rare beast of sorts, something that was neither familiar to us, nor familiar with us.

Chapter 28

We were often approached by people with strange requests. To help their kid brother who had a problem with a bully (they assumed we were intimidating), or how they could be more badass (they assumed we were cool).

One day a thick redheaded boy approached us as we were leaving school. I recognized him from my Spanish class. Cody was his name, I think. On the quiet side, wore camo a lot. Had a lower-class southern accent.

He seemed uncomfortable. That wasn't unusual for people asking things of us.

"I don't mean to bother you," he began, not making eye contact. "You know Abi Drake?"

"Yes," Rob said dryly. Lesa and I stood a little ways behind him.

Cody fidgeted with the zipper of his heavy camo coat, then he looked up suddenly at Rob. "Are you and her a…." He trailed off.

"No." Rob neither smiled nor seemed particularly upset. There was only a cold calm about him, as usual.

"Oh! That's good, I mean, that's— I was wonderin' if you'd be okay w'th me askin' her out, y'know. I mean, I thinks she's a real special—"

"You may ask her. Whether she does is up to her."

"Sure, sure, of course. I just—I wanted to invite her huntin' w'th me this weekend, and I figured she'd wanna go, only I didn't wanna step on any toes w'th you and your lot, seein' as how she talks about you so much and all."

Rob nodded conclusively and walked past the redhead who looked as confused as ever.

Rob stopped suddenly and turned. "Did you say you were going hunting?"

Chapter 29

Rob was very excited about his new gun. It was an old shotgun. The wood was worn and the metal was slightly rusted, but to him it was power. He even got a new duffel bag big enough to accommodate it.

"You can't bring that to school!" Lesa declared.

"Watch me." He had to take some of the books out so it'd fit.

Abi wasn't in a particularly good mood at that point either. "Why did you tell that guy he could ask me out?" She questioned Rob on another occasion.

"His right. I didn't endorse him one way or the other." Rob went back to cleaning his gun.

"Rob's blind," Lesa said to me when the two of us were alone together.

Her room was full of colors. Soft pinks and yellows. She talked often about redecorating it, making it "more mature," but I liked it. There was something calming about being there. Just me and her.

I ran my hand along the quilt on her bed. It was very quiet, except for the hum of a fan on out in the hall.

"Would you date Abi, if I wasn't here."

I studied the weave on her quilt. It was very small and tight. "I wouldn't date anyone if you weren't here." It was an effort at a romantic dodge, I suppose. But I would not have dated Abi anyway.

"Do you think Rob likes her?"

"How should I know?" I lay back on top of her made-bed and closed my eyes, my hands behind my head. Lesa sat in front of her mirror, fidgeting with makeup and brushes and the like.

"Oh, come on, James. You know, don't you?"

"They're friends, aren't they?"

"I mean does he like her the way you like me?"

"No."

I opened my eyes and gauged her response. She looked a little dejected.

"No?"

"No."

"That's too bad."

"Why's that?"

She picked up her purse. "Come on, our reservation's in 15 minutes."

Chapter 30

"James and I saw Burason at the restaurant last night."

It was break. I leaned against the wall, light streaming in from the window behind me. Tommy was there, and Rob and Lesa of course. Abi was eating rice cakes, and the less common Anne was there as well.

"He was with a woman," Lesa continued. "Curvy, blonde hair. A little younger than him."

Rob said her name was Hunny. "She pretended to be his wife when Burason filed to get us. They don't like giving kids to single men." He turned and looked out the window.

"It's Friday," Abi said changing the subject. "What're we gonna do tonight?"

That we were expected to do something was a mock assumption, but we all played along.

"Why don't we all meet by my car after school," suggested Lesa, "and we'll see if we can't find something fun to do!"

I heard long toe nails clicking on the synthetic tile floor.

"Sounds good," said Abi. "Is everyone in? Anne?"

Anne hadn't ever hung out with us outside of school, but she smiled a little. "Sure" she said with a shrug.

I know Rob was glad Anne was coming, but he was too distracted to say anything. I looked and saw it too: A large German shepherd walking down the line of lockers towards us. Attached to him, by a thick black leash, was a tall cop, studying the lockers as though he could see through them.

"Fuck," I said. "Is there shit in yours?"

"Come on," Rob said, neither nodding nor shaking his head. Anne was one of the few people in the school that didn't know, and he wanted to keep it that way.

We ran to Locker 99 and emptied it into Rob's extra-large duffel bag.

"Now what?" I said looking up at him.

The dog appeared at the other end of the hall, coming towards us still. The hall was a dead end. We walked past the dog, it would smell what we had. We stood there, the dog coming closer. Every step, every click of its claws, and I felt myself falling into the abyss of the lost persons. It was then that I began to realize that I, unlike Rob, did have a future to lose. I thought of the cold walls of a jail holding cell, my mother being disgraced, my ambition to go to college dashed—

"We can't get caught, Rob. I can't get caught."

"No shit." He glanced around. Grabbing me by the collar he half dragged me into an adjacent classroom.

A wrinkly faced older teacher, a woman, in a frumpy flower print dress, sat at her desk. I didn't know her name. I was on the edge of a breakdown, a fucking breakdown. I was gonna go up to the cop and spill all of it on the floor. I was gonna tell him—

"No students during break!" the woman declared, irritably.

I was gonna tell him how I was sorry, that I was from a good family. That both my parents had been to college, that I intended to go, and had the grades for it, and this had all been some crazy game that I hadn't understood. A game. Yeah, that was it. That's what it had been. Just some kids trying to be Al Pacino. A game. A game that—

Rob pulled out his gun. He aimed it right at her head.

The old teacher's mouth opened. She tried to speak, but for once she couldn't.

"You say anything," Rob said coldly, "I swear I will cover these fucking walls in your brains.... You yell, I ain't got nothing to lose. Not nothing to lose, not nothing to gain, except revenge. And that is the one thing I'll have before they drag me off."

She gasped for words.

"Not nothing to lose...."

It was very still. Very quiet. Only the sound of the dog's claws clicking across the fake tile floor. Rob and I didn't sit down, the lady didn't stand up. We just stood there. Rob watched the lady, I watched Rob. I had never seen him like that before, not all the way. Life had turned him cold. No sympathy shown in his eyes, no shutter in his hands. His hands were steady, his gaze un-flinching, and I honestly believed he might kill that woman for nothing but a little cry of fear. But she remained silent, so Rob just kept watching her, studying her. Understanding her, in an awful sort of way.

Finally the dogs were gone, and I started to breathe again.

"Let's go, Rob," I said. "Let's get out'a here."

He didn't look at me. He kept his eyes on the woman. She tried to look calm, kept her hands in her lap, but she was afraid of us. I could see it in her eyes, in her little quick movements that I don't think she could've helped.

Rob saw it. I know Rob saw it, and probably much, much more. But he didn't seem to care. He walked straight up to her, ran his hand along her desk. Her forehead would've touched the barrel of the gun had she only leaned forward.

"Come on, Rob, they're gone. Let's go." I pleaded.

But he didn't look at me. He was looking at several little picture frames on her desk. One that I figure to be from the late 80s, one that was more recent, of her, with her three adult children. They were smiling and they—

"Your kids," Rob said. "I suppose you love them, and take care of them, like my family, my family" (he nodded towards the hallway), "loves and takes care of me.... If anything happened to me, or to him" (he nodded towards me, now) "they would be sad, I think." (He leaned in towards her.) "Mad even. Mad. Mad at you?" (He put the newest of the pictures in his backpack.) "A crew mate for a crew mate." (He walked towards the door.)

Then turning back to her one final time: "Don't give them a reason."

And we left.

Chapter 31

"Fucking Hell, Rob! Fucking Hell!" I couldn't even put sentences together. Couldn't stand still. I—

"Calm down, James." He was surprisingly relaxed.

"I didn't sign up for this, okay! This—this isn't me. I'm just some kid, I got a future you know? I'm a—I'm a pretty nice guy! I don't go around blowing people's brains on the wall!"

He grabbed me by my shoulders. "Calm down." He was stern, and I fell quiet.

"I did not kill her. I did not intend to kill her, even if she screamed. But between scaring an old lady a bit, and going to jail, I did make a choice. If that is not the same choice you would've made, then I'm sorry—but, to be honest, I don't really give a fuck."

Chapter 32

The rest of the day passed like a hazy dream. There were colors and sounds, but it was as though I was an observer rather than a participant.

It'd all been pretend for me up to that point. I'd had some diamond studded fantasy, I suppose. Nice clothes and Escalades. The respect of women. *Pineapple Express* was a comedy, but Larry Hoover, Carlos Lehder, Frank Lucas: they were all killers. The blood made them shine, but I didn't know if I had it in me. If I'd been in Rob's tattered old shoes, no future if I put the gun down, no future if the fat lady yelled, what would I have done? Would I have pulled the trigger if she'd made a sound? Would Rob have?

These hard, rough-textured questions haunted me as I sat through the remaining classes. The lessons, the teachers, the pretty girls who were still innocent enough to smile, with their pastel camisoles, and their whispered jokes. People ate and talked, and did work now and then to fill the time. But I now occupied a different world from them. I knew not if it were above or below them, or perhaps only on a different plane. But we were different, and I no longer knew how to speak and be with them.

Chapter 33

We met by Lesa's car, after school. The others hadn't heard what'd happened, and I didn't tell them. What was I to say? Rob hadn't shot anyone. He hadn't hit anyone. It was just something in his eyes that haunted me, something I couldn't possibly describe.

So I met the rest of them at the car, in accordance with the casual plan. Lesa smiled in a friendly, bored sort of a way. Tommy grinned. Anne had an anxious smile; we were a new crew to her. And Rob looked calm as ever. Calm because he was distant.

We piled into the little sedan and rolled off, aimless in direction.

"So what you guys wanna do?" Lesa fingered the wheel lightly.

"Something fun for a change." Abi looked out the window coolly. Even after our recent discoveries, our invigorating plans seemed to deteriorate quickly into nothing.

"Like what?" Tommy looked at her. "We could go to my house and play some games?"

"Games? What, like video Games." Abi smiled at him sarcastically. "No, Tommy! Come on, we have to do something fun!"

"We could go to the tower," suggested Lesa.

"We always go to the tower," Abi whined. "Let's go to the river."

It was a dark slow-moving river, not far from the tower. The water was deep enough to swim, and tall trees kept it well shaded from the outside world.

"We could go to the river," Lesa agreed. "That okay with you guys?"

"What're we going to do at the river?" asked Tommy.

"Go skinny dipping." Abi responded immediately, without really thinking, I figure.

Lesa laughed uncomfortably. "Oh, that Abi. Always trying to get her clothes off!"

Anne glanced around, a slight smile. Trying to tell if it was a plan or a joke.

"Come on!" Abi justified. "It'll be fun! It's something you should do at least once in your life. Who's in? James? Rob?"

"Look, if we're going to do it, we should wait 'till it's dark," Lesa stated.

Abi agreed. So we went back to Lesa's house, and baked cookies, and waited for the sun to fall.

Chapter 34

The moon shown blue-green through the tall old trees, providing just enough light for us to slide down the muddy path that led to the water. The woods where lush. Ivy and ferns covered the ground below us, and the hard old trees formed a canopy above us, lending a tent like feel. The water was black, but for little patches that caught the shine of the moon.

It was an usually warm night. Abi was the first to slip her shirt off. Her breasts were large, and she held them in place with a large plain white bra. I knew not whether to be awkward in looking at her, or awkward in not, so I tried for some faux-casual combination of the two.

Crickets and frogs sang around us, and I stared off into the night for a moment, trying to see what it was Rob saw when he became lost in the shadows. I heard a zipper. Abi's thick brown skirt came down. Her panties were similarly conservative, but soon they were off too, revealing a small patch of blonde curly pubic hair. She reached to unclip her bra. "Rob, can you help me?"

Lesa stepped in before he could respond. "I'll get you, Abi." She did the deed and Abi's boobs fell several inches.

Her skin was rough, like her clothes, and she stretched in the warm night air. Stepping forward she eased her weight, one foot at a time onto the thick mud of the river bottom.

"Come on, guys!" she was waist deep.

I hesitated. I'd had a boner since Abi's shirt came off, and I didn't want

Lesa to see it. She looked at me and shook her head to say she wasn't going. That meant I wasn't either.

"What is she doing?" I heard Tommy whisper to Lesa. I didn't hear what Lesa said back.

"Who else is coming in?"

We all looked at the ground uncomfortably.

"Rob?"

"Maybe in a bit."

"Anne?"

The night sounded very much alive. Crickets and frogs sung everywhere, as though the very air were vibrating.

"Okay," Anne said softly.

"Yay!" Abi exclaimed, splashing the water a little. She let herself fall back into the river, and treaded water so that she appeared to be neck deep. I was half relieved her body had disappeared into the water.

Anne glanced at us, not saying anything. She didn't feel comfortable with this, but that was exactly why she wanted to do it.

She wore a white ruffled blouse. Even in the dim moonlight, I could see her hands were shaking slightly as she reached up to undo the first button.

Rob glanced at me. There was something strangely present about him, all of a sudden.

Anne slid her buttons from their holes slowly, carefully. Not allowing the sides of her shirt to gape until they were all free of each other. Finally the soft white cloth fell down like a picked flower to the mud behind her.

She seemed somehow more exposed than Lesa, more vulnerable. Even in her small lacy green bra she seemed somehow more naked than Abi who had nothing on at all.

Her soft white skin shone contrasting to the roughness of the black. Everyone, even Lesa and Abi stared at her.

She was quite thin, and moved gracefully, though we could all tell she was uncomfortable. She unfastened her jeans and allowed them to slide down her legs. She stepped out of them, and, seeing that we all stared at her, forced a sad pleading smile.

I looked away. It seemed a sin, almost an insult, for me to look at her a moment longer, when she was in that position.

But soon she was in the water, and the vigor of the cool river and the warm night air, and the crickets and frogs singing, and the moon shining overhead touched her, and she looked up at the night sky, like some primal she-wolf. A smile shone on her face, as pure and as genuine as African ivory, and she laughed at the absurdity and wonder of the world.

She gave a little yell, a battle cry, that was not directed at me, or Rob, or Abi, or any of us. It seemed to me a secret conversation between her and the world, between her and life.

That was what was wonderful about Anne, I suppose. One of the things anyway. She was not afraid to live. When she was sad, she was not afraid to let you see her cry, when she heard something funny, she'd be the first to laugh. And now, that place and that night, she saw the world through rose colored glasses, and she looked around at us and smiled, as though everything were right in the world.

"Who else is coming in?" Abi yelled at us excitedly.

Rob shifted his weight slightly, moving almost imperceptibly closer to the water.

But Abi saw it: "Rob! Why don't you come in?"

He waved his hand, dismissively.

"Come on, Rob! Anne and I are both in!"

"Only if he wants to, Abi." Lesa gave me a sideways hug as she said it.

"Rob, we can see your boner from here! Better come in the water to hide it."

"Abi!" Lesa released me.

Anne looked uncomfortable again. This was a sex game for Abi. I don't think it was anything of the sort for Anne.

I tried to step back more into the shadows. It made Rob uncomfortable too, I think. But he tore his clothes off as quickly as possible and slid into the water.

"Tommy? James? Lesa?"

Lesa shook her head.

Rob and Anne didn't look at each other. Only Abi seemed comfortable. The rest of them didn't know what to do with themselves.

"Toss me my purse, will ya' Lesa?" Abi cried.

It was flung to her, and she pulled out a lighter, some paper, and a bag of leaves. Standing chest deep, she rolled one and handed it to Anne, then one to Rob, then one for herself.

I could tell, even from the shore, that Anne had never smoked before. She held the joint with discomfort, with years of health class in her mind. That wasn't living to her, but there was a place of mind one reached, especially when with friends, that led you to do more than when you were level headed. So when Abi approached her with the lighter, she did not protest.

It seemed wrong to me, but I didn't say anything.

Abi splashed Rob in a flirty kind of way, when she lit his.

Soon smoke rose up from the water.

Anne wasn't inhaling, but again I kept quiet.

"Let's swim to the island!" Abi yelled suddenly. There was one just past the middle of the river, with trees on it, and a good bit of underbrush.

"Okay!" Anne agreed. And they all doggy paddled out into the darkness.

Lesa, Tommy and I were left alone on the bank. It seemed very quiet, and almost lonely at first.

"Was this the night you had in mind?" Lesa smiled up at me.

I patted her on the back tenderly.

I found Abi's lighter after a while and built a little fire.

"It'll help them find their way back," I gave as an excuse, but mostly I just wanted something to busy myself with.

It felt good, even in the warm night. We sat and talked, asked Tommy questions about his past.

He was a good kid. As I always said, he was more of man than me. I'd been good, before this year, but wanted to be bad. Now I was bad, but wanted to be good. Either way I was nothing but a pussy. Tommy. He never seemed to want anything but what he was, and he never seemed to pretend to be anything else. I respected that about him.

"Did you think they were sexy?" teased Lesa. "Abi and Anne?"

"I don't know," Tommy said smiling. "I guess so."

"Do you want their bodies?" Lesa gave a little laugh. She was joking.

"I don't think they like me like that."

"But do you like them like that?"

Tommy covered his smile in mock drama.

"Well, do you?"

"No!" he exclaimed finally.

"No? I don't believe you!"

We all laughed. Then Lesa suggested we sing campfire songs, and so we did.

Chapter 35

We were singing when we heard splashing and turned to see Abi emerge from the water violently. She ran to warm herself by the fire. She was very wet, and it was very dark, but I thought she was crying slightly.

"What happened?" Lesa asked. "Where're Rob and Anne?"

"They ditched me!" She said it like she was kidding, but I could tell she really did care. "They swam fast, and left me behind."

"That wasn't very nice," Lesa said sweetly, draping a towel over Abi's shoulders. "They should've waited for you."

We waited for hours, sitting there on the bank, with the little fire, talking about our pasts and our hopes for the future. We spoke of other things, but whenever the air grew quiet we looked back out, peered into the darkness, asking the unspoken question.

They might have drowned, I thought to myself. Or might've ditched us all.

The moon had fallen from the sky, and we were on the verge of going for help, when finally the two of them emerged from the water.

"Where the fuck have you been!" yelled Lesa, as they grabbed towels and dried themselves. "You ditched Abi! She could've drowned! And then you left us waiting around for you for half the night! We were worried sick! We were about to go call the cops or something, and we all would've gotten in trouble, 'cuz we thought you'd drowned or something."

"Sorry," Rob said without really looking at her. "We swam to the island, and lost track of time."

Chapter 36

Dear Anne,

I wanted to write.

As I sit here, though, I'm afraid I don't know what to say.

How do you feel about last night? I don't think it was right of me, seeing as you weren't in a clear state of mind. To be fair, though, neither was I….

What can I say? If you want me to forget, I will do my best. But irrelevant of what happened last night, and what happens in the future, I want you to know that for today, and for many days in the past, and no doubt for many days in the future, I admire and respect you very much. You have been a light atop a tower for me in these dark times, have guided me, inspired me, captured my very imagination. I feel so deeply in awe of you, and all that you stand for. I would stand by you, through danger, loss of life, loss of youth, happiness, and sadness. I don't pretend to think you feel the same, that you would desire to welcome someone imperfect into your world. But know that, whatever you decide, I love you.

Kindest Regards,
Rob Tenebris

PS- I wanted you to know: the tragedy with Burason is over. My sister and I are free, and I hope and pray now for her speedy recovery. The other of the two great women in my life.

Chapter 37

Dear Robert,

Thank you for your sweet letter. I lay on you no blame for what happened this weekend. It was unexpected, and completely new to me, but I was as much a participant as you.

I don't regret it. But, I don't want to do it again for a while. It's just too soon.

I was very glad to hear you and your sister are reunited! But how? Did the courts take you from Burason's care? Or was it his own doing? Please write with details (or tell me in person).

Much Love,
Anne Dawson

PS- I like Italian restaurants.

Chapter 38

Robert acted odd after that weekend. He'd always been odd, I suppose. Always a little aloof. But now he stared off into the distance more than he was present. And he was jumpier. You brushed him accidently when he wasn't looking, and he'd flip before he knew who you were.

He and Anne became a couple, which did him some good.

It was a very confusing period for her. In crazy times, guys like Rob suddenly seemed stable, when they would've seemed quite the opposite under different circumstances.

The first part of the week, I thought a lot about extricating myself from the whole thing, but I didn't know how, even if I wanted to. Lesa was in, and I didn't want her to think I was pussy. Even Tommy went along with it, though he did not actively participate. I couldn't do that, though. I was already too involved. It was either all the way in or all the way out.

Then there was the money. We were making a good bit of it. Sometimes in the good weeks Rob and I would both make almost a thousand bucks. Silva was a big market. Everyone, it seemed, smoked, and only a handful had the balls to buy from Escobar. So at times there seemed no limit to the amount we could make.

I was getting my license soon, and already fantasized about a car.

Something sexy. Something fast. My parents must've noticed the change. I was better dressed, I went out more. But they didn't ask any questions that couldn't be handled with a simple dodge. Occasionally, when times were tight, I even slipped them some money. When they were asleep, in a place they wouldn't think anything of. It was like Rob said, you took risks so your people could prosper.

I lived in fear for a short while that the old woman would expose what we had done, and that Rob and I would be swept away by well-armed cops one day. But it didn't happen. In time that memory became less vivid. The life we led no longer disgusted me, and again I was proud to be on top, raging against the system, earning money and glory.

So we kept the racket going, and it grew. We gained new customers, and began selling booze and even a little coke. It was crazy times.

We had more money than we knew what to do with, especially those of us with parents (we didn't want to raise suspicion). We'd go out a lot. See movies, concerts. That kind of thing, whenever we felt like it.

Rob was the primary puppeteer. Abi and I were key players. Lesa and Tommy didn't get involved, at least not directly, but we treated them as though they were in all the way. Most people thought they did as much as me.

Chapter 39

Dear Anne,

That sounds like a lovely garden. The deer do seem to cause trouble for gardeners here. In Centennial, it was the lack of water. Here: the deer. I guess everywhere's got something. But I think you should grow violets all the same. They're pretty flowers, and they're what you want to grow. Roses are also nice. Either of those would be lovely, I'd say.

Felicity is feeling better. Her legs were a bit shaky, at first, but today we went outside and I helped her walk around the back yard. The birds were singing, and one of the neighbors a little ways off was mowing his lawn, which smelled good. It was very peaceful.

It was the first time I've seen Felicity really smile in a long time.

This afternoon, I need to help Burason send some emails. To his former employer, friends, family, etc. Just letting them know what's going on. Once that's done with, Felicity and I will finally be free.

Also, in regards to your bedroom door: I agree, you should be able to keep it closed if you like. You're obviously old enough to have that right. Good luck.

-Rob

Book II: Anne Dawson

Chapter 40

Every little girl dreams of the man she will one day love. Charming princes, with great white horses, ready to ride off with us on some glorious Romantic adventure. Mysterious masked men, that will never be tied down, but that would no doubt fill our lives with excitement and passion. Men like our fathers, hardworking, subtle in their affection, but with as big a heart as any of them.

The men and boys we date are inevitably compared to these archetypes, and I'll admit, usually come up short, particularly in middle school. In those four years I dated exactly three boys, and went on exactly two dates between them. It was silly. I knew it even at the time. But it was practice, I suppose. All of us, boys and girls alike (though many of us didn't really know it yet), were waiting for that day when we would really, truly fall in love.

Sure, the boys liked to be above it all. Like in high school, when they tried to sleep with everyone, but care for no one. I've always had a theory, though, that most of them would've given that up in a blink if they'd only met the right Juliet. And the girls, well, they weren't much better really. They either were like the boys, after commitment-less sex, or else thought themselves too progressive to—

Dear God, I sound like my mother…. I guess I'm just a hopeless romantic. Always trying to convince myself that everyone wants what I want, or should want what I want, so I feel like less of a naïve little wet sock.

Maybe that's part of why I went out with Duncan. I guess a part of me wanted to see if there was anything to it, that lifestyle they all talked about. The drugs, the alcohol, the wild sex. That was what they all seemed to want, what they said they wanted. Perhaps I just didn't get it, though.

I met Rob soon after that. He seemed like a nice guy. Handsome. We talked in art class. I didn't realize, though, until later, how he'd prove I was right about all of it. He was my charming prince, the man I could see fathering my children, and perhaps most of all he was the masked man.

I sat in my bedroom. It was a little girl's room, I thought. Too much pink and too many stuffed animals for high school decency. There were violets by the window that Rob had sent me. The ground was too hard and frozen this time of year to plant anything. You could barely break the surface with a shovel.

There were lots of pictures around. Me with my family, me with my friends, me with Rob. Those first few months were good times. I don't think I realized, beforehand, how much you could fall for someone in such a short time.

He became such a wonderfully significant part of my life. It became almost hard to imagine him not there. It felt as though I'd known him for a long, long time, yet also, when I looked at the facts, there was so little I really knew about him.

Rob was a foster kid, I knew. Lived with a man named Burason, or didn't, I was never really clear on that. He had a sister Felicity, to whom he was very close. She was ill in some sense, but again I knew not with what. I didn't know what had happened to their parents. I knew Rob and Felicity had lived in Centennial at some point, probably after their parents died. Were they dead? Perhaps they were just incompetent. Drug addicts, or schizophrenics, or something like that. I really didn't know.

All I really knew was that when we were together, it felt right. As right as it ever had with anyone. We both liked Italian food. That was the first date we ever had, and we went back often. "Lady and the Tramp," he used to joke. Often, though, I felt he was more worldly than I was. But perhaps that's the way it is with tramps. In any case, he was always finding little shops, underground shows, the most colorful people I'd ever met.

Incipien was not a particularly big town, and I figured I'd seen everything worth looking at or doing, but Rob proved me wrong. We had such adventures; sometimes I felt as though I were in a completely new city.

I was so very much in love.

Chapter 41

It was an overcast Friday afternoon. The clouds, which had once seemed like seals and rocket ships, now took on far more ominous physiques.

We were in James' car, a small Volvo SUV, parked in front of the Icarus Department Store, on the less popular side of the parking lot. We were waiting for something, but they wouldn't tell me what.

"Is he coming?" Lesa asked.

"He's coming." Rob was faced out the window, squinting, looking for something through the slight fog that gave the parking lot a desolate, isolated feel.

"There he is," James said, just above a whisper. "He's right over there."

I rubbed my hand across the cold glass, wiping away some of the moisture that had accumulated there, so that I could see the dark haired man limping towards us. His clothes, like his hair, were tossed and hung haphazardly from his body, like old shirts struggling to hang on their line during a hurricane.

It began to rain slightly, but the man's gait did not change. He ambled slowly towards us, seeming almost undead as he did so, as though each step required great exertion and personal sacrifice.

"This is stupid." Everyone ignored James at first. "This is stupid," he said again, looking around at the others desperately.

I didn't understand.

"He's got money, like the others, doesn't he?" Rob was calm. He barely glanced at James. His attention was focused on the strange man still shuffling towards us.

"He's a fucking adult," James whined shaking his head slightly. "Sorry Anne."

"I'm not 12." But I was too confused to say anything very convincingly.

"We sold to Cody's uncle once," Rob said matter-a-factly.

"Yeah, and that was stupid, but at least he—"

The hurricane man was at Rob's window now, staring in at us with distant blood shot eyes. The window fogged and cleared as the man breathed, and I had the odd sense that we were suddenly in some inescapable cavern in which every shadow was occupied by things that I did not understand, but that posed a great threat to my life.

"Roll down the window," Rob ordered.

Lesa looked at me, frowning slightly.

The window moved very slowly, it seemed, sinking lower and lower into the car like the setting sun.

Finally it stopped, and there was only the sound of distant children coming out of the store.

The hurricane man stared at Rob expressionless, as though very far away. Suddenly, almost aggressively, the man raised an envelope up from his side and handed it to Rob.

Robby took it, and, keeping an eye on the hurricane man, looked into the envelope. He then lifted an old paper bag from the floor, and handed it through the window.

The faraway man stared for a moment, glanced in the bag, nodded to us, and then disappeared back into the wispy fog.

Chapter 42

"How you like them apples?" Rob grinned, passing the envelope over to James, who whistled.

"I ain't Matt Damon, but I can do that math."

Tommy looked at me uncomfortably.

"The math tells me, that we need to expand." Rob had a glint in his eyes I hadn't seen before. "Expand supply, expand sales, expand profits."

The truth was beginning to sink in now. I was jittery, because I hadn't seen it coming. And I was angry at myself for not figuring it out sooner.

"Lesa," he finished, as James turned the car on and threw it into drive. "I think you'll be able to pay for college."

James looked uneasy as he drove, but he didn't say anything else about not selling to grown-ups.

Chapter 43

As the front door of my house swung open, there was Rob, grinning at me through the bright sun of the early morning.

"Go for a drive?"

Behind him was a shiny new chrome-colored coup, with Abi, Lesa, and James in the tight back seat.

A bumble bee hovered over them for a moment, then flew away.

Robby drove fast. Who could blame him in a car like that?

I leaned out the window, and let the warm air rush over my skin and blow my hair crazily behind me. Seeing me, Rob smiled, and sped still faster.

Finally we came to a stop light. I half expected Rob to run it, but he didn't, and I fell back upon my seat. My hair was whipped to pieces, but I was grinning nearly a full half-circle. The air was warm, the places were beautiful, and we were alive!

It was that time in the start of Spring, when the weather could go either way.

"We're on top, you guys!" Rob yelled as the light turned green and we shot forwards across the intersection. "The fucking top!"

It was as though the very air were charged with excitement and possibility.

We parked on the road, and walked through the woods to an old fire tower that the others had evidently been to before. We sat up top, and looked out over the pine trees, bees, and birds, and flower petals dancing through the heavy air.

It was quiet for a long time. We just ate, and looked, and thought about things.

"So, we work through the end of the year," Rob said finally, finishing his sandwich. "We sell outside the school, we can make—I haven't done the math yet—but enough to, you know, make some opportunities for ourselves next year.

No one said anything for a while.

"I think I'll go south." Rob was still looking out over the trees, speaking as much to them as any of us. "Go somewhere warm. Me and Felicity. Run away from all this bullshit. The pants suits, and the Burasons."

He was quiet for a bit, then turned suddenly to face me. "She really wants to meet you, Anne. I was telling her about you, and she says we must have you over sometime.... Actually," he turned back to the woods. His shoulders were tense. "Actually, I had thought... maybe you could go south with us, when this's all over. We could get a house somewhere. On the beach maybe. A quiet little town, where we could rest, or a city, maybe, if you and Felicity prefer. We could...."

"What about Escobar?" James interrupted him.

"What about Escobar?" Rob again turned back to the trees aloofly.

Chapter 44

Dearest Anne,

Felicity is doing much better. Thanks for asking.

She's almost a hundred percent, I'd say. Next year she'll be able to go back to school. I think that'd be good for her. She stays in good spirits, but I know it must be hard for her, staying in the house all day by herself.

It'll be good for her next year, having as close to a normal life as she's ever been able to remember. Staying in the same place for more than a few months. Being able to go to school steady. Only difference is it'll just be me instead of Mom and Dad. But she doesn't much remember them anyway.

I told her what you said about Saturday, but she insists I go anyway. It is your birthday after all. So I'll see you then.

Much love,
Robby

Chapter 45

The morning was warm and humid. The trees had turned to full fledge green almost overnight. The new leaves felt soft and cool to the touch. Rob and I brushed them gently with our hands as we walked down the little trail to the old fire tower.

The rusty construction that seemed harsh and domineering in the starkness of winter now seemed calm and strangely paternal. Like some Saint that watched us all through that year, saw the good and the bad, but reserved judgment from both. It held us up either way, took us a little closer to God. It was my birthday and Rob was carrying take out from the Italian restaurant, and a cake from the grocery store that he wouldn't let me see yet.

We ate that first, however, (Rob was concerned the icing would melt) and then moved on to spaghetti and garlic bread.

It was very peaceful there, and we sat quietly for a while, and listened to the birds singing, and the peepers singing, and watched the clouds floating slowly past us. The day was bright and vivid, and it was as though you could see every detail on every blade of grass if you just allowed yourself to get close enough.

"Have you thought any about what I said?" Rob asked after a while.

I looked at him.

"About going south with Felicity and me."

Two bees chased each other near the edge of the clearing, and I watched them for a time.

"Somewhere it's warm like this all the time. We could get a house there. On the beach maybe. We've made enough money to start something legitimate, of course. And we wouldn't have to work too hard. We'd swim, and walk on the beach, and go to movies and plays, and eat good food, and make love."

"Do you love me, Rob?"

"Of course I do," he said softly, kissing my neck gently as he said it.

I pulled away. Subtly. Almost imperceptibly.

"Do you think that, do you think that you will love me always?"

"I do think that." He smiled hesitantly, unsure of my meaning.

"Let's have some more cake," I said after a moment. "Before it melts."

We sat on the edge of the platform, dangling our feet into the full spring air, the empty space between ground and those that tried to be above it.

"They say you end up loving as your parents did."

Rob looked at me thoughtfully.

"Your parents fight often, and so you are afraid that's how we will be, some years in the future."

I looked at the trees. The bees were still chasing each other. I was never sure if they were fighting or mating.

"No one seems to last anymore," I said. "I hate to see people fall out of love. I think perhaps it is the saddest thing I can think of."

Rob nodded. "Everyone's so damn modern now."

"Lesa doesn't believe in marriage."

"No, lot of people don't these days. They get married for fucking tax benefits."

"Do you believe in marriage, Robby?"

"I believe in marriage with you."

"And do you believe love can last a lifetime?"

"With you I do."

"But how do you know?"

"I don't."

"But—" That hadn't been the answer I'd expected.

"That's the trouble with people now-a-days. They try to figure it all out. You've just got to live while you can, and love while you can, because you never know what beast is hiding right behind the corner."

The tower creaked slightly in the wind, as though it were saying something profound that we couldn't quite understand.

Chapter 46

Rob took me back to his house after that. He wanted me to meet Felicity.

It was a small brick house, with faux-shutters that needed replacing, and old flower print curtains drawn in all the windows. In the front, there were overgrown box hedges. The grass was rough, and craggy, and pallid, and had extended into the cracks of the old cement driveway that rose up twenty feet or so off the main road in such a way that a parking brake was required for older cars. The yard was small, however, and similar houses stood all across the street and on either side.

Everything there was faded and dry and harsh.

I stepped through the doorway, unsure of what I would find. Everything was very dim at first. As my eyes adjusted I saw old sofas and arm chairs, some still with plastic on them. They were arranged in a semicircle around a dusty old rear-projection TV with rabbit ears on top. Faded paintings and posters hung on the walls and scattered about were plates of half eaten food, old newspapers, and cigarette butts.

"Sorry, I would've cleaned up more if I'd known you were… it's not really my house, of course." Rob scratched his head. But I was squinting away from him, still deeper into the shadows. There were two eyes shining back at me reflecting the light from behind us. As I stared a girl emerged from the haze-like darkness. She was thin and very pale, but there was something strangely beautiful about her. Almost as though she were made of porcelain.

She walked very slowly, as though going too fast would snap her slender legs. She smiled as she approached me.

"You must be Anne," she said.

"Felicity? Yes, yes I'm Anne. It's nice to meet you."

She smiled at Rob, then back at me.

"Robby's told me so much about you. He seems to like you very much."

"He's told me a lot about you as well."

We all sat down on one of the sofas.

It was quiet for a moment.

"This plastic is atrocious, isn't it?" She was referring to the wrap on the couch.

"Oh, it's alright," I said, not wanted to offend them.

"I suppose," she looked down at the plastic again. "I suppose we could've taken it off. But as Robby must've told you, it's not really our house."

"Yes, he mentioned that."

"Someday we're going to have a lovely house," Rob cut in. "With big white columns, and a pool, and at least one balcony."

"Robby's been telling me all about our new house lately. It really sounds quite fantastic." She was smiling at me again. Other than Rob I think I must've been the first person she'd talked to in some time. "He mentioned," she chose her words carefully, "that you might come with us."

"It's possible."

"I hate this dreary old place." Felicity looked around at all the mess obscured only partly by the shadows. "We must have some big picture windows in our new home. Would that suit you Anne?"

"Sure, big windows sound fine."

It was quiet for a bit. The wind was blowing outside, and you could hear it subtly when everything else was quiet. A dog barked somewhere off aways.

It seemed so very lonely there. We were in a neighborhood, but that room, with its thick curtains and dim lighting, seemed as isolated as any desert.

"Felicity," I began with a start.

She looked at me calmly.

"Why don't you… go to school like Rob?"

"School? I can't. No one knows I exist."

"No one knows you exist?"

"What I mean is, the government doesn't."

"Why not?"

She seemed truly uncomfortable for the first time. "Rob's told you about Burason, hasn't he? How handy he was with computers?"

"He's mentioned it."

"Yes, he was very good, I think. Could've made a lot of money if it hadn't been for his record. Anyway, he killed me off. In terms of paperwork, at least. The schools wouldn't know what to do with me."

I gaped at her slightly, not fully understanding.

"He showed me, soon after I came here. Showed me how this house was the only place I still existed. How to everyone else I'd look like an undocumented worker. And no one would remember me, of course. Robby and I are quite alone, I'm afraid."

"Couldn't you go to the police? Couldn't they give you back your… identity?"

"It's better if they forget about us. Soon we'll leave this place and buy a big house on the beach, with a pool and at least one balcony, and it won't matter anymore about Burason or any of them." She smiled at Rob again.

"So," she stood up as she spoke. "We've just got to avoid being found out for a few more months, and then we're free. Won't that be something Robby? Finally free…. Would you like something to drink Anne? I think I'd like a glass of water."

"I'm fine, thank you."

"Robby?"

"No thanks, Lisy."

"Rob, can I talk to you a minute?"

"It's fine, Lisy."

"There's a car outside. It's been parked across the street all day, and I don't think it belongs to any of the neighbors. It's probably nothing, but I thought you ought to take a look, just in case it is police."

Rob walked over to the window and pulled the floral print curtains apart just enough to peep through.

"It's an Escalade. I don't think they use those for cop cars." But he looked concerned after that.

Felicity got her water and sat back down on the plastic wrap. I touched it gingerly. It got sweaty when you sat on it too long.

"Rob tells me you garden, Anne."

"Yeah, I try to. Grow some flowers. A few vegetables."

"I've been working on a garden in the back. There's a nice big fence that keeps the deer out, you know, but I've had a terrible time with the soil. It's so hard here. You can't dig more than an inch or two. It's solid clay."

"Very true. I should give Rob a bag or two of good soil for you."

"Yes, that's a good idea. That would be very nice."

My cell phone rang. It was Lesa and I picked it up.

"Anne! Are you with Rob?"

"Yeah, what's up?"

"Tell him to get over here! James got caught!"

Chapter 47

We sat around Lesa's room tensely. Rob paced off to one side.

It was a fairly good sized room, with a colorful quilted bed spread, and big bean bags lying around that were comfortable to sit on, but seemed all too colorful for the situation, like reminders of an innocence we once had, scolding us silently. On the walls hung vintage-style posters of the great American icons—James Dean, Marilyn Monroe, Audrey Hepburn, and the likes.

Beside the bed lay a stack of newspapers. Lesa must've been one of the last people in the country under the age of 50 who still read her news on printed paper.

She was the tensest of any of us. Babbling nervously. James was her boyfriend after all. And though she liked to act like it at times, she was never the badass that Rob was. He was quiet, calculating. Slightly anxious, if you looked him right in the eye, but mostly calm and composed.

Tommy was solemn. Abi seemed almost to enjoy the excitement of it.

Felicity had stayed at Burason's house. She'd said very little after the phone call. Just hugged us sympathetically as we left.

"We've been treating this shit like a game," Lesa was saying without looking at anyone in particular. "A fucking game. And now what?"

"Lesa!" Rob cut in. (She glanced up at him.) "It's never been a game for me. It was a business on day one, it's a business now. We're having our first hitch, that's all."

She stared at him, almost blankly for a moment before reacting. "Rob, his whole life is fucked! You think he was some fucking thug like you? No! He was a smart kid, Rob! He had a future! We all could get dragged into this, guys. Rob, this was your world, I guess. You knew what you were getting into. You knew what you were getting us into. But for us it was a game. We were playing Al Pacino, like James said, trying to be cool. We didn't need this Rob! You needed this! But we didn't!"

"Lesa!" I squeezed her shoulder trying to make her be quiet.

"She's mostly right about me," Rob said calmly. "Only you don't give me enough credit."

It was quiet for a bit. Tommy looked scared.

"How far are you willing to go to save James' ass?"

"How far is necessary?" Lesa was cautious.

"I don't know yet. Talk to me about details."

"James was closing a deal around 4:00. Nobody was around. Just him and whoever it was, some underclassmen boy. Anyway Dr. Chua came out of his office and caught him there. The underclasser ran, and Chua comes over and grabs the stuff from James. Says he's gonna call the police."

Dr. Amos Chua was a strict principal, famous for his speeches on the failings of the American education system, and millennials in general.

"Was it weed?"

"No, coke. And a lot of it."

Rob cringed.

"Does anyone know if he's filed a report yet, called the police, anything?"

"Not last time I'd heard," Lesa said. "It's his kid's birthday, so he may not wanna deal with it 'till tomorrow. But of course I don't know."

"We can think our way out of this." Rob ignored the skeptical looks of the other. He was getting fidgety like the rest of us. Flipping through the old newspapers, one caught his eye and he picked it up.

Zimmerman Acquitted the headline read.

"How do you like that?" Rob said to no one in particular.

George Zimmerman was a household name at the time. The old skinhead had gained fame for the killing of Trayvon Martin, the young, black, hoodie-sporting teenager who had reportedly "threatened" him. The case had torn the country apart on issues of race, self-defense, and gun control.

"Asshole," mumbled Lesa, referring to the front page.

"Do you know anything about the case?" Rob studied her.

"Trayvon Martin was just walking around, and Zimmerman shot him because he's black!"

"Have you watched a single day of the trial? Or read a single deposition? Or full statement from a witness?"

"No. I don't have to! What's your problem?"

"Shh.... I think Zimmerman probably is an asshole, but I'm making a point. Tommy? Where do you get most of your news?"

"Uh, ... I guess the headlines come up when I check my email...."

"Do you read the whole article usually?"

"No, not usually. Sometimes I read the first paragraph.... My parents watch CNN. Sometimes I'll pay attention if it's something interesting."

"Tommy, can you name one specific way that Obamacare will impact your life?"

"Fuck, Rob!" Lesa cut in. "I don't want to talk about politics right now! Tommy has his head up his ass, what's your point?"

"That news is entertainment! The General Hospital for people who like to think they're educated. Nobody goes in depth any more. Half of what you hear is bullshit. All the stations are trying to be the most exciting, the most up to date." Rob was up on his feet now, gesticulating angrily. "They report things without ever looking too hard to see if they're true. It's just 'according to this organization' or 'this statement from this person says.' It's all just he said, she said bullshit!"

He took a deep breath.

"O.J. Simpson was almost certainly guilty, too. But 90% of the population had already decided that before the trial even started."

"You sound like Dr. Chua," mumbled Lesa.

"You're right, I do." Rob spoke softly now, looking out the window as he talked. "I asked you how far you're willing to go to save James."

"Pretty freakin' far," Lesa said not looking at him.

"Then let's use our times to our advantage...."

Chapter 48

The old north wind whipped through Incipient like a frozen strip of leather to a camel's back. The weather had suddenly turned cold again. Lesa and I huddled outside the school by the dumpsters waiting for Rob.

Lesa was nervous, I could tell. I squeezed her hand, trying—

"Where the fuck is he?"

I shook my head.

Then, there he was, emerging from the mist, walking slowly, confidently.

There in front of us.

It was freezing. Lesa and I were huddled together for warmth and still our hands shook, but Rob— he just stood there. Uncovered, unaffected. I wasn't sure anymore if he were even human.

"I asked you how far you're willing to go to save James," he said again.

"Pretty freakin' far," Lesa repeated, more cautiously this time.

"Good," Rob said curtly and handed her a shoe box.

Lesa opened it. "Rob...."

"It's Chua's rubber. I found it in his trash can."

"His secretary..."

"Right. Listen, Lesa. You need to put it inside of you. Go in the bathroom now and do it. Come right back, and you and I will have some stops to make."

"Rob, I don't know if I can...."

"Lesa...." He looked at her sympathetically, like a child about to get a shot at the doctors. "Lesa, this is not just about James, you know. James is first but if he goes down it's dominoes and sooner or later we all get caught. Even you."

"I know, but—"

"But what? Everyone knows you and James are together. You're the perfect person to do it."

"I know."

"Go and do it now."

She went inside.

Rob and I didn't speak. His mind was far away and I knew not what to say to bring him back, or even if I should.

And then Lesa was back and I squeezed her hand once more for good measure. And Rob said they were going to the Police station for a little while and then he was going to make some phone calls while they were waiting for the tests to come back, and Lesa's eyes were looking very far away like Rob's had all along, and then he was ready to go and they disappeared off into the mist.

There I was. Alone in the cold. I wanted to go back inside.

Chapter 49

Dear Robert,

I feel like we haven't seen each other lately. We've been together, but we haven't seen each other. I know things are crazy right now, but I really miss you, Rob. I really, really miss you.

Maybe we could have dinner Friday? Forget about it all for even an hour, just you and me— and Felicity, if she wants to come. Our last meeting got cut short, but she seemed like such a lovely girl.

Anyway, I hope you're well Rob. You always act so tough and brave and calm on the outside, but I know you must be worried like the rest of us.

Forever yours,
Anne

Chapter 50

"What do the people love even more than a story about teenage coke dealers?" Rob gloated.

None of us answered.

"A story about teenage sex."

It had worked. It was almost painful how easily it had worked. The SBI labs had confirmed that it was indeed Chua's semen inside of Lesa. It was still unclear how much legal trouble Chua was in, but his reputation was ruined.

Rob had fanned the flames as far as the news people were concerned and all of Incipien was now convinced that Chua had been seducing underage students for years.

In fact, the news people took it even further than Rob had, proposing direct exchanges of grades for sexual services, and girls as young as fifteen being exploited. It was sickening, really. All of it was sickening.

But the news people got their ratings. James got off the hook. Lesa was taken good care of by everyone involved and Chua was fired and disappeared off into shame and oblivion.

That was how things worked nowadays. Once the newspapers convicted you, it didn't matter what anyone else said, you would lose your job. Especially anything related to schools. They just couldn't take any chances.

Rob was beaming. He was a genius, in a twisted sort of way. "Let's go out tonight." But he'd saved his friends, so what could I say? "Let's go to Finnegan's."

"Isn't it twenty one to enter?" Lesa asked naively.

"I have a relationship with the owners," Rob said casually. "We'll have the place to ourselves."

Chapter 51

Inside Finnegan's was as dim and hazy as the whole situation. It was empty, as promised. Just us and old Finnigan himself.

"What'll it be?" he asked and poured us vodka and rum the rest of the night.

Soon we were feeling good. Dancing. I'm not sure if there was music on or not, but there was dancing.

"Oh, Robby, we're having so much fun, aren't we?"

And he nodded and smiled at me.

James was there with us. He was quiet that night. Still had a lot to process, I suppose.

Abi. She always had to be the most wild. Next thing we knew she wasn't wearing a shirt, then she was wrapping her bra around Rob's neck, which even in his drunkenness made him very uncomfortable.

"What're you doing, Abi?" he asked. "You can't do this."

She ignored him, now easing her hips closer to his, sliding her body snake-like along his chest.

"Abi, I'm telling you no! I don't see you like that!" he pushed her away and she stumbled in drunkenness, or perhaps just embarrassment.

For a moment, she stared at him, with sad whipped-puppy-eyes. Then she pulled her shirt on over her head and without looking back walked out the door.

I looked back at Rob. Rob looked down at the floor.

Chapter 52

"We have to go after her," Lesa stepped towards the door.

"It's a bad neighborhood," Rob cut in.

Lesa hesitated.

"Stay here." Rob put his jacket on and walked towards the door.

The night was cold and dark. That time of year the weather was still bipolar. Clouds engulfed the city, suppressing everything to a slumberous state of pause. Everything was dead or dormant but the cold young man that walked confidently, or perhaps uncaringly, across the concrete jungle.

We watched him from just outside the bar.

And there she was, stumbling across the dim orangey light of cities at night. Still crying a little. For a moment, she was an injured gazelle and he the lion that had done it to her.

Rob stalked her like an animal, watched her involuntary flinches, predicted with his eyes what she would do next.

"Why did we let him go?"

Lesa and I stood a little ways off. We were scared of him now. That was why we let him go.

Rob saw it before we did. His animal instincts, no doubt. The big, dark shape emerging from the shadows. Moving slowly closer to him. Then it was there, right beside him and all focus on Abi was gone, snapped to the three men that stepped from the haunting black Escalade.

Abi disappeared into an alleyway just as the men grabbed Rob and slammed him against a wall. I thought I saw the glimmer of knives, but Rob did not scream. Only in his eyes would he scream. And in that moment, for the first time in weeks, he was human again, and I was in love with him, and all I wanted to do was drive those men away.

But my legs were frozen, and I knew there was no good I could do anyway.

Then the men left. And Rob stood there for a moment, breathing aggressively.

Lesa and I rushed to him.

"You should not have followed me," he said coldly, but unsurprised by our presence. "This is not a good neighborhood."

"Who were those men? What did they say?"

For a moment he just breathed. Shut his eyes and breathed. For only a split second, then he was back.

"It was a warning. Next time it will not be."

He walked back towards Finnegan's.

Chapter 53

Abi wasn't in school the next day. It was probably a good call. Things were going mad. As soon as you stepped through the door you could tell. The office was swarming with a crowd of angry parents.

And there was Rob, standing just outside, listening casually.

"You had a monster in the principal's chair!" one of them shouted.

"How could you expose our children to this?"

"And how about this drug problem? Every day my little Sammy comes home talking about all the druggies taking over the school!"

"Are you giving our kids an education? Or an introduction to a life of crime?"

"We demand massive changes in the way this school is run!"

Chapter 54

We didn't do anything in any of our classes that day. Everyone was too shaken up about Dr. Chua. But Rob and Lesa and I knew Dr. Chua was just the beginning.

I knew the dark side of Rob now. Knew he would keep this thing going 'till— well, I didn't know what it would take. Strangely it didn't occur to me to walk away at that point. That just never even seemed like an option.

And when we met in secret at lunch and Rob declared, "We need more power," none of us even looked up. "We need to take the board!"

It was all happening so fast now and none of us really understood it anymore, so we left it up to Rob to lead us, to make the decisions. Not because we trusted him, but because we had no other option.

In some ways it was beautiful how calculating he was. How his mind worked. How he always thought three steps ahead of everyone else. But then again, perhaps it was all a show. You could see it in his eyes, in the subtle gestures when he thought no one was looking. It was not as it was before. He was not a perfect machine.

The way he paused as he spoke to us now. It was confidence, but it was... it was a show now. I had never been sure before, but now it was definitely a show. He was trying to make us feel safe and confident in him, but you could see it in his eyes. He was afraid, and worse than that alone, he was also reckless.

"We need to take the board!" he declared decisively, and I couldn't help but to look away.

"If we don't, they'll get someone who's worse. Someone who'll actually crack down on everything we're doing."

"Everything we used to do," Lesa corrected.

Rob considered her words. "We'll start again when this mess dies down a little. In a few days."

"Rob, how can you say that?" Lesa exploded finally. "You've got Escobar breathing down your throat. The parents are practically rioting! How can you not see that this has gotten way out of hand?"

"Lesa," he began patronizingly. "If you didn't know what you were signing up for then I'm sorry, but all large-scale operations have hitches when they're getting up to speed. I anticipated that we would have... difficulties, and I also believed, and still do believe, in us, and our ability to overcome."

"Overcome for what goal?" Lesa was practically shaking. "Wha—what's this about a large-scale operation? Is that what we're calling ourselves now? I thought we were just some crazy kids messing around while we were in high school?"

Rob sighed. "Fine, Lesa, what is it exactly that you propose we do?"

This caught her off guard and she stuttered for a moment, then found her words. "Destroy everything, destroy the evidence."

"The evidence?" he raised an eyebrow.

"You know what I mean, Rob," she shot back. "The drugs! We have to destroy the drugs."

"You think the drugs are the only evidence?" He stood and looked down at us like children, children that'd just done something very stupid. "Lesa, what did you see when you walked into school this morning?"

She didn't answer.

"What did you see?"

"Angry parents."

"Yes, angry parents. They were very angry, weren't they?"

"Yes."

"Demanding an investigation, I heard. Silva High's turned into a hotbed of crime these past few months. You think they're going to let that go? They want to know why, but more than that they want to know who. They want to know names!"

He slammed his fist on the table.

"Would you like to give them your name, Lesa?"
"No!"
"Nor would I."
He walked out.

Chapter 55

It was Tuesday. Cold as dry ice, and almost as foggy. There was a storm blowing in. You could see it in the corners of the sky.

Rob and I walked arm and arm towards the doors of the school. He'd asked me to come with him. "I need you there with me tonight," he'd said.

The front of the school was abuzz with people. Most seemed solemn. A few of the parents picketed with signs. The old Vietnam generation.

The local TV news had even sent a van out to cover the event.

"Thanks everyone for coming," the chairman said when we were all inside. "The emergency school board meeting is now in session."

Rob and I sat near the back. Wrapped in woolen winter coats.

"What're all these homeless men doing here?" I whispered in Rob's ear. They were easy to spot. I recognized them from street corners and beneath bridges. Their unkempt beards. Their ragged clothes. Their hungry eyes. But what was really shocking was how many of them were there. They filled the room.

"They're citizens too, aren't they?" Rob said.

I leaned back in my seat.

"As you all know," the chairman continued, "under the pressure of recent events, more than half the board has unexpectedly resigned."

Rob nodded subtly. A cold shiver ran down my back.

"Tonight," the old chairman said solemnly, "we must select their replacements. I shall now read the candidates."

And he did.

"We shall now have discussion regarding the aforementioned candidates."

"Most of them are not even parents!" one blond, young father declared, as part of a painfully long winded speech.

"That is not a requirement in this county," the old chairman clarified.

There were more speeches. Many more speeches. And then the candidates gave speeches. And then there was voting. The room voted, as was the legal procedure with charter schools in the state.

When the speeches happened, I saw why the parents were mad. We all watched perplexed as homeless man after homeless man rose and spoke.

It was the homeless men that ran. It was the homeless men that voted. And it was the homeless men that won.

"They're citizens too," Rob whispered with a smirk. "Let's go find the others to tell them the good news."

Chapter 56

Necci was an upscale Italian restaurant in downtown Incipien. Mahogany paneling on the walls. White linen tablecloths. The whole deal. Rob and I had been there once before, but tonight he booked the whole place. It was just the five of us in the grand, huge, restaurant. Two waiters per person.

But Rob wasn't enjoying it. It was solely for our benefit. Rob's attention was elsewhere. Perhaps a dozen elsewheres that night. He looked off into the distance and clutched his leather messenger bag.

Everyone was tense, but I was glad to be with them anyway. My parents had been fighting more and more and I needed to get out of the house. These were the people I wanted to be with right then.

We sat at a long wooden table and ordered gross amounts of pasta and garlic bread as well as Fragolino and Limoncello.

"A toast," Rob said, "to us." We drank.

"To you, I say," said Lesa dramatically. "You control the school now. I would not have thought you could do it, but you have. You, Rob—a few months ago you were this shy, quiet high school kid, we would barely have thought you could speak, but now—geez. This man is the king of our school."

"And you my noble knights!"

We drank again.

Rob leaned in closer to me. "Have you heard anything from Abi?" She was the only one of our usual group still missing. Even Tommy was sipping fragolino tonight.

"No, I haven't."

When we finished eating they brought out the sambuca shots and I could tell it was going to be another one of those nights.

Soon they were dancing on the table, stomping their muddy shoes all over Necci's fine white table clothes. You could see the waiters a little ways off looking bothered, even hurt, but they didn't dare interfere. They knew Rob too well for that.

"You control the school!" Lesa shouted. "You control the school!"

"Next we'll control the whole damn city! Then maybe the country!" Rob was high on it all. That was what made them dance on the tables even more than the sambuca.

Outside it was raining as hard as it ever does. It rained in sheets and blankets, covering the whole world in an inch of water.

"I want to show you all something." He unzipped his leather messenger bag and let us all look inside. It was full of twisted, green money.

His audience cooed approvingly.

"I must've recruited a dozen new customers today," he muttered. "We're back in business now."

"All that from a dozen new customers?" Lesa asked. "How much were you charging?"

"Fair market value. We're big shots now. No more weed. Well, maybe a little on the side. But, you know, to fund the takeover. To protect all of us, I had to expand into some more serious stuff. That's where the real money is. Do you have any idea how much these Incipien businessmen are willing to pay for a little bam bam?"

The group was silent for a moment.

"Rob," Lesa began slowly. "I had my doubts. I was against all of this, against expanding, against continuing at all. But now I see, you're smarter than all of us. More importantly, smarter than all of them. You can work them all like puppets, and from now on, I trust you."

I couldn't believe what she was saying. She'd been the biggest critic of his expansion plans, and now she yielded to him like—

Rob smiled. "You're as good a friend as a guy could ask for. All of you are." Then to the wait staff "more sambuca!" They jumped.

Shots, shots, battle cries and shots.

Tommy threw up. It was the first time he'd really drank.

"I'm gonna go for some fresh air." He stepped outside. I decided to follow him.

It was quiet outside by comparison. Just the sound of the rain crashing like waves on the asphalt and concrete. I patted Tommy on the back sympathetically.

"How you doin' with all this?"

He looked up at me studying me. Then relented. "I don't understand it all. They seem crazy."

"Yes, they do. I guess a little money and power will do that to a person."

"Maybe so."

He threw up again, over the curb and into the street. I held his shoulders and pulled him back beneath the awning.

A big, dark mass emerged from the shadows. Moving slowly along the yellow lines of the road, like a spectre you could make disappear if you only blinked.

We blinked. But that big black Escalade didn't disappear.

There was something mesmerizing about it. The way the lights shone off it. The way you knew immediately what it was. I understood all of a sudden the way Lesa was mesmerized by Rob. I couldn't turn away. Even though I knew it was dangerous I—

"We should go inside," I whispered.

"Yeah..."

I snapped out of it. Grabbed Tommy, "Come on! We have to go now!" I ducked and dragged him towards the door. It was locked.

I started banging on the glass.

The rear window of the Escalade started rolling down.

The wait staff saw it was us and came to unlock the door.

I banged harder, as though it would make them come faster.

They unlocked it. The door fell open just as they started shooting. White light flashed through the rain. The sound of a hundred and ninety decibels deafened the night. I fell through the open doorway. There was blood on my hands, blood on the floor.

"Come in!" yelled Rob. He grabbed me and pulled me the rest of the way through the door.

And behind me, Tommy's hand lay limp on the sidewalk. Rob sat me down in a chair and pulled Tommy through the doorway as well. Then the door was shut and locked.

The Escalade kept shooting and we all lay on the floor against the wall as the glass shattered from the windows and rained down like bombs all around us.

Rob army-crawled over to me. "Are you okay?" He tried to act calm, but you could see the fear in his eyes. It was there for sure now.

"I dunno." Everything was ringing, everything was crashing down around me. I couldn't tell if I was in pain or not. Everything started drifting away and I began to sink back into blackness.

Rob shook me. "Come on Anne! Stay with me!"

He ran his hands over my clothes, checking for injuries.

"You're gonna be fine. A few cuts from the glass, but you weren't hit. You're just fine."

Everything was hazy. I was just an observer now. I couldn't move.

They kept shooting for what seemed like an eternity. The wait staff was screaming. Then we heard sirens in the distance and the SUV screeched off. And Rob was up on his feet again yelling at us "We have to go! We have to go!" And then we were moving. Running over the broken glass, through a dark alleyway. Across some old lady's lawn.

We had to leave Tommy behind. That was the hardest part. Looking back at him that last time, his broken body sprawled out bloody and lifeless in all that broken glass.

"We've got to get to my house," Rob told us. The rest of us were too scared to speak.

Chapter 57

We all filed into Rob's little house. Wet and scared and buzzed. Felicity came out of the back and went wide eyed at all of us. It was probably the most people she'd seen in months.

Rob hugged her. "I had to make sure you were all right."

"What happened?" she whispered.

"Escobar hit us hard tonight. Tommy's dead." He turned to us. "Please, everyone, sit down. Make yourselves as comfortable as possible."

We sat tensely on his plastic wrapped couches, unsure of what else to do. It was hot and musty in that room. The air closed in around us, trapping us, making us feel as though the very world were after us. My ears rang. My muscles pulsed. I wanted to fight, to run, to do something other than sit.

The rain stopped. The quiet was suffocating.

Lesa burst into tears. She was sobbing. Screaming a jumble of stuff I couldn't understand. With a flinch she ran out onto the back deck.

"Will she be okay out there?" James asked Rob.

"There's a high fence. They won't be able to see her if they drive by. We can give her a few minutes."

Felicity came out with ice water for everyone. Unsure of what else to do.

"Come on, James." Rob was walking down the hall. "Help me get the guns."

"We should board up the doors and windows as well," James said.

Rob shook his head. "It isn't safe to stay here."

Rob and James went in the back.

Felicity noticed my torn, bloody clothes. "Come on, Anne, let's get you fixed up."

She led me to the back of the house, gave me clean, dry clothes. And bandages and antiseptic for my cuts.

"Did you see him die," she asked quietly. "It must've been really terrible."

I started crying for the first time. She just hugged me, held me.

"How could they do that to someone? How could they just kill someone like that? I could never kill anyone."

"That's right. I know you wouldn't." Her voice was soothing, sympathetic.

Then there was a scream. Lesa. And we all ran to see if Escobar was back.

They weren't. Lesa stood alone in the back yard. Screaming and staring at the ground.

Cautiously we stepped out onto the back deck to see what it was.

"Monster!" she was screaming. "Monster! Monster!"

We followed her accusing finger to the ground and there, protruding from the half frozen soil was the sunken shape of a human face.

Book III: Rob Tenebris

Locker 99: Chapter 58

The door closed behind them. It was silent in the little living room. I'd thought it was silent before but now it really was silent. Deadly silent. And I realized in that moment that silence, that isolation, was what terrified me far more than Escobar.

"They left—" Felicity started. I just hugged her.

"They're pretty shaken up. It was a rough night for all of us." I tried to seem calm about it. "Get your stuff together. We better go somewhere else."

We went to Target. I know that may seem strange at a time like that. But I decided it'd be better to be in a public place, and Target was too close to the Police station for Escobar to try anything. I hoped. Besides, the bright lights were comforting. Something about big box stores like that. They felt strangely safe to me. Strangely connected. Having other people around all night long. I needed to be around people right then.

It was being alone that terrified me far more than Escobar.

"Will the others be okay?" Felicity asked. We sat in the small furniture section towards the back of the store. They had a few soft lounge chairs that we could curl up in.

"I think so." I really wasn't sure.

"Monster!" Lesa had called me. "Monster! Monster!"

I could still see Anne's eyes. The way she looked from Burason's rotting face back up to me, eyes wide. She was thinking 'Monster' too. "Monster! Monster!" They didn't like people like me. Didn't like thinking about how people like me existed. They liked the clean, polished version of guys like me that they saw in movies and on TV. But in the flesh it was too gritty and real for them.

Felicity closed her eyes. I knew she wasn't asleep. She just wanted to pretend she was for a little while.

"Monster!"

I couldn't stop thinking about the way Anne had looked at me. Right before they all left. James had tried to calm everyone down, but they were too shaken up after they found Burason, and he had to take them home.

Tommy.

Tommy looking over his shoulder. Pausing. That loud, awful, ear-shredding sound of gunfire. A flash of white. I was on the ground. "Get on the ground!" Tommy was on the ground, but not in the same way we were.

The way the blood started seeping out from his wrecked body. They'd really torn him to pieces.

A security guard came over and glared at us. "Asset Protection," his uniform said. What the fuck was that? I was tired but also buzzed. Buzzed out of my mind, but ready to sleep. That damn copper kept glaring at me.

Felicity opened an eye.

"Wanna walk a bit?"

She nodded.

Through the frozen section. Accessories. Trying on some sunglasses. "Monster! Monster!" The lingerie section. (What would Anne look like in one of those? (felt guilty)) Sports, auto, grocery—pushing a shopping cart down the aisle. Toys. I liked the toy section. Those were things that were meant for fun. All the ingenious things people came up with.

The way she looked at me. Like she was dying inside. Like I'd killed her instead of fucking Burason. Burason! It was guys like that that'd made me like this.

Who the fuck did they think they were?

"Who the fuck do they think they are, Felicity?" I wasn't loud about it. I was contained. I was always contained. Always under control. Always—

Burason. What he'd done.

"They've been fucking us for years. For as long as you can remember. In Centennial. In Incipien. And then they get mad at us when we finally fight back? When we finally defend ourselves?"

I pushed over a display stand of books. They fell all over the floor and everyone turned to look at me. Looking at me. Me. Always the problem. Always doing the wrong thing. "Rob, are you okay?" She touched my arm. "I'm fine!" And walking back to furniture.

I couldn't even walk straight I was so tired. I was too buzzed to sleep. I was always too buzzed to sleep. Fucking Burason. What he'd done to us. What he'd done to Felicity.

I'd liked it. I'm man enough to admit it. I'd liked killing Burason. Best damn thing I've ever done.

There's only so long you can let them fuck you in the ass.

Chapter 59

"Are you sure I should go?" There were bags under my eyes. My skin was papery. I hadn't slept any.

"I'll be fine," Felicity said. She touched my hand. "Go."

I passed the back to school section. That's where I was going. Back to school. Why was it still out this time of year?

I didn't like leaving her alone. Not with everything that was going on, but I'd stayed up all night thinking about the way they'd looked at me and I figured any last hope I had of pinning things back together with them was dependent on me doing it today. Before their imaginations made me any more evil than I really am.

I walked along the sidewalk. You could see everything when you were tired. You couldn't process it, but you could see it. The sidewalk, I kept staring at the sidewalk. Nodding off, coming back. Everything was hazy in my mind. My ears rang, my head ached.

I made it, though. I made it to school. And they were actually there. Surprisingly. I guess that meant their parents didn't know and they wanted to keep it that way.

I sat in the back of class and struggled to stay conscious.

There was Lesa in the hallway! I tried to catch her, but she walked faster and disappeared into a crowd of people. Had she seen me? Was she avoiding me?

James— "James!" I touched his shirt and he turned. He looked at me— he looked at me the same way Anne had. That scared, disdainful— like I had killed something inside of them, destroyed a part of who they were—they, shit, I couldn't stand them looking at me that way. "James, it's me! What's going on?"

"I dunno, Rob." It was silent. We were both silent. A sea of people moved past us and it was just him and I looking at each other. "I can't do this anymore, Rob. I don't want to have anything to do with any of it. I just— can't see you for a while."

"James!" He turned. "James, don't do this! Please, don't do this! We can get through this together, but we need each other!"

"I'm sorry." He didn't look at me again. Just turned and disappeared into the crowd.

An ocean of people, and I was completely alone. That was the only thing that really scared me. I didn't mind anymore if Escobar killed me. But what destroyed me was the thought of them killing me and— my ears rang even louder, the world was swimming around me, that ocean of people was sucking me up and drowning me like a tiny seashell—

Floor. Hands and knees. Panting for breath.

They'd look at me, but they'd turn away if I looked back. No eye contact. Never make eye contact. I'd die there on the floor and they'd pretend not to notice.

"Pull yourself together Rob." That damn pulsing headache.

I made it outside. The cool air did me some good. I leaned against a tree and took some deep breaths.

Felicity. What mattered now was Felicity. She was always the one, really. Always the one that really mattered. I had to get her, take what money we had and go south. We'd start a new life. Start over completely. We didn't have as much saved up as I'd hoped, but we would make it work. There was nothing left for us in Incipien. Nothing left— not for her anyway. For me, I still cared about them. Despite it all, I really did still care about them.

Anne. If I've ever loved anyone that way, Anne was the one. I thought about her all the time. I'd lay awake at night thinking what it'd be like to be with her always.

If she would only come with us. Me, Anne and Felicity. It would be perfect. I'd have everything that really mattered.

But the way she'd looked at me— I'd never forget that. That would haunt me for the rest of my life. I had to see her one last time.

Maybe I'd ask her to go south with us. Just in case. Maybe she'd say yes. Maybe. There'd been times. Moments, at least, when I'd thought she loved me too.

I'd wait for her after school. Ask her to go south with us. See her one last time.

Chapter 60

I leaned against the wall by the entrance to the school, waiting for her. And there she was, after a while. Coming out the door. Walking to her car.

She really was the most beautiful creature I'd ever seen. Even like that. Even when she had bags under her eyes, when her hair was a mess, her face pale, no makeup and an oversized sweatshirt on— she really was the most beautiful creature I'd ever seen.

I watched her for a few moments before speaking. Whatever else happened, whatever else was said, I wanted to remember her like that. Remember her the way she was before I ruined her.

"Anne." She turned. Her face sank. Her skin turned even paler.

We were alone in the parking lot.

"I— are you doing okay?" I didn't dare get too close to her. "I mean, after everything that happened."

She studied me for a moment, reflecting, I think.

"I'm okay, Rob." She started to turn.

"And your parents?"

"My parents?"

"I mean, they're not fighting too much, are they?"

She looked at the asphalt.

"They're okay, Rob," she said very quietly.

She looked up at me—

Was she crying? I couldn't tell.

"Robby, I'm sorry, but I just can't see you anymore."

"Anne, it's been a bad spell, but it's gonna change, I'm gonna overcome my past, an—" Even coming out it sounded dead.

She was crying.

"I need more good in my life. I just can't do this anymore."

She turned and ran towards her car.

I just watched her go. Watched her getting farther and farther away from me. Slipping away like a diamond ring down a manhole.

For a moment, I'd thought it would be peaceful. Thought it would be closure or some bullshit like that. But it wasn't. It hurt like hell.

And then there it was— the executioner coming to the funeral, that shady black entity that had chased me everywhere I went since Tommy died.

The doors opened. Anne saw it. She started to run back towards me, but it was too late. They had her in an instant— like a raptor catching a mouse, scooping her up and flying off with her. Her lover running helplessly after. Me, running helplessly after.

I kept running long after they were gone. Just kept running and running in the direction they'd gone, hoping I'd see them down some side street, or stopped at a traffic light.

I kept running 'till mucus formed in my mouth gagging me and my legs started to give out and my chest burned. I could hear my pulse in my ears. I stopped. My eyes still darting around.

This was on me. This was all on me. Whatever happened, it was all on me.

Chapter 61

It was just before sunrise when I finally found her. She was stumbling down an alleyway. Stripped down to her underwear, bruises all over her body, breathing like she had the devil himself inside her.

She stopped when she saw me, but I couldn't tell if it registered who I was or not. She was standing there wheezing, knees bent, legs like saplings that could snap at any time under the weight of what had happened. I reached out for her, because I was scared she'd fall if I didn't.

She flinched when I touched her, but then I pulled her to me and she melted into my arms, letting herself collapse and depend on me.

She had blood on her forehead and I looked closer at it. I realized it was words carved brutally into her flesh. I squinted to read it through the blood. "Sell again, all die."

They'd left her there for me to find. They knew where I was, knew where I was looking.

It was terrible seeing her like that. If those Escobar bastards where there now I'd've cut their hands off, shot them in the gut, done anything I could've to make them suffer.

And then I looked down at the poor crying girl in my arms and I knew the time for war was over. At least for now. What mattered now was getting her warm and safe and comfortable. That was the only thing that mattered right now.

Chapter 62

I took her to the hospital. They cleaned her up, and took pictures in case Anne decided to try and press charges.

She insisted her parents not be called. I didn't understand it, but she was eighteen so apparently she had that right.

There were no serious injuries, at least not of the physical kind, and soon they had her cleaned up and she came out in her little blue hospital gown and sat beside me. In a sombre, uncomfortable kind of way.

For a long time neither of us said anything. It was good just sitting beside her.

"I only did it because he was hurting Felicity."

She looked at me. It was the first time since I'd found her that she'd really looked at me.

"He was still hurting her," I pleaded. "He was going to keep hurting her until I did something about him."

"I know," she said softly. "I understand."

We sat for a little while longer, just being beside each other. Then she turned to me and asked if I could drive her home.

Chapter 63

She wanted to go by the tower one last time before I took her home. I stopped the car by the side of the road and we walked down the little trail through the woods like we had so many times before. I remember how it'd been the first time. How excited we'd been, going down the trail like a tribe of Indians, like kids on an adventure. But that was gone now. Now we were grownups, and when we walked down the trail, we were focused only on stepping in the puddles as little as we could. That and everything behind us.

We sat up top, dangling our feet over the edge. Funny how that'd seemed daring at one time. But that was a long time ago.

I stared at Anne when I thought I could get away with it. She really was the most beautiful creature I've ever seen. Even like that, with an ace bandage around her forehead, bits of blood still in her fried hair, bruises on her neck. Even like that, she really was the most beautiful creature I've ever seen.

"What will you do now?" Her eyelids were heavy now. I could see, but she had something to finish before she slept.

"Felicity and I will go south. I don't know after that. Set up a new life somewhere."

She nodded.

"You could come with us."

"No I couldn't."

I nodded.

"I do love you, Rob. I really do love you, but I can't go south with you. I just can't."

(The wind blew in the distance. I thought I could hear it whispering something to me.)

"I understand."

I looked out at the woods. How vast they seemed. How many places a person could hide in woods like those.

I tried to explore the woods with my eyes because I knew if I looked at Anne my heart would stop right then and there.

"Why couldn't we have had an innocent love?" she asked. "Why couldn't you have asked me to prom? Instead of fucking me there in the mud."

I nodded.

"I guess I'd better get home." She looked away.

FINAL TREE

It is sad to be the last,
To think of those from the past,
Here a thousand trees once stood,
To see them again; I wish I could,
But now it's just me, I am alone,
The seasons keep spinning, like a gramophone,
And as my leaves come and go,
My time runs thin, like phylo-dough,
For when there is no one with to stand,
Sometimes I think I ough't to just land,
In the back of some old lumber truck to be,
Like the others that once shook with me,
No longer a tree.

The Truth About the World

All the world exists on a turtle's back,
Which in turn lives on a turtle stack,
How do I know this, you ask of me?
It's been passed down my family tree,
Along with hepatitis B,
Discovered by my great uncle Schmi,
He was a biologist, or so I'm told,
The type to do tests on things like mold,
As well as his famous tests with acapulco gold,
But his real passion was the turtle,
He was the top dog in the turtle scientist circle,
And one fine day in the month of June,
He went too high in a meteorological balloon,
Higher and higher he continued to fly,
Through birds and clouds and wind and sky,
Till like ants looked the human race,
And next thing he knew he was in space!

"By George!" he called to his assistant,
(though of course the man was far too distant)
"The water wet, the ground so fertile,
but it all exists on a giant turtle!"

Superstition

Prologue

As all who have lived through it know, hatred is a force more corrosive than acid. It trickles down through the bowels of domestic and public affairs, burning and eating away at the bonds that once held people together, at the very foundations on which a family is built.

What was once a peaceful, edenic coy pond becomes a seemingly inescapable and turbulent sea, murky and dark in its uncertainty and violent and unpredictable in its passion.

Men and women cast into that vast ocean cling to remains of their once glorious ship. Bits of unstable driftwood and broken beams become their home as they stave off death itself. Yet, nurtured deep inside their hearts, is an ambition beyond mere survival. It is predictable, for those in their state. For all cast into the great unbalance, the huge uncontrollable uncertainty, crave the same thing: The escape from instability. Control of themselves and their own lives. Power.

Chapter 1

Sometimes, June Lacon liked to feel normal.

After school, she would sit by the playground, or go to the library, or, more often now, take a bus to the local mall, with its bright lights, its perfect, pretty, clean and clean-cut clothing stores. She was *intrigued* by the other twelve year olds, with their over-priced clothing, their cell phones and brand name shoes. The other twelve year olds whose parents wore button down shirts and blue tooth headsets and had vague but important sounding job titles.

Yes, she was *intrigued* by them. But the older she got, the more she was glad to be different.

For as long as she could remember, she had lived exactly 32 miles outside of town in a place called *The Farm*, a small collection of haphazard shacks made of plywood, corrugated metal, stone, and whatever else residents could pull from dumpsters or salvage from the side of the road.

It was a mecca for "the poor, the eccentric and the wonderful" as June's father liked to say. And the Lacon family fell into at least two of those categories, if not all three.

June was an only child. And like most children, she'd grown up hearing stories about how her parents had come to know each other. Jerome and Tisha, her father and mother, had met in 2004 at a supernatural conference in Chicago. Tisha had been there as a protester, on behalf of her conservative Baptist church. Jerome had been there as a keynote speaker.

They met by accident in a broken elevator, thus beginning several years of torrid courtship and passionate fights, climaxing, ultimately, in the birth of June.

Jerome increasingly dictated how the family should live, and they soon moved to *The Farm* when June was learning to walk. While Tisha, isolated by her new home, began to struggle with bouts of depression and general anxiety, Jerome flourished, gaining increasing respect, if not wealth, in the small world of specialized shamans-for-hire, of which The Farm was a Mecca.

But above all else, he took great pleasure in giving private lessons to his daughter, who, he quickly decided, was the most gifted child he had ever met.

*****

Sweat dripped down June's forehead. It was hot and stuffy in the dark closet.

She tried to move, to shake out her legs, hoping that would help, but the industrial vacuum behind her didn't leave much room.

For a moment she watched the dust dancing in the little streams of light creeping in through the slats in the door, then she leaned forward again, pressing her face to the light, carefully looking out into the school hallway.

Nick was at his locker, absentmindedly running his fingers through his soft brown hair, unaware that she was watching him. He was like the mannequins at the mall, June thought. Perfectly proportioned, Abercrombie shirt, Levis and Jordans.

He'd spoken exactly two words to her since they'd been in school together. "Excuse me." (He'd bumped into her in the hall.)

June was usually good at getting the things she wanted. Or at least asking. But even the thought of talking to Nick made her hands sweaty and her tongue swell up.

Thus the closet.

Brittany swaggered down the hallway towards him. Aeropostale shirt. Perfectly straight blonde hair. June was always in awe of how a girl her own age could sway her hips like that. Like a grown woman.

Brittany poked Nick in the stomach. He grinned and poked her back.

June threw up a little in her mouth.

The poking continued.

June reached deep into her bag and pulled out a little homemade doll, with Aero written across the chest (Brittany's uniform).

She reached into her bag again. She had to dig a little longer this time, before… she found it. A shiny three inch sewing pin.

She would see about poking.

*****

Her teacher handed her a hall pass.

Without smiling, June left the room. Outside, the hall was quiet. The interior of the middle school was painted with bright colors. Children's artwork hung on the walls (*most of it's terrible,* June thought) as did a variety of inspirational posters about things like becoming a teacher, drinking milk and getting HPV vaccines.

June stood over the water fountain and took a long drag.

Where to now?

Outside it was a warm day, the last before summer break began. The trees, now a lush green, danced in the gentle afternoon breeze.

She tossed her hall pass on the ground and walked outside.

Brittany's mom was helping her to the car. (*The bitch now had an ace bandage on her knee!*)

"This is the second time this week!" exclaimed Brittany's mom with great gesticulation.

But June's mind was on other things.

The sidewalk in front of the school was crisscrossed by a ridiculous number of cracks. June had to be careful, so as not to bring any bad luck on her poor mother.

The woman had told her several times now that it was nonsense, superstition, and that June could step on as many cracks as she wanted or walk under as many ladders as she wanted and nothing bad would happen. Still, it made June uncomfortable. Her mother could be naive about things like that. And if June were to step on a crack and anything bad *did* happen, she would regret it for the rest of her life.

Despite the cracks, she eventually made it to her destination. An old gas station two blocks away.

Inside, the cashier, a frumpy lady in a corporate polo shirt, smiled at her.

June mumbled something under her breath to make the cashier go in the back for a while, which she did. Then June strolled over to the ice cream freezer and picked herself out a nice big cone, the kind with caramel and chocolate and nuts that would be just perfect for the hot weather.

It was almost time to catch the bus, so June headed back towards the school yard.

*****

June hadn't tended to be glad to see her mother in recent months. She loved her, in a prolonged sense. But lately, the woman, Tisha Lacon by name, had invariably been a herald of bad news or, more often, unnecessary worry. Usually some vague but damning complaint regarding June's father (the two had been fighting like warhawks lately).

Unfortunately, this Friday afternoon was no exception. There was her mother rudely blocking her path to the school bus.

June tried to duck behind a building, wiping the sticky ice cream off on her pants.

"Honey, where are you going?" Tisha ran after her. "I'm giving you a ride home!"

(By that she really meant her friend Mr. Johns was giving them a ride home. Tisha didn't drive.)

"Ahh! Mom! I'm just going to ride the bus."

"No, come on, June. There's something I need to talk to you about. A surprise!"

June stopped. She didn't buy the surprise bullshit for a second, but there was nowhere else to run to, really. The bus was already pulling away.

*****

Mr. Johns was a tough, wrinkly, seventy-seven-year-old codger with a kind heart and a mean tongue. His stories were better than his waffles and he drove a rusty old moving truck in which June soon found herself, crouching in the back with her mother and several suitcases.

She thought they were her mother's suitcases, but she wasn't sure. It was quite dark in the back of the old truck once the doors were closed. Just a bit of light coming in through small holes in the roof.

The truck pulled away from the school, and they quickly found themselves sliding back and forth across the metal floor.

June grabbed the side of the truck to stabilize herself.

"So, what's the surprise?"

Tisha slid forwards. “Um… your father and I are getting a divorce.”

It was a terrible surprise, and not really a surprise at all. June felt her little heart sink and her stomach tie itself in a knot. Her hands shook slightly. It was not a surprise, but somehow that didn’t make it any easier.

June sat in silence for the rest of the trip.

*****

The truck ambled along a winding country road like an old bear looking for a place to rest. That place was *The Farm*.

The moving truck pulled off onto a dirt road, sliding down along the gravel track through the woods. On the right ran a collection of small shacks, built by hand from rock and earth, corrugated metal, and second hand wood. Each was unique and beautiful in a haphazard sort of way. On the left, through a small buffer of pine trees, stood the great expanse of a Southern tobacco field. And at the end of the old, gravel road was the rocky spring that spewed forth the special deep earth water that was so treasured.

That glimmering, cool mineral water had in it the chemical compound fortitide which the mystics of The Farm believed would much ease their connection with the supernatural. Unfortunately, it was also physically addictive, which made it difficult for anyone living there to ever leave.

Though Tisha had lived on The Farm for some years now, she only drank bottled water from the store. June, however, had drank the deep earth water since infancy.

As the truck continued down the gravel road, people of all ages and races milled about on the edge of field and forest, their clothes worn and caked with earth from years of hard work, and carefully patched in all manner of colors. Their hair was wild and their gait slow and calm. June couldn’t see them from the back of the truck. She could only hear them calling out to their old friend Mr. Johns, but they were as familiar to her as her own two hands.

Finally, the old truck coughed to a stop in front of the gnarly old shack in which Mr. Johns had lived for nearly twenty years. Behind it, up on blocks, was an old yellow school bus.

Chapter 2

June sat outside the bus with her best friend of ten years.

Tim was a baby faced eleven-year-old, with greasy, black hair that hung in front of his eyes and a careful, precise way of moving.

He was on the ground, playing marbles by himself, as June sat nearby on a log, acting very solemn-like, and her mother busied herself with lord-knows-what inside the bus.

"You think they really mean it this time?" Tim asked.

June shrugged. "Mama says they filed the paperwork and everything. Makin' it official and all."

Tim won the game of marbles and set up a new round.

"They do some crazy stuff sometimes." June had her hands in her pockets. She was being stoic, as Jerome called it, but Tim could tell she was upset.

"Turd, I'm bored. Can't we go to the river or something?" He wanted to distract her. (As much as someone in her situation could be distracted.)

"Mom says I can't go more than one hundred steps from the bus."

"Your folks are crazy. No offense."

"I know it." She sighed.

Tim stood up.

She leaned back against a tree. "I'mma have to figure out some way o' straightenin' it all out," she said.

"Yep, I reckon so. Come on, let's see how far we can make it."

He touched the side of the bus, then leapt as far as he could.

"One," he said, pleased with himself.

He leapt again and made it even further than before.

"Two."

June smiled.

Tisha appeared like a ghost over them. She stood, pale and somber, at the top of the stairs that were connected to the back of the bus.

"See ya', Tim." June slid off the log and walked gracefully towards her mother, not quite looking up at her.

June's curly brown hair danced in the breeze, and Tim was suddenly very sorry to see her go. She was the most wonderful girl he'd ever met, but he didn't dare tell her that.

Chapter 3

The rows of seats that had once filled the old bus had been gutted, and in their place now were the various makings of a simple house: a makeshift kitchen with a propane camp stove, a basin for water, an old refrigerator with magnetic lettering on it, a couch, a few beat up chairs, and a saggy mattress in the back for sleeping.

The sun was setting as June entered the old bus following her mother. She'd been in it once before when visiting Mr. Johns. Apparently his mother-in-law used to live there, many years earlier.

Tisha began cooking dinner, and June looked out the window at the setting sun. Night made her nervous.

"Did you remember to bring the bone meal?" She asked her mother.

"I didn't bring it."

June looked concerned. "Whul, what're we gonna do?"

"Pray, I reckon."

June raised her hand, irritated. "I mean, that's good n' all, but what're we gonna do if, like, an evil spirit turns up or somethin'?"

Tisha took two mismatched (chipped) ceramic plates from the cupboard and began scooping pasta onto them, then turned to face her daughter, the fringe of concern entering the edges of her eyes.

"Your father…."

June raised an eyebrow. She was playing with the word magnets on the refrigerator.

"My father what?"

Tisha glanced uncomfortably at the naked Barbie laying on the coffee table near the couch.

"Don't make him out to be a god."

June's mother brought the food to the table and they began to eat.

Tisha flashed a smile. "Maybe I can do your makeup after dinner. I could show you how. Maybe it could help with impressing that boy at school—"

June glared at her.

"Not that you need it or anything, of course. Just if it helps you, you know, feel beautiful… or whatever."

June used her fork to move peas and bits of noodle around on her plate. The butter and tomato sauce left thick trails on the old ceramic.

"Give me something, honey!" Tisha burst out suddenly. "I can't live in this bus all by myself, with you completely ignoring me! I'm trying to be there. I'm trying to help! Just, let me do your make up! It's one small thing I'm actually good at."

June pursed her lips, then shrugged slightly. "Fine."

Tisha continued eating somberly.

Tisha had obtained an airbrush many years earlier while doing makeup for Monsignor Elslander Jr.'s Traveling Roman Catholic Circus. In those days it was necessary to apply quite a lot of makeup in one night, as she routinely did near-full body make up for two dozen adults. And so, she had purchased, with her own money, an exceptionally large liquid makeup canister to use with her airbrush, allowing her to refill far less often and to more easily buy in large bulk quantities.

Despite occasional ridicule from her daughter, Tisha had continued using the large canister because she was used to it and because the makeup was cheap compared to other airbrushable makeups, and it lasted a long time.

It brought her great joy to do her daughter's makeup, a wonderfully feminine connection with the girl she loved so much.

*****

June couldn't get to sleep in the old bus. It was too quiet, and there was a slight smell of something beginning to rot that gave her an uneasy feeling.

She closed her eyes and tried to think of nothing. She thought she could hear a clock ticking, but she wasn't sure.

That was a thought. She let go of it and returned to thinking about nothing.

She focused on her breathing. Inhale, exhale, inhale, exhale.

It was dark and quiet and there was only the sound of her breathing.

She thought of nothing. Just inhale, exhale, inhale, exhale.

June nodded off. She wasn't sure how long she'd been asleep, maybe a few hours maybe a few seconds. But she woke up suddenly—

There was a crashing. Glass breaking.

Her mother awoke violently beside her.

It was still very dark and June couldn't see what—

"Hide," Tisha growled.

June could see the moonlight coming in through the front door. The slight glint of smashed glass and, as her eyes adjusted—

Her mother grabbed her arm and half dragged her to the cabinets at the side of the room. It was dark and small inside, with too many pots and pans, but Tisha pushed her through the cabinet door and soon the two were crammed together in the dark box.

June went over what had happened in her head. There was the slight glint of smashed glass in the moonlight, and as her eyes adjusted, the silhouette of a man emerged. She wasn't sure. Had there been someone there?

There was a slight crack at the edge of the cabinet and June was able to peep through and see—

There was a man. June couldn't see who it was, but there was an arm reaching through the glass, reaching for the doorknob!

June's heart beat fast. Her hands were shaking. Her head swam.

The arm was hairy and muscular and strangely confident. Confident and unafraid.

"Who is it mom?"

"Shh, baby. Just keep quiet."

Then the door swung open. Slowly, because the man's arm was still in the door and he was controlling it.

And then there he was, inside.

Dressed in denim and grey and old work boots, tall and muscular and confident. There in all his glory. The man to whom June owed her creation.

Jerome Lacon.

"Daddy?" it was little more than a whisper. Everything was still so strange. She didn't understand. But it was him, wasn't it?

The gas light flicked on, flooding the place in detail and clarity.

It was definitely him. The man who had hoisted her to his shoulders, had taught her how to climb a tree, how to ride a bike. The man who'd taught her magic. The man who'd told her every night that he loved her.

Yes, it was definitely him.

She reached out to push the cabinet door open.

Suddenly Tisha grabbed her with both arms, covering her mouth and pulling her back. For a moment, June struggled, out of reflex. Then she was still.

She could still see through the crack in the cabinet. Her father pacing through the bus, looking in this basket, throwing everything off that little table, kicking this box over, smashing that, just because.

"June?" He asked the night. "June?"

She could see, even through the crack, that he was becoming increasingly frantic. Checking everywhere, however illogical, trying to find—

He found a picture.

She knew from the frame that it was one of her, taken several years earlier.

He stared at it. It was the first time he was still.

Jerome slipped it out of the frame and into his shirt pocket.

Then, for a reason June did not know, he looked up suddenly at the cabinet. He stared at it for, oh, two seconds, then stepped slowly towards it, like a mirage. Unsure whether or not he wanted to break the illusion. Unsure for the first time that night.

Suddenly, something else caught his eye and he stopped. A light had come from behind the neighboring shack. A lantern. It was coming towards the bus.

Quickly, Jerome put out the gas light. Then disappeared into the darkness.

June could feel Tisha relax.

June didn't understand.

*****

June didn't particularly like going inside Mr. Johns' outhouse. It was full of little piles of animal bones, with just a little flesh left on them, and faded old maps that smelled like moth balls. The dried snake skins and old postcards from Vietnam were certainly intriguing, but didn't necessarily set the mood well for taking a dump. So June was relieved to escape back into the fresh forest air outside.

The kind old bear was primarily known locally for his waffles and his stories. That morning, he provided Tisha and June with both.

"Radios'd gone dead, uniforms trashed. We'd been stuck there better part o' three days. Was a Charlie nest up top of the hill, rainin' fire and hell down on us every time we showed our sorry faces."

They sat on fresh cut logs between the bus and Mr. Johns' shack, eating syrupy strawberry-topped waffles off styrofoam plates. Waffles made with corn meal instead of flour.

June played with her food, her mind (aspiring to be) elsewhere.

"A boy from Saigon was with me. Spoke only about three words of English, but shot like he'd been born with an M1 instead of a pacifier. Him and I rushed it with everything we had. Laid waste to the whole place 'fore we even saw 'em clear."

Tisha stared at him with a strange expression: half horrified, half mesmerized.

This made June smile.

"People at the bottom cheered," he continued, "'n we thought for sure we'd won a medal of honor or some such thing. Then we went up there, checkin' for survivors. Not one survivor, but a few o' their faces were intact enough to make out."

June finished her waffle, her stomach a little unsteady, either from the story or the thick red syrup. She wasn't sure which.

"Seems we'd gotten turned around in the jungle, lost track of who was who."

June put her fork down.
"We won no medal for that escapade."
He was solemn for a moment.
Then "I'mma get you another waffle, Ms. June," and he went inside.

There were peepers singing a little ways off.

"How many times you think we've heard that story now?" June said, looking up at her Mom.
"Shh. Mr. Johns is very good to let us stay with him. An' I like hearing his stories."
June was skeptical of that, based on her mother's facial expressions. "He's gonna tell the gross one about the little girl next."
Tisha finished her waffle as well.
"When'm I gonna see Dad again?" June asked suddenly.
Her mom crossed her legs uncomfortably. "It's not a good time for you to see him right now."
She wouldn't look at June. It was irritating. She would look everywhere else.
"He's very angry. Because of me, I think. N' it's better if you stay here for a while."
"He needs to give me lessons."
"That needs to stop as well. What your father does is not good for the soul. I don't want you ending up like he has."
"Why? What'd you think's wrong with him?"
Tisha played idly with the syrup left on her plate.
Then Mr. Johns returned with another waffle and the conversation was over.
"Thanks," June said, taking the second plate.
Mr. Johns sat down.
"I ever tell y'all 'bout the time I accidently slit a Charlie girl's throat with my buck knife?"
June grimaced.

*****

It was empty on the bus when June snuck back in that afternoon. She checked around first to make sure, then climbed up onto the counter to reach something on the top shelf.
She brought a creased and faded shoebox down and stood by the bar to open it. She'd hidden it there as soon as they'd moved in. Inside there were many

odds and ends: sewing things, feathers, metal pendants. She rummaged around a bit until she found a doll, then another. Dolls of her parents.

She went back into the shoe box and found this time a bit of red string which she used to tie the two dolls together with a floppy bow.

Then muttering. "Let my wand form cupid's bond, let hate turn to restored fate, faction back to attraction."

She kissed each doll once on the head, then returned them, still tied, to the box, and the box back to the top shelf.

Then, with a satisfied nod, she went back outside.

Chapter 4

Tim was sitting on the forest floor, playing attentively with a little snake he'd found. He let it crawl over his hands, one after the other, and slither in between his fingers.

He heard the crunch of dead leaves and looked up to see June.

"That's some big steps," he said. They were well over 100 paces from the bus.

"Mom went shopping. Mr. Johns fell asleep."

She sat down next to him. Her shoulder brushed his.

"You figure anything out about your parents yet?" he asked.

"I did somethin' this mornin'. Should take about three days to take effect, long as nothin' interrupts it."

"That's good."

He let the snake slither away into the dry leaves.

"You seen your dad yet?"

"Nah. Not really."

They were high enough up the hill that they could look down on the little shacks and see all of them as a bird would.

"Oh, I got you some bone meal," Tim recalled after a bit. "Not a lot, but some."

"Yeah?"

"Yeah. It's in the tree house."

*****

The treehouse was as high as any kid could ever hope for. Tucked among the trees towards the top of the hill, you could look down on the occasional passersby and remain completely unseen.

It was a sturdy structure, perched at a ridiculous height. Easily six stories up, Tim thought, with a crude but effective rope ladder connecting it to planet Earth.

Wrapped around the tree house was a thick handmade rope, strung all around with dream catchers.

June sat on the edge, dangling her feet over the abyss.

Tim brought a mason jar from inside, extending his arm to hand it to her.

"Dang, we probably shouldn't've built this thing so high." Tim maintained a careful distance from the edge.

"Thanks." June took the bone meal and placed it carefully beside her.

"What's Mrs. Lancraft doing in her backyard, you think?"

Below them and a ways away through the trees was the house of Mrs. Lancraft, a hunched-over old lady who always wore a shawl. At the moment, she was standing in her backyard, digging a hole.

Mrs. Lancraft's mystique was greatly advantaged by the ten foot fence which surrounded her cabin, as well as by the reclusive disposition with which she led her later life. It had been a great excitement when, after completing their tree house, Tim and June discovered they could stare down into the old woman's back yard.

They would've felt too guilty to ever *plot* to spy on the poor old woman, but as it was a happy accident, they relished it.

The digging holes in the backyard, however, June had not yet seen.

"Burying her money," Tim said. "I watched her do it the other day, too."

"How much she got?"

"I heard she had a million dollars."

"A million dollars?"

"Yep. They say she's some kind of black widow or something." Tim leaned forward to see her better. "She marries men and then kills them for their money."

"Oh man."

Mrs. Lancraft dropped a rusty old box into the hole and began to bury it.

"Oh, there was another thing." Tim popped up and headed back into the interior of the tree house. Reappearing a moment later, clutching a little resin statue of a man only two inches tall.

He handed it to June, then sat down again a little ways back from the edge.

"My dad got it 'n ah antique store 'n New York," he explained. "Check the bottom."

On the bottom was a symbol—three vertical lines crossed by one horizon line—the symbol for The Farm.

"That's weird. What'd you think it is?"

Tim shrugged.

"I should ask my dad about it." She handed it back to him. "Whenever I see him again."

"Three days, right?"

"Three days."

She looked out at the woods. The leaves danced slightly in the wind. A lone bird glided between the trunks of the trees. In the distance the sunlight shone on the young tobacco. It really was an incredible view from the tree house.

"Sometimes I wish we could just hide up here forever," she said after a while.

"Well, climbing down freaks me out, so that may end up happening."

Chapter 5

The red-orange of the sun was just visible through the leaves when June finally returned "home". Tisha was standing, arms crossed, in the kitchen with Mr. Johns. They were standing very close together when June first opened the door, but immediately, her mother turned to face her.

"You're back," said June innocently.

"Where were you?" asked Tisha.

Mr. Johns looked a little uncomfortable.

"With Tim," said June. "He was showin' me somethin'."

"What were you thinking? We thought Jerome kidnapped you!"

"He's my dad…" June didn't know what her mom meant by it. She glanced at Mr. Johns uncomfortably.

He glanced once more at Tisha, then started towards the door. Paused uncomfortably. Left.

"I found this!" Tisha held up the dolls. The red string had been severed.

"You cut them!"

"I can't believe y— you tried to put a spell on me! Like your Father! It's all silly, crazy, and not real, but— I can't believe you'd— oh, June!"

Tisha gently touched June's shoulder and led her over to the couch where they sat down.

"I know it's been hard for you, leaving the house so suddenly, and your father and I— I feel just awful about it because I know how it's been hard on you, but—"

June hated these "heart-to-hearts".

"We're not getting back together. It's just not gonna happen at this point. I need you to respect that, and I need you to…"

June was stoic. She would never let them see her cry.

"Let go of the things your father taught you. I know it's hard to understand, but... you just have to believe me that it's not good for you. It's not good for you believing that stuff."

She couldn't hold it in any longer.

"Mom! You have to respect what I believe!"

June didn't cry, but she—

Well, she didn't understand all this, to begin with. Her mother had gone—

Her mother turned away. June could tell she was on the verge of crying.

"I raised a sinner," her mother said, not looking at her. "I raised a rotten sinner, who loves her father more than her mom."

Tisha collapsed into tears, letting herself fall into a ball against the side of the couch.

June tensed her shoulders and looked away. "I don't love dad more than you."

Her mother kept crying.

"Sheesh, Mom! What're you trying to do?"

Tisha turned even further away, face still in arm.

"Fine! I'll quit! Is that what you want?"

She only sobbed louder. "I'm such a wreck!" Then turned, and hugged June very forcefully.

Chapter 6

The gas lights flickered in the darkness. Tisha and June were still sitting on the couch somberly. Neither spoke for a while.

"I'll tell you a story," June said after a while, not looking at her mother. "To help you sleep. Like Mr. Johns does."

"Okay, sweetie."

June looked out the windows into the blackness that surrounded the bus.

"Once upon uh time there lived a king an' queen, and they ruled over a happy an' prosperous kingdom. Everyone was happy. Even the peasants were happy."

Tisha let her eyes fall shut and leaned her head against the back of the couch.

"And the king and queen loved each other very much. At least that's what they said. But they'd fight sometimes. Over silly stuff, mostly. But very loud and angry like."

June looked again out into the blackness, deciding whether or not to continue.

"And sometimes when they fought, they'd get so upset, that they'd go out into the woods, because they were so full of anger that they didn't even want to be in the same house together. The same castle, I mean."

June pursed her lips.

"And one day when they were each out… in the Deep Dark Forest… a demon came and told them he would take their fighting away, but in return he wanted a piece of their hearts to live in."

June turned the light off and let the darkness envelop them.

"The king and queen were weak. And the demon took over the kingdom. He made them do mean things, wicked things, even though they were good people, because he was controlling them. And the kingdom stopped being happy and everything got sad and dark and grey."

Tisha started crying again.

June just stroked her head gently, as her mother had done when she was little.

Chapter 7

Tisha lay asleep on the couch, her eyes still a little red. June lay awake beside her, listening to her breathing. Listening to be sure she was asleep.

When June was sure, she arose slowly and slipped out into the darkness.

She walked fast through the woods, the sounds of the night ringing in her ears, until she came to a clean and tidy little shack near the heart of The Farm. The lights were still on and a bit of smoke rose up from the chimney.

June climbed the two steps and walked past the rocking chairs on the front porch. She knocked on the heavy, familiar front door and a moment later there was her father standing in front of her.

"June," he said with a kind sort of smile. He hugged her. "Come in."

They sat together at the kitchen table. (Where June had her first solid food, lost her first baby tooth.)

"Want some tea, sweetie?"

They had some. With milk and honey.

He studied her, as though looking to see if anything were different.

"I'm glad to see you." He let his head rest on his hand. It was late, but he didn't seem sleepy. Tired, but not sleepy.

"Me too."

"How's your mom doing?"

"She's okay."

Jerome studied his hands. June liked looking at her dad's hands. They were much bigger than hers and there was something comforting about that. Or at least sometimes that was comforting.

"You guys need to make up," she said suddenly. "Even if you're not married again. Just, get along so I don't have to hide and Mom doesn't have to…."

June fell silent. Jerome frowned slightly.

"You know I tried to make it work, don't you? I really did."

June nodded slowly, unsure of herself.

"She's been difficult to live with for a while now," he continued.

June gripped her tea a little tighter. It was warm in her hands.

"It's better this way. You staying with me."

June's gaze darted up. "I just came for a visit."

Jerome played with the skin between his fingers.

June began to look sleepy.

"I should go soon. I just wanted to—"

She bent forward and laid her head on the table.

"I'm…" she tried to continue.

"Shh," Jerome said. "Just go to sleep. We can talk about it all in the morning.

Chapter 8

June sat in a small rowboat, drifting aimlessly across a vast, dark lake. She turned, trying to get a sense of where she was, and found that she was not alone. For behind her, looking at her, sat a skeleton.

Just as this registered in her mind, she noticed something else. A light, coming towards her from across the water.

Then, there it was. There she was. The most beautiful woman June had ever seen, floating winged beside the boat, glowing golden with her own radiance. She smiled at June, and June thought that must be the best feeling in the world.

The woman extended an arm to June, offering her an olive branch. (June knew somehow that it was an olive branch.)

But she didn't take it. Why didn't she take it?

June found herself instead, turning back towards the skeleton, who now offered her a wand.

Slowly, but inescapably, June found herself reaching out to take the wand. The skeleton's hand: firm and unflinching, alluring. Her fingers brushed the tip of the wood, then clutched it. It was cold and firm in her hand.

It was hers, it was in her hand—

Fire sprung up around the boat. The woman was gone.

It was a sea of fire. With a shudder, she realized she was standing on an awful, giant, fiery, grinning face.

Chapter 9

June awoke with a shutter in a room filled with stuffed animals, dolls and other toys. There was a peaceful still in the room that did no justice to the feeling June had in her gut.

She lifted herself out of bed.

Downstairs the house was still and quiet. She could hear the floorboards creak with every step she took.

All around her were familiar things. The setting of her life thus far. Yet there was an uneasiness about the place. Something about it was not quite right. She had to get back to the bus.

She tried to open the front door—a flash of green light. Jerome must've done something. The door would not open.

Maybe the window would—another flash of green light.

She stood by the kitchen table. Desperate. Quick breathing.

There was something on the table. A drawing. A house, she saw. Her childhood house. The house she was trapped in now. There was a box around it. And scrawled out beside it: "securum spud exire non".

A spell, June thought.

She tried to rub it off. But of course that didn't work.

She scrubbed harder… stopped.

Desperate. Quick breathing.

Jerome appeared on the other side of the room.

"June! You're awake! What would you like for breakfast?"

"Let me out!"

Desperate. Quick breathing.

Jerome bit his lower lip.

"I was thinking of French toast, maybe."

"You put a spell on the door! You're kidnapping me!"

"You're my daughter. I'm not kidnapping you."

He put a frying pan down on the stove, added oil, then flipped the element on.

"I just think it's best if you stay here for a while." He took out a bag of bread. "I told your Mom already. That you'd come here. That you were going to stay for a while. She understood, I think." He took eggs out of the fridge.

"I'm in a better place to take care of you right now. She knows that." He started cracking eggs into a mixing bowl. "How many pieces can you eat?"

Chapter 10

June sat on her bed, fidgeting idly with a naked Barbie doll. Her mind was in a million places.

She let the doll fall to her bedspread.

Her window curtains were open and outside, beyond the glass, it was a lovely day.

She crossed the room to a little desk, messed with childhood things. She reached into the mess, like a butcher into the innards of a fat turkey, and pulled forth from it a tiny wand, the one from the dream.

She held it like a trophy, like a key to a forbidden garden.

Under her breath: "Sorry, mom."

She was in the hallway, downstairs. There was a thick brown spell book and she took it down off the shelf. It was heavy in her hands and she bent her back a little to accommodate its weight.

She was in her room again, with the book and with the wand, crouching by her bedroom window. It was a nice day outside and the leaves blew a little in the wind. She was in her room again, crouching by her bedroom window, trying one last time to open it—a flash of green.

She opened the thick brown book.

Outside it was a nice day. Again, the leaves blew in the wind a little and everything seemed very alive.

Inside it was very still and quiet.

She flipped through the book, looking for—she picked up her wand.

"Libre obsidem!" she enunciated. There was a ringing, an ionization of the air. She lightly tapped the glass with the tip of her wand. The ringing disappeared, the glass did not. But a slight hairline crack appeared where her wand had touched.

She slammed the glass with her hands, trying to break it, but—the flash of green light.

June sighed.

She couldn't think. She was hungry, maybe that's what it was. She went down to the kitchen and made herself a peanut butter and jelly sandwich. Then headed towards the living room to sit and eat, but—on the way, the table again caught her eye.

On it this time were a new set of drawings: stars, scepters and other demonic symbols drawn in crude chalk. In the center of the elaborate illustration were three photographs, two of Tisha and one of the bus.

June was transfixed by it for a moment, staring off into emptiness as it's meaning set in. Something had to be done.

She went under the sink for cleaning supplies. She sprayed everything, scrubbed till the rag had holes.... Nothing.

Back to the cabinet, looking desperately for something stronger, pure acid if that was what it took.

There was a pile of plastic grocery bags in one corner and she rummaged through them, checking for something she may have missed. A little brown spider scurried out across the floor. She followed it with her eyes as the thing hurried up the chimney back into blackness.

She'd found a way out.

Chapter 11

When June finally made it back to the bus, she found the place encircled by what the children of The Farm called a *witch's ladder*, a thick rope, stuck full of feathers, twigs and other such things. Used in the execution of horrible curses. She had never actually seen one before, but she knew all too well what it was. It sat there, thick and rough, like a huge serpent surrounding its prey, ready to constrict it to oblivion.

June's heart beat a little faster and she broke out into a run towards the front door.

There was her mother inside, laying on the couch. Very pale, her hair very dry, her eyes somewhere far away.

"Mom!" But she heard her name, she was there enough for that.

"Sweetie….." Her voice was rough and frog like. "I was so worried about you…." Her body was limp on the couch.

"Are you okay, Mom?"

"Yes."

June didn't sit. Her little heart was beating like the wings of a hummingbird.

"I just don't feel so good," her mother said.

"Dad put a curse on you!"

"Is that was he says?"

"There were marks on the table. And right now, there's a witch's ladder wrapped around the house!"

Tisha's eyes were far away again. "I'm sure it's just the flu…." She nodded off.

"Mom! Wake up!" June was shrieking now. She shook her Mom with all she had.

Her eyes flitted open momentarily. "I just need to sleep, sweetie." Then she was gone again.

June bolted out of the bus. She ran straight through Middle Farm and didn't stop 'till she found Tim, standing on the edge of the tobacco fields. There was a little apple tree there. Tim was so calm. He picked one, slow as a box turtle, and let it slip into his mouth.

"Hey June." He bit into the apple again.

"He put a curse on her." June was out of breath.

"Are you sure?"

"I saw the marks and the rope."

Tim lowered his apple.

"She's very sick." June was pale with fear. Her arms hung limp by her side.

Chapter 12

Tisha was very tired. Dead tired. Tired from the tips of her fingernails to the marrow of her bones.

She had always been a good housewife, though. A good mother. And there were things 'must be done.

She rose, slipped on a bathrobe and limped into the kitchen.

"Enough sleep for one afternoon, even if you do have the flu," she told herself.

Suddenly, there was a knocking sound coming from the very walls themselves. It came thrice and made Tisha freeze in her own shadow. Something in the corner of her eye caught her attention.

The word magnets on the refrigerator were moving, rearranging themselves. Shifting and lurching horribly like a rabble of thick, white maggots.

LEAVE THE FARM NOW

Tisha's legs gave out and she collapsed to the floor. She hung on the cabinet, staring up with terror at the words that were still moving.

FIRST OF MANY

June and Tim rushed in and Tisha let out a little cry.

Chapter 13

June and Tim sat on the logs outside the bus. Tisha and Mr. Johns stood just a little ways off.

"I can't do this! I just can't do this!" Tisha was saying. And Mr. Johns was trying to calm her down.

"You don't have any choice about anything. Just go sit with them. Try to seem calm. Try to make them calm."

Tisha went to sit with them and Mr. Johns followed.

They sat in silence. Tisha looked very small and afraid.

"Maybe I should leave for a while. Till things blow over." Tisha crossed her hands in her lap.

Mr. Johns fidgeted with a stick. "I dunno if that's such a good idea, Ms. Tisha. You'd have to leave June behind. She's drank the water all her life. The withdrawal could be dangerous."

"You can't leave!" June cut in with disbelief. "Mom, don't leave me!"

Tisha looked down, not at anyone.

"That's how we lived all these years," she said. "He's the best around. He could charge anything he liked."

"There's no one that could match him?" Mr. Johns frowned solemnly.

"Not in this area."

He let the stick go.

"Do you think he'll kill me, June?"

"N-no—" everything was crazy and June didn't have any idea what was coming. "He just wants you to go away."

"And what if I don't?"

Tisha hugged her daughter. It was an awkward sort of hug, laced with elsewhere minds and very fake confidence. It was supposed to make June feel better, but something about it made her realize for the first time what a really nasty situation they were in.

"You're my daughter, and I'm going to do my best to protect you."

"You can't leave."

"Okay, I'll stay. I'll—"

Tisha teared up again.

Mr. Johns stood. "Just try to calm yourself down." He walked away.

Chapter 14

The sun burned golden orange as it fell away. June watched it go through the foggy bus window by their bed. That was always how it was with things dying. Near the end, that was when they struggled the most, when they burned the brightest, when they gave that final moment their all before being snuffed out and forgotten.

Chapter 15

Baths always helped Tisha calm down.

Behind the old bus, beneath a dim electric light, sat a dense and rusted claw foot tub, guarded by some thin wooden walls that, while sufficient to keep out wandering eyes, still allowed entry to a pleasant evening breeze.

And so, when dinner was done, Tisha distracted herself by carrying heavy buckets of hot water out to the tub. When it was adequately full, she slipped her clothes off and let her aching body ease into the warm, clear water.

It was dark by that point and she closed her eyes and listened to the crickets singing in the night. Several candles sat beside her, casting the little open air room in a flickering otherworldly light that mixed with that of the yellowed electric. It was steamy and delicious and she thought about the wax melting down and forming alien like masses on the beam beside her.

Her mind was far away when she heard the walls tap thrice, when she felt the slight tingling sensation at her knees. She thought it was her imagination at first, yet there before her was a small cloud of blood. There in the water. Small, but growing and thickening.

Within a moment she lay in a bath of thick blood and gore.

She screamed and threw herself from the bath, threw herself from the makeshift room, and ran naked out into the darkness.

There was June, standing on the front steps, looking worried.

"Am I okay?" Tisha shouted. "Am I okay?" She must've been cut. She hadn't felt it, but she must've been cut very badly.

"I don't see any cuts," little June said.

Tisha grabbed her. It was a hug, probably.

*****

Tisha was yelling again. Not at anyone present, or anything present. Just yelling. Perhaps at her father, June thought. Why was she yelling?

She fell quiet… but the yelling continued. It echoed through the trees, and came back to her from every rock and every branch. The night was yelling an awful, terrified, otherworldly yell.

Then growing out of the yell, part of the yell, was an awful, eerie, otherworldly voice. The kind that sent shivers down your back, and made June want to run inside and cover herself in blankets.

"You who give your heart to me…." And behind it an echo: *"Odium, odium, odium…."*

June wanted to go inside. With everything in her, June wanted to go inside. But her mother didn't move and June wouldn't leave her.

The voice welled up again from the yelling.

"The more you give, the closer I come…."

("Odium, odium, odium.")

Then the scream finally faded away and June and Tisha were alone together in the quiet darkness.

"We should go inside," Tisha said, to June's relief.

The bus felt very small in the great, wide night.

Chapter 16

Things felt a little better with sunlight. But there remained a somber still over everything that kept June from ever forgetting that night would come.

June kneeled just outside the bus, collecting dirt in a little velvet bag. The dirt was very dry and faded in her hands.

Tim ambled up the hill, sheepishly carrying a bouquet of wildflowers.

June frowned. "Hey."

"Hey." Tim held the flowers out to her. "I picked these for you." There was something dry and faded about them, though they were not wilted, and were very pretty in a wild kind of way.

June pulled the drawstrings of her bag shut and stood. "How come?" she asked.

"I thought'd you'd like them, an, I dunno." He was fidgeting, which June found strangely irritating. She caught herself, she was being—

"They're pretty. Thanks, Tim." They *were* pretty and he was being sweet.

"Any problems last night?"

"Bloodbath."

"What?"

"A curse, but nothing too serious yet."

Tim held out a mason jar full of an ashy powder, which June took with a polite smile.

"He's not gonna give up." There was worry in Tim's eyes and she knew that it was genuine.

"I know," June said. "Walk with me."

He followed her obediently around the side of the house.

"It's so silly really." Tim fidgeted nervously with his pants pocket.

"It's not gonna seem silly if someone gets hurt." Maybe that was the wrong thing.

"True."

Tim frowned thoughtfully. "Speaking of silly, you've been wearing the same make up for like three days, haven't you?"

June grinned and rolled her eyes. "Oh, Tim! You're such a girl."

"Seriously! It's gonna clog your pores and give you blackheads!"

"Clog my pores, huh?"

"I'm just worried about you. That's all."

"Oh, Timmy!" She pushed him playfully. He grinned.

She stepped back and leaned her face into the bouquet of flowers, then inhaled deeply. They still smelled sweet in a wild and free sort of way. They had seemed so out of place, but perhaps out of place was what she needed.

"Tim, there was something else besides the curse."

"What?"

"Afterwards…." She lowered the flowers. "We heard a voice. Coming from the forest. It didn't sound good."

Tim looked concerned again. "Do you think—"

A sick looking Tisha appeared at the door, waving at her weakly and rasping.

"June, come back inside."

The girl glanced at her old friend once more, then started up the stairs towards her mother.

It was musty inside. Everything was damp and muggy.

Tisha collapsed back onto the couch and returned to making odds and ends out of plastic beads and nylon line.

"I don't want you going out anymore."

"Mom, we can't just stay inside all the time!"

Tisha gave her a look.

Or can we? June thought.

She walked over to the couch and sat down a little ways off from her mother.

"You're making handicrafts again?"

"I'm gonna try and sell some to raise some money. I'm done being pathetic."

"Don't we still have some money left over from the last check?"

Her mother worked faster. "Not gonna be enough to satisfy Lester Topshun. We barely had enough for the deposit."

"Who's Lester Topshun?"

"A shaman from Louisiana. Mr. Johns found him."

"And you gave him all our money?"

"As a deposit. We have to come up with the full $3,000 in a week." Tisha had circled the day on the calendar.

"Or what?"

"We lose the deposit."

June was speechless for a moment. "Damn it, Mom! You gave all our money to some sham you've never met?!"

"Hey! Don't curse! You're too young. And I'm doing what I can, June. Your father is very good at what he does, and I need help protecting myself, and protecting you."

"But how do you even know this Lester guy's any good?"

"I'm doing what I can do, June. That's all."

June crossed her arms, unimpressed by her mother's efforts.

Tisha went back to her handicrafts.

Time passed like cars on a highway. Tisha toiled hour after hour producing more and more of the thing-i-ma-bobs and whatcha-ma-call-its. By the time the sun had been reborn and was once again a young adult, Tisha had a basket all but overflowing with her creations.

June lay asleep on the couch beside her.

"I'm going to start selling, sweetie," Tisha whispered. "I'll be back in a bit."

Chapter 17

June and Tim sat cross legged together on the floor of the tree house.

"So, first order of business. My mom gave all our money to some random shaman. We need to find out if he's any good."

"Your family needs less cursing each other, not more."

"I know my mom's crazy and all, but she's trying to protect herself. And me too, really."

Tim ate his sandwich.

June glared at him.

June sighed. "You can't expect her not to fight back."

"Yep. Everybody'll kill each other in the spirit of fighting back. I get it."

"Whatever. His names Lester Topshun. Have you heard of him?"

Tim shrugged dismissively, still a little hurt by June's harsh response.

"You have heard of him, haven't you? Tell me!"

"I really don't know if your Mom bringing him in is a good idea."

Now he had her attention.

"Why? Is he weak?"

"Nah, he's pretty strong." Tim fiddled absent mindedly with the brown paper his sandwich had been wrapped in. "He's like sixty-five, but he doesn't look it. Done some crazy spells. Back in the 60s, when he was a kid, the NAACP hired him to protect one of their sit-ins. Just protect them, mind you. But as soon as he got there, the Klaners started dying right and left."

June looked away. A cold tingle had just gone down her spine.

"'Till the white people gave him more money. Then he crushed the sit-in within an hour."

"So he's powerful."

"That's all you got from that story?"

June stood up. "Look, obviously he's not loyal. He's work for hire. That's why we have to come up with the money."

"We?"

"Well, obviously my Mom can't do it." June rolled her eyes.

Chapter 18

Tisha had a lot of time to think, walking quietly from house to house. Time to think about what had been, what it had become.

Friends and lovers make the worst sorts of enemies, she thought. They understand us more than any stock villain ever could. There is a piece of us in them, and even when we win, we lose, for every time we stab them, so too do we stab ourselves.

Tisha could not afford to think like that. Not at this stage. Of course there were moments, far more often than she would ever let on, that she remembered.

The times back when the passion took a different form. Those early days. Those early nights. When she and Jerome had wandered deep into the woods to be alone. His smile, illuminated in the full moon, grinning wildly. His entire face, his entire body, focused only on her. Everything on her, and she on him. There was no one else in the world, just the two of them alone in that clearing in the woods.

Her slipping her clothes off. Like Adam and Eve, the only two people in the world, alone in the moonlight.

Then came June, and they were young parents together. Oh, how wonderful that had been! Now there were three people in the world that mattered. But of course it hadn't always been easy. There'd been sleepless nights. Time's when they worried about paying the bills. And Jerome, sometimes he wasn't the same man she'd made love to that night in the clearing. There was a frustration about him now. Perhaps it had always been there, but it grew more and more prevalent.

At the same time, he was becoming more and more powerful. But there was always more to achieve. The stronger he became, well, the stronger he became. And perhaps she wasn't the same woman she'd been that night in the meadow, either. Perhaps she was less splendid, less fun, less young and beautiful. Perhaps he didn't love her quite so much as he had before. Perhaps she was no longer his complete world.

She didn't know. But there was more yelling. Definitely more yelling. And sometimes worse. Sometimes he scared her. Sometimes she thought about leaving him. Sometimes she thought about running away. But that wasn't easy, either. She had no money, of course. No job experience in years. There was June to think about. And despite the yelling and all of it, there were still days when he was like he had been. When he was charming, when he gave her that look again, where she was the whole world. She longed for that look, she lived for that look. Sometimes she thought about leaving, but she didn't, until she did.

*****

Tisha knocked thrice on one of her neighbor's front doors. Mr. Lafayette, a bald man with an impressive mustache, answered.

"Hello, Mr. Lafayette. I'm selling some jewelry I made—"

"No more of your knick knacks, Miss Lacon!"

He slammed the door.

Another front door opened:

"They're really quite well made, all with—"

The door slammed.

The next one had an animal snarling on the inside. *Best not to even get involved.*

Six dollars. All day and six dollars was all she'd made. Tisha put it in a shoebox under the sink. That circle on the calendar was getting close.

Chapter 19

June sat on the couch reading a book. Or pretending to read a book, at least.

There was food cooking on the stove. Smelled like cumin and garlic.

Tisha went in the back, behind the curtains at the rear of the bus and June jumped up immediately and grabbed some stationary from the cabinet. She slid it under the couch just as the timer went off.

June dove back on to the couch and returned to "reading."

She waited for Tisha to return.

"Mom! Food's ready."

June kept reading.

"Mom?"

She got up and walked to the back, then carefully lifted one of the curtains. There was her mother, sitting limply in an old chair, her eyes dark and distant, staring somberly at a picture of Jerome.

Chapter 20

It is not a pleasant feeling to awake from fright. Usually this happens because of things in our heads, but that night, June awoke because of something on her chest.

She felt something poking her and she squinted in the darkness to see what had woken her. Her mind was still somewhere between dream and awake, and at first she thought she was still asleep, but no, sure enough, there standing on her chest was a naked Barbie doll. The doll was staring at her, moving her head slightly and—

June jumped from bed, throwing the doll back onto the floor. June yelled in surprise and ran out of the bus.

She stood just outside, panting. Perhaps it had been in her head after all?

Then, there was the Barbie standing in the doorway, still staring at her.

*****

A rock hit Tim's window. With June, he was used to that sort of thing.

"Okay, I'll be right there," he called down to her, just quietly enough that his parents wouldn't hear.

He closed the front door behind him. "Sheesh, what time is it?"

"I don't care what you think of Lester Topshun, we're getting him as soon as possible!"

She turned on her heels and walked away. Tim rubbed his head sleepily, then followed her.

*****

They sat cross-legged on the floor of the tree house, a melted wax candle flickering between them. They stared at each other solemnly. It was too dark to speak loudly.

"Got any ideas? Tim asked finally.

June shook her head.

The sun came up. The candle melted down and went out. June held a pad of paper and a pen. She and Tim had bags beneath their eyes and wore half-present-half-asleep looks of slight discomfort.

"Let's go through the list one more time." The energy was gone from her voice. It took great effort just to sit up straight. "Okay, lemonade stand."

"No. The going rate is fifty cents. Even if everyone on the farm bought a cup, it still wouldn't be nearly enough."

"Girl Scout cookies?"

"You have to be a Girl Scout."

"Penny stocks?"

"What, is that seriously on the list?" Tim let himself fall back so he could lay on the floor. "These are all crap. We're screwed." He closed his eyes.

June frowned. "I should get home before my mom wakes up." She stood and went towards the door, then, looking out into the morning, she stopped.

"Tim?"

"What?"

"Could this work?"

Tim opened one eye. After a moment, he stood with a groan and walked over to stand beside his friend. She was staring out into the forest, into Mrs. Lancraft's back yard.

*****

The thick rope with the dream catchers hit the ground with a thud.

"I don't feel good about this." Tim fidgeted. "Isn't there another rope we can use?"

"Can't think of one." She didn't even bother looking at him.

"Without the charms we're gonna start getting demons in the tree house."

"We only need it for tonight. We'll put it back up tomorrow."

"I also don't feel good about, you know—"

June scratched her head uncomfortably.

"Look, neither do I. But my Mom really needs the money. Speaking of which, I gotta get back. If she's awake already, I'm dead."

Tim looked at his shoes. "Okay, see you tonight."

"Bye."

Tim watched her leave. Nobody else could've gotten him to do something like what he was about to do.

Chapter 21

When June got back to the bus, the naked Barbie was still standing in the doorway. June stopped and crossed her arms defiantly as she stared at the doll, who was raising her arms above her head and waving them dramatically, as though warning June not to go inside.

June grabbed a large stick and prepared to strike the Barbie with it. The doll shuddered and quickly jumped out of the way.

A cold chill ran down her spine as she entered the bus. There was something in the air, a tingling, a vibration that made every hair on June's body stand on end.

Then she saw her mother— unconscious, floating in thin air over their bed.

June stepped towards her, uneasily. Unsure of what to do, or even what was happening. All of a sudden there was a massive gush of wind and Tisha fell gasping onto the bed.

June rushed towards her. "Mom, are you okay?"

She was groggy, uneasy, lost. "I just had the most awful nightmare."

Her mother wouldn't look at her. June felt very uneasy.

"I don't think I can keep doing all this, sweetie. I just don't know if I can go along any more."

"Mom, listen to me. It's not—you're just feeling weird because of the dream. You have to keep on going, because we haven't got any other choice."

"I just need to sleep, for another day or two...."

June's hands were shaking. "Come on Mom, you've got to go sell your handicrafts or something."

There was a sort of metallic noise, a small, subtle banging and clicking. June turned to see a ragged, vintage monkey toy standing on the kitchen counter, clapping its cymbals. As June looked at him, the monkey gestured sideways. To a jar. The sugar jar.

She cautiously approached him. (It isn't wise to trust monkey toys you don't know.)

Tisha retched and coughed up a thick wad of green slime.

None of it felt real. It was like being in a dream, a nightmare. None of it made sense. What was this? A monkey toy, a Barbie, green slime. Was her mother dying? Everything was out of her control. Her mother wasn't there, not really. It was just her. She was alone with the monkey and the naked Barbie and the green slime.

Her mother's life depended on her, and maybe her own life as well.

Although it isn't wise to trust monkey toys you don't know, June was out of options. Out of ideas. The monkey toy continued gesturing unequivocally at the sugar jar. Finally June stepped forward decisively raising her shoulders, took hold of the sugar jar and extracted from it a perfect spoonful of sugar and fed it to her mother.

Tisha looked at her, breathing deeply. June checked her mouth to make sure she'd swallowed. Tisha seemed very tired, but slightly better, slightly more present.

"Why is this happening to us, June?" her mother said. "Why is this happening to us?"

"I don't know, Mom."

"Your father is an evil man, June. An evil, evil man who—"

She was interrupted by a scream, echoing back and forth in the woods. Then there was the voice again, deep and otherworldly, booming, drifting, reverberating from every direction at once. *"Odium, Odium, Odium"* it said.

The scream shifted up, increasing its pitch to an earsplitting ring.

For a flash Tisha looked a hundred years old. June was screaming as well now. Her's was absorbed into the scream of the forest, became part of it, bounced back at them like bullets from every crevice of every tree, every leaf, every rock. It was as though the air itself were shaking in fear.

"A piece of your heart I have," the voice said. "The rest shall I take." *"Odium… Odium… Odium."* The voice was as deep as the ocean and rough as pine bark.

With the last word all the sound faded away and everything in the morning air was silent.

After a moment, June fell upon her mother, embracing her, burying her face in her mother's arm.

Chapter 22

The next time her mother went out to sell handicrafts, June gave her a small bronze pendant.

"It's a charm-charm," she said. "Not as good as the ones daddy makes, but it's something."

Tisha put it on. "Thank you, sweetie." She smiled sadly, hugged her daughter, then walked off towards the other shacks.

Chapter 23

"Thou shalt not steal," Tim muttered as they stood outside the fence surrounding Mrs. Lancraft's home.

June looked at her feet anxiously. "My dad'll kill her if we don't get the money."

"Shit, shit, shit, sh— " It was difficult to see his expression in the darkness.

"Stop making noise." She threw the rope from the tree house up over a branch near the fence, then handed both ends to Tim. "I'll go first."

She pursed her lips.

Tim held the rope tight as June climbed up it, pushed herself off the tree branch, and landed with an ungraceful thump on the other side.

"Your turn," she whispered.

He tossed the ends of the rope over the fence and she held them as Tim scrambled over, dusted himself off and stood before the girl he cared for more than anyone else in the world.

He looked around and remembered with a sudden jolt where he was and what he was doing. Not that he'd ever really forgotten. But somehow it felt more raw now. Felt more real, now that they were standing here, standing on the other side of the fence they'd only ever seen from one side, seeing every blade of grass, every rock, the house only a few hundred feet away. It was a real place, and they were there, and they were there to rob an old widow lady.

"She buried the boxes over there," June whispered, pulling him from his anxious revery.

Suddenly a light came on in the house and they froze. It seemed to last six days. An owl cooed. Sunday came and the light went off.

June motioned for Tim to follow her and army-crawl across the yard to the designated spot. But before they made it, a dog ran from around the corner of the house. Again they froze, with panicked faces like the Hellenistic statues from art history class.

For a moment it stood over June, close enough to drool on her, just staring at her.

Then Mrs. Lancraft appeared in the doorway. "Axel!" she called. "Come on, Axel!"

Tim's whole body was tense. He wasn't sure he'd be able to move when the time came. There was no way they'd be able to make it over the fence fast enough, and he had a vague idea what Mrs. Lancraft, despite her age, was capable of.

"What are you looking at, Axel?"

The dog stared at her just a moment longer, then turned and ran back to his owner. Woman and dog disappeared into the house and the lights went out. Then, without missing beat or measure, June and Tim crawled the remaining distance and, with two small garden shovels, began to dig.

Chapter 24

They dug and dug like lost souls in Anarak's desert. It was slow going. The soil of The Farm was lined with dense red clay.

"Maybe she moved it," Tim whispered anxiously. His hands were shaking slightly, but perhaps that was just from the digging.

The owl crowed again.

"We just need to keep digging." June was completely focused.

They kept digging. Now the red clay was tangled with thick roots and rotting branches. They could make out the slight movement of disturbed roley polys and worms scurrying away in the darkness.

Tim threw his shovel down. "We've been here too long already."

Just then, June's shovel hit metal. They glanced at each other, momentarily savoring that joyous metallic clang they had craved since their feet hit the ground in that mysterious yard. With restored energy, June pulled aside the last of the dirt and clay and, with a sense of awe, removed a worn metal box from the ground.

She looked up at Tim, expecting to see admiration, but instead she found him looking past her, distracted by something else.

"We have to go."

"Yeah, just a minute." June looked back down at the box. "Let's just look inside first."

"No! We gotta go now!

June looked up just in time to see the silhouette of Mrs. Lancraft appearing in the illuminated doorway, this time brandishing the long, harsh shape of a shotgun.

"Go!" June cried and they took off across the yard. There was no secrecy now. They were found out. It was just about getting out before the hammer clapped. Before—

A loud shot cut through the night. Everything was ringing. There were no individual rocks now. No blades of grass. Just a blur of color and sound—the one loud sound in particular, and that ringing.

She could see Tim in front of her. He had to get over first. They were running and she could hear the old woman re-loading. And it was a blur of black and greys and moonlight. They were running. Breathing fast. Running.

They made it to the fence and June flung the box over. Later she would be surprised at her own strength, but in that moment it was simply what had to happen.

Tim seized the rope and two more shots rang out. A flash of light illuminated the darkness. They hit the fence nearby and they both knew their odds of escaping ungored were decreasing by the second.

Tim was nearly to the top of the fence now. June seized the rope to climb after him.

The old woman was coming closer, re-loading.

The two kids flung themselves over the fence like long jumpers. Without stopping a moment June grabbed the box and the two ran off into the night. They looked back only once, just in time to see the thick rope disappear behind the tall, tall fence.

Chapter 25

The two kids dragged their stolen box back up to the relative safety of their tree house. Tim collapsed against the wall, exhausted. June studied the lock on the box. It was still dark and she couldn't see it clearly. She groped around with her hand for a moment and found a large rock in one of the corners of the little room.

"That was too close," Tim said. "Way too close." He was fidgeting with the little figurine, turning it over and over in his hand.

June lifted the rock into the air and brought it down hard on the lock. Again she slammed it. She continued the assault for several more moments until finally the rusty old lock broke. Excitedly she pulled the box open.

Her heart sank to her stomach. Even in the darkness, Tim could see it immediately in her figure. He put down the toy he'd been holding and stepped over to see what she saw.

Inside was not a dime nor dollar. Instead, the box was filled to the brim with little orange pill bottles.

"Damn," June said.

"Damn," Tim said.

June shut the box. She tried to keep from crying.

Chapter 26

"Still no!" Mr. Miser said. He was a skinny, snobby looking man and Tisha was standing on his front step.

"But please, Mr. Miser, if you would just buy a bracelet or a necklace for your daughter it would help me so very much!"

"I told you no the past two days, Tisha. Leave me alone!"

He slammed the door in her face.

Chapter 27

The sun was setting as Tisha walked morosely up the hill toward the front door of the bus.

She stood in the kitchen, pen in hand, staring forwards. She crossed the last day off the calendar. The last day for the deposit.

June watched her from a distance, only looking away when her mother collapsed onto the couch and closed her eyes.

*****

June was cleaning the kitchen when the tapping noise came back. Three times. She listened for a fourth, but it did not come. She glanced around the bus. Waiting.

Suddenly, the walls of the bus began to move. Not to shake, as in an earthquake, but to bulge and distort, as though they were something organic. As June watched in horror, thick, sagging pores opened up all over the interior of the bus. They were huge, swollen, fleshy pores and from them oozed a thick oily black tar.

June panicked as it began to cover the floor. A drop of the stuff fell on Tisha's forehead and she woke up.

"Get outside!" June shouted.

June rushed to the door with her mother close behind, but the door would not open. Each time they tried to leave, there was a flash of green light, just as there had been in Jerome's house. But the bus had no chimney to climb out of.

They were stuck inside, and the room was quickly filling up with the suffocating grease.

June tried the windows without success. The stuff was up to their knees and rising fast.

Tisha zoned out, her eyes un-focused, her body swaying slightly on her feet.

"Mom! Mom, what're we gonna do?"

Tishas eye's remained in a far away place. "I'm sorry, sweetie. I just can't do this anymore." She closed her eyes. "I'm so sorry I let you down." Then Tisha let herself collapse into the tar.

"Mom! Mom!" June shrieked. The tar was up to her waist now, and it was becoming difficult for her to move, much less find her—

Something moved. She thought she'd seen— for a moment, there—a huge worm surfacing from the gloop. But then it was gone and she wasn't sure if—

"Mom! Oh my God! Mom, don't do this!"

June reached around, frantically trying to put a hand on her mother.

All it would take was a few moments beneath the surface and she would be dead, June kept thinking.

Then she felt something.

June pulled her mother's head from the gloop. The woman's skin was covered in the thick blackness, and she was unconscious but she seemed to still be alive.

"Mom, I need you to be strong! I really need you to be strong!"

Tisha didn't wake up.

June carefully dragged her mother through the gloop and lifted her as best she could onto the kitchen counter. Then June scrambled up herself. It would buy them some time, but not much. The levels were continuing to rise.

She was inky black from the waist down. The thick stuff would soon engulf them. They would be smothered and drowned in the blackness. The curse had sealed the bus perfectly. There was no way out this time.

June curled up in a little ball and waited for the blackness to reach the top of the counter. She wished her mother was there to comfort her. Really there, and not just passed out. Not just an empty body.

Just then she felt something tapping her side. She looked to see the Barbie, standing beside her, holding a tiny makeup kit.

It took June a moment to realize what the doll meant, but when she realized she jumped up with renewed vigor. She jumped off the counter back into the abysmal gloop and rushed over to the nearby cabinet from which she took her mother's industrial makeup sprayer.

She hurried through the bus spraying makeup in each of the pores. Each clogged and ceased to ooze the sickly gloop.

June breathed a sigh of relief, then tried the door.

No luck. The shield was still there.

As she turned around, the gloop splashed up before her and from it emerged the fatty, sun starved white body of some giant boorish worm. It knocked her beneath the surface so that her whole person was submerged in the terrifying blackness.

She surfaced a moment later, gasping for breath, but the thing still had a hold of her and was trying with all its considerable might to drag her back to the depths.

Just as she was dragged back below the surface, June managed to catch hold of a worn old kitchen knife. Then she was gone. Back beneath the bitumen.

A moment passed.

Another.

Again the mucilage bubbled up and this time June emerged from it, unrestrained.

Once she'd caught her breath, she took her wand from her pocket and after a bit of mumbling and wrist flicking she was finally able to open the door.

No doubt the spell had been weakened by the death of its boorish worm.

Chapter 28

June stood on the doorstep, looking out into the night. Gloop splattered out on the ground before her.

"You can't get her this time, Mr. Odium!" she shouted. "She's not even conscious!"

June stopped to catch her breath.

"What am I doing?" she thought suddenly. "It's starting to get to me...."

There was a scream in the distance. A strange, otherworldly scream that grew louder and closer from every direction until it filled up the night air completely, pulsing and reverberating from every rock, every branch, every leaf, every mysterious and haunting shadow.

The scream was all around her, and for a moment, June was 80 years old. Her back hunched, her skin sunken, her eyes tired. She felt what it was to be old, to be close to death. For a flash, and then she was a little girl again. But the scream was still there. She was still inside the scream, and then there was that voice again. That terrible, deep, haunting voice.

"Four more days," it said. *"Odium, odium, odium."*

Then the noise faded away and the forest was silent.
Four more days? June thought. *What happens in four more days?*

She rushed inside and closed the door.

Chapter 29

The next morning June busied herself cleaning the bus. She carried the thick, black gloop out in buckets, two at a time, and dumped the cursed substance a sufficient distance from where they lived.

Her mother appeared in the doorway. "Come on, honey. Get ready. I want you to come with me!"

*****

Just outside the farm was a little country church that many Farm residents went to on Sunday mornings.

Tisha and June sat together in the waiting area, outside the minister's office. It was a simple church. Worn antique wood, with flower print cushions. Little religious statues sat here and there between lace laden lampshades.

Tisha was staring at her daughter, looking at her deeply, somberly.

"I can do this," Tisha said.

"You can do this?"

"A little more optimism would be nice, but…."

June looked away.

A church secretary appeared in the doorway. "Mrs. Lacon? Minister William's will see you now."

*****

It was Sunday morning. Wanda Williams stood at the front of the room aiming a piercing stare at her congregation. She was a small woman, in stature and build (although age had contributed some mass in certain areas). She had short thick dreadlocks that didn't quite reach her shoulders. She spoke with a Caribbean accent and wore glasses, which didn't hide her eyes. Big eyes, the kind of eyes that always told you exactly what she was thinking.

Today, her eyes were narrowed and careful.

"There is evil in the world," she began. "Sometimes it tempts us with promises of great power. But I promise you, just as the Lord promises you, that no good will come from dealings with the devil."

Tisha and June sat in the audience, June watching her mother, Tisha considering her own expressions carefully.

"Someone in this community has utilized unholy powers. Someone in this community has given a piece of his soul to the darkness." Minister Williams spoke with passion and subdued fury. "You know who you are. And you will be damned to eternal Hell."

June gaped in shock.

"Today's collection plate goes to the victims of this atrocity. I ask you all to give as generously as you can. For these women truly are in need of your help."

Two silver platters began to circulate the sanctuary.

*****

The sanctuary was mostly empty. Wanda Williams was standing near the front, organizing some papers when June approached her cautiously.

"June. Come here, my dear," she said sweetly.

She obliged.

"Your mother told me how bravely you protected her. With your brains and your spells."

June frowned. "Is all magic a sin?"

The woman considered carefully. "We believe it is sinful because it comes from the devil, or pagan spirits, rather than from God."

She finished a stack of papers and went on to another.

"Sometimes in life, though, we are faced with complicated choices. You had to choose between using magic or letting your mother be harmed, which would've been far more of a sin. Intentions matter in situations like this."

June nodded, still looking very solemn.

Tisha approached the two, and Williams handed her an envelope.

"Thank you so, so much." Tisha stared at her, wide eyed.

"Good luck to you both."

Wanda Williams turned and left, leaving June and her mother alone in the sanctuary.

"You're going to use it to hire Lester Topshun?"

"That's right."

"Does she know?" June nodded after Wanda Williams.

Tisha studied the cross at the front of the room. "Come on," she said finally. "Let's get home."

Chapter 30

June awoke to the sharp, startling feeling of a hand pressed tight over her mouth. She shook violently for a moment before realizing it was Tim, crouching in the shadows beside the old mattress she and her mother shared.

He uncovered her mouth.

"What're you doing here?"

"Remember how I said taking the dream catchers down was a bad idea?"

*****

Tim and June looked up at the treehouse as they walked out from the flickering shadows. A fire was burning inside the structure, though the wood itself appeared undamaged.

"Fire spirit," Tim mumbled.

"Damn." June pursed her lips.

"Too many demons in these woods to leave a structure as high as that one unprotected."

"Yeah, I know. Let's go get some water balloons."

"I already got some."

June flashed a quick smile. "Nice."

Tim grinned sheepishly.

Then she was back to business. "Alright then, I guess I had better start climbing."

"You want me to go?"

June paused for a moment, considering. "Nah, it's fine. I got it."

With a bucket of water balloons in one hand, she began to climb the ladder. She climbed higher and higher as Tim became more and more nervous down below. Finally, she neared the top.

Suddenly a tail of flames spat from the door of the tree house. It cracked and swung, like a bull whip soaked in gasoline. She dodged it but it came again.

She retreated down the ladder.

Tim sighed as her feet hit the ground.

"We'll have to go the back way."

"I'm coming then," Tim said. He tried to sound brave and chivalrous.

"Suit yourself."

The two kids climbed through a hole near the base of the tree. The inside of the tree was hollow, and slowly but surely they began to shimmy up through the inside of the trunk.

"You're not claustrophobic, are you?" June asked.

Tim stuttered.

"When we get inside, aim for its heart."

*****

By the time the sun came up, the inside of the tree house was littered with the colored remains of broken water balloons and the harsh black of ash and soot. Tim and June busied themselves cleaning the mess up.

Tim had been of actual help to June in the fighting, and he felt more confident than usual.

She had been so brave, fighting the fire spirit. He knew there was no other girl like her in the world, and even though she was sweaty and shaky and covered in charcoal, he couldn't take his eyes off her.

"June, um, can I talk to you about something?"

"Yep, I'm listening."

"So…." He fidgeted with the broom he was holding. "I really like you."

She looked at him, raising an eyebrow.

"Like me?"

"Um, yeah.."

June looked away uncomfortably.

"You're pretty much the coolest girl I've ever met. I love spending time with you. When we're having adventures, or just hanging out. And, you're really pretty. So, I thought—"

"Tim, just, no!" she interrupted him. "I, I like hanging out with you too, but I just don't see you like that. I just see you as a friend."

Tim was speechless and embarrassed. He sputtered again, before finding his words. "Oh, right. Okay. I'm sorry, June. Nothing weird, right?"

June noticed something on the floor and picked it up. It was the statue Tim's dad had brought back, only it had started growing in certain places, and gaining color.

"Must've been the water," June muttered.

Tim looked away.

Chapter 31

June and Tim walked the little statue down to the edge of the lake and dropped it in so that it was submerged completely in the cool forest water.

"What do you think it is?" Tim asked.

"I dunno. We'll have to come back tomorrow and find out." She turned and started to leave.

"June?"

She paused.

"June, you're not mad at me, are you? For what I said in the tree house?"

"No, why would I be mad, Tim?" She didn't look at him. "Just don't bring it up again, please."

*****

Tisha was busy cleaning when June walked back through the door of the bus.

"It's hopeless trying to get you to stay in, isn't it?" Tisha asked.

The bus was cleaner than June had ever seen it, and Tisha was in better spirits than she had been in some time.

"I guess it'll all be over soon enough anyway." She was dusting. *Her* mother was *dusting*?

"What's going on?"

June put her stuff down.

"Go put your stuff away. Lester Topshun's coming tonight!"

"Lester Topshun? Already?"

"I told him it was an emergency."

June gaped for a moment, then scurried off to put her stuff away.

*****

Tisha and June sat anxiously outside the bus, waiting.

It began to get dark. The crickets came out of hiding.

Finally, a bright red truck pulled up the rough gravel road, and June and Tisha rose excitedly, nervously.

Like a lumbering giant, the truck rolled to a halt mere feet from the bus. The huge mass of shiny red metal and plastic seemed otherworldly in the run down hodgepodge of The Farm. Dust radiated from the wheels. The windows were too tinted to see inside, and for a moment, everything was simply still.

Then one of the doors opened and a fifty-something-year-old, big-gutted, swaggering good ol' boy with a patch over one eye and a belt buckle big enough to kill someone stepped down as though he were getting off a horse at the rodeo.

"Lester Topshun?" Tisha asked nervously.

"That right!" he boomed. "You must be Tisha."

They shook hands.

"And this is my daughter, June."

"How you doin' little lady?" He shook her hand as well. "Let me be the first to tell you ladies, your troubles with your former husband, father, are officially over. I am the best paranormal provocateur and soldier in the southern United States." He bowed dramatically. "You've hired just the right man."

Tisha stared at him in awe.

"Well, how about you show me where my bed is?"

Tisha looked uncomfortable. "We have only one bed.... But you can have it. I'll sleep on the couch."

"That'd be fine."

Lester started towards the bus and they followed.

"Not much privacy here." Lester Topshun set his stuff down beside the mattress on the floor. Tisha and June stood a little ways off, watching him carefully.

"Yes, sir. We're a little hard up right now." Tisha rubbed her hands slightly.

"Long as you're not so hard up as to not pay me."

"No, sir. We have the money. As I said before we really appreciate you coming on such short notice."

He finished unpacking and turned to face them.

"Well, sure! I always try to help people in need. Anyway, this fellah' Lacon's been a bit of a rival ah' mine for some time, as it were."

June stepped forward suddenly. "I do magic too, sir," she said.

Lester laughed. "That right, little girl?"

He took his shirt and pants off to reveal pajamas underneath.

"We'll get it all figured out in the morning." And with that he climbed into bed.

He lay still for a moment, his eyes shut. Then, "Turn the lights off, please."

Tisha was a little taken aback, June thought, but she obliged.

Chapter 32

It was morning, barely. Lester Topshun was standing about nine feet off, blowing a whistle to wake them. They looked up at him groggily, Tisha from the couch, June from the floor beside it.

"This is war!" Lester bellowed. "And we will treat it accordingly. Up! Both of you up! I wanna know everything there is to know about this fucker Lacon. Where he sleeps, where he pisses, his hopes and dreams, his worst nightmares. We're gonna destroy him cell by cell!"

June frowned. "We don't want to destr—"

Tisha cut her off with a glare and she fell silent.

Lester gestured for them to come and sit with him at the kitchen table.

"Y'all ever hear of a fire spirit?" he asked.

June nodded.

"Well, I got a whole family of 'em." Lester grinned wickedly.

Chapter 33

June stood with her father in the ashes of her childhood home.

"I came as soon as I could get away," she said.

He nodded slightly.

After a moment he gave her a hug.

The two walked together through the woods, slowly, not saying much at first.

"I heard about what happened with the pores, and the bloodbath, all of it," he said.

June looked around at the scenery. The forest was lush and cool. Moss grew on the huge old trees. Little pockets of sunlight danced down through the leaves.

"I didn't mean for it to happen like that." He had stopped walking now. For some reason she couldn't look him in the eye. "You know," he went on, "I'm not great like Lester Topshun. I cast generic spells. I—I put everything I had into one that was supposed to bring you back to me. But, you know, those kind of things never turn out like you expect."

June nodded slightly.

"I'm so sorry." He pleaded with his eyes. He was tearing up now. She still couldn't look at him.

"Tell your Mom I'll leave The Farm. I'll let you two be."

"No, Dad," she said finally. "I don't want that! I just want you two to get along!"

"I don't think that's going to happen at this point."

He walked away, leaving her alone in the woods.

Chapter 34

June flew into the room like a storm. Lester and Tisha were sitting at the table, planning another offensive.

"Stop!" the little girl demanded. Pleaded. "It's over. Daddy says he'll leave us alone."

Lester and Tisha glanced at each other.

"It's over! We can all be done with it now!" June's hands shook slightly.

"Over? Already?" Tisha seemed uneasy. Cautiously optimistic, maybe. But uneasy.

"It could be a feint." Lester's countenance was solemn and calculating.

"A feint?" The color drained from Tisha's face.

"Feint deceive," Lester explained. "Fencing term. You think he's here," Lester gestured with his hand. "He waits 'till I'm out of the way, then bam, he stabs you in the heart."

"You think he's calling ceasefire so you'll leave?"

"Seems like a strong possibility to my mind."

"Makes sense."

Now it was June's face that sank. "No! That's not what it is! I talked to him. He—he just doesn't want me to be in the middle anymore. Doesn't want to put us in danger an—"

Her mother stood and embraced her.

"Why don't you hang out with Tim for a bit?" Her mother's voice was sugary sweet, in a cold, dismissive sort of way. "It's probably better, like you say, if you don't have to be in the middle of this."

June was on the verge of tears now. "Just think about it, Mom. You used to love him. He used to love you. The least you can do is leave each other alone."

Chapter 35

Tisha was only twenty when she became pregnant with June. She used to like to lay on the floor, staring up at the stars through the skylight, her eyes damp with tears.

Now Tisha's eyes were dry and full of fire, full of spunk and of life. She stood with Lester atop the bus, only now, the old yellow thing floated, turning ever so slightly just above the tops of the trees. The wind rushed through her hair, blew her skin dry.

Two weeks ago she would have been terrified, but now she found it exhilarating. There was a carnal rush to it, an almost sensual immediacy. She could see forever, and she surveyed the forest as a queen would her subjects.

"I've never felt like this before!" she shouted above the rush of the wind.

"Free?" Lester asked.

She took a drag from a cup of sweet deep earth water.

"Better than free." A bonfire danced in her eyes. "Powerful!"

Lester lowed himself to one knee. "Majesty," he said in a deep, hypnotic voice, "Your wish is my command!"

He bowed and Tisha's face contorted into a broad, wicked grin.

Chapter 36

"We're being destroyed by our own hate," June said. They were sitting on the edge of the treehouse, staring off into the verdure.

"They are." Tim was, as always, careful of the edge. "I don't think you have a mean hair on your head."

"I'm sure I do." She didn't look at him.

Tim fidgeted with a stick. "You can stay at my house 'till it all blows over if you want."

"I'm afraid they'll kill each other before it all blows over."

Tim nodded slowly. "So what's the plan?"

"I need to find my dad."

"I'm coming too, then."

"I think it's better if you don't."

June stood up decisively.

Tim stood as well.

She glared at him for a moment, then just shook her head and started down the ladder.

Chapter 37

Lester lay three identical briefcases down on the kitchen table where Tisha was sitting. He popped one open to reveal rows and rows of little figurines, each unique, each representing some man or beast.

He offered the briefcase to Tisha, inviting her to choose. She carefully selected a figurine depicting a bulky, mean looking troll of a man, taking it from the case with a grin.

"We *will* find him, Majesty."

Chapter 38

"He may have gone to the old oak by the lake," June said. "It's one of his favorite places to sit and think."

She was walking fast through the woods and Tim struggled to keep up. Finally they reached the grand old tree.

"Dad?"

"Mr. Lacon?"

June began to circle the tree, but before she'd made it 200 degrees, she found herself face to face to with a hulk of tan flesh. The troll of a man roared upon seeing her, and droplets of saliva and bits of undigested food splattered themselves upon her terrified face.

The two took off down the hill.

"Can you do anything about it?" Tim yelled.

"Trolls are almost impossible to kill. Just run!"

They flew down the hill towards the pond, the troll man in hot pursuit. Finally they lost him by jumping down an embankment, but they knew full well he was not far off.

When they reached the water, however, something caught their eye and they could not help but to give pause.

In the shallows of the water there sat a life-size version of the stand their figure had stood upon. The man himself, however, was gone.

A stick broke overhead and they looked up to see, perched precariously on a branch over their heads, a twenty-something-year old young man dressed in vintage Victorian era clothing that matched his greasy black hair.

June took a step back. "He's the—"

The man looked confused.

"What're you doing up there?" she called to him.

"Trying to see where I am," he said. "Who are you?"

"I'm June. This is Tim."

"June? Why are you wearing boys' clothing?"

The man half jumped, half fell out of the tree and landed with a thump near where June and Tim stood. He stood and dusted himself off delicately.

"What do you mean boys' clothing?" June asked, a little offended.

"Britches," he explained. "They're not very flattering on a girl your age. Even way out in... wherever the hell we are. Where are we by the way?"

"The Farm."

He seemed oddly reflective upon hearing that. "That's interesting," he said, then turned and began walking up the hill.

June glanced at Tim, then followed the strange man.

"Look, I think you really should be more appreciative considering we just freed you from that thing you were in. And anyway, I think it's perfectly fine for me to wear jeans if I want to. I mean, it's not the 1800s or something like that."

The man turned suddenly. "Is it not?"

June was a little taken aback. "No…"

"Damn it, fucking hell!" the man shouted suddenly. He then turned and continued up the hill.

"I mean, we don't know who you are!" June stayed on his heels. "Maybe Tim and I have done something awful by setting you free. Maybe you've got an evil side."

"I will gladly show you my evil side if you don't leave me alone."

Suddenly they heard a roar, and smelt the sweet odor of warm breath and decomposing flesh. They turned to see the troll man a little ways back, towering over a terrified Tim.

June rushed towards him, flicking spells at the troll man, but it did no more than to annoy the monster further. The thing grabbed Tim and it seemed he would rip the poor boy in half.

The strange man from the lake rolled his eyes and finally stepped forward towards the thing. One flick of his wrist and the troll thing began coughing up blood and it's own guts, dropping Tim as it grabbed at it's stomach. A moment later, it was dead on the ground.

Tim and June stared at him dumbfounded.

The strange man shook his head, then turned to continue, once again, up the hill.

"Whoa…" June said under her breath. She shot Tim a rotten look, then ran up the hill after their rescuer. She managed to get in front of him, then she stopped.

He raised his hands in annoyance.

"I mean, that was unnecessarily brutal and all, but you're really powerful! You could help us!" June was practically bouncing with excitement.

"Why would I want to help you?"

June looked a little taken aback.

"I've only known you for about thirty seconds, and I've disliked you for twenty-six of those seconds." He began to walk past her.

"We could pay you!"

The man stopped, mildly interested.

"How much?"

"Oh, never mind. I forgot we already gave it all to this other shaman who's—"

The man kept walking.

"Where're you going anyway?"

The man stopped suddenly, considered for a moment, then turned to face her.

"What's around here? Is there a stable or something?"

"A stable?"

June smiled slightly, considering something.

*****

The strange man and the two kids stood outside the bus, staring at Lester's shiney new truck.

"Horses are obsolete, unfortunately," June said. "But now we have these. Cars."

"How do they work?"

"Something to do with explosions and gears and whatnot."

The strange man grunted. "Well, I don't see how this is going to help me. I need to get back to New York."

June shook her head. "These things go seventy, eighty, even a hundred miles an hour."

"Really?" the man seemed shocked.

"Sure! But you need to know how to drive them."

The man stared at the truck, fascinated by it.

"I'll teach you how to drive it," June said, "if you teach me to do magic like you do."

"Like I do? That took years, darling."

"Just teach me what you can in the time it takes me to teach you about the car."

The man crossed his arms. "I hate teaching."

"Worse than you hate walking all the way to New York?"

The man grimaced. "A hundred miles in an hour, you said?"

"Yep!" Grinning, June extended her hand for a sealing shake.

The strange man just grunted and walked away, leaving her hand floating.

"Do you actually know how to drive a car?" Tim asked.

"How hard can it be?"

Chapter 39

Lester Topshun lounged on the couch, his eyes closed, snoring, while June and Tisha cleaned up from dinner.

"He's going to teach me magic!" Tisha whispered excitedly. She was smiling like a schoolgirl.

"Why?" June scraped a plate.

"Because he's a nice man who wants to help."

"No, I mean, why do you want to learn all of a sudden? I thought you said it was a sin. You never had any interest when you were with dad. You never had any interest when I tried to teach you."

Tisha frowned, pursing her lips carefully. "Since I left him… I've realized how… influential it can be."

"Influential, huh? And how about this Lester. What's he getting out of it?"

"Like I said, he just wants to help. Some people are like that, believe it or not."

June crossed her arms. "Are you paying him extra?"

"No. He just wanted me to sign some contract."

June nearly jumped out of her own skin. "A contract!? What did it say?"

"Just like, don't use it against him, or—you know, inform to his enemies…."

"His enemies! You don't know, do you? You didn't even read it?"

Lester bolted up from his nap with a gasp, glancing around a little embarrassedly.

"Damn inquisition," he mumbled before walking out irritably.

"You've never done anything strong before in your life! What makes you think you can start now?" June put down her dish rag and walked out as well.

"June!" Tisha called after her. "June!"

Chapter 40

Tisha walked angrily, but with resolve, through the forest. She came to an old, ivy covered tree by a pool of water.

"You knew where I was all along, didn't you?" a voice said from above.

Tisha turned to see Jerome perched on a tree branch behind her. He was in bad shape, haggard looking, his clothes in rags.

She struggled to seem calm. "I've come to—to tell you that you have to leave The Farm, and June."

"I already said I'd do it. For June's sake. Not for you."

"I'm going to make you do it." She tried to stare him down.

Suddenly she flickered her wand at him aggressively, and he, with reflexes built over years, flicked his wand from his pocket and blocked it.

"Did you come here to kill me?" He smiled slightly.

"I'm not as weak as you think."

This time he stared her down.

"Lester's been teaching me!" She tried to sound confident. "I've become—I've become stronger than you! You can't treat me like you used to, because I'll—"

Jerome tapped his wand and Tisha's eyes glazed over.

Everything was hazy. She could see herself in their old home. She was on the floor, writhing. Jerome was standing over her, wand out.

Then it was a different day, and she was up against the wall in the kitchen, shaking slightly, her face puffing up in bizarre boils. Jerome stood there, watching her, wand out. "Please—" she gasped. A five-year-old June peered through a crack in the door, watching in horror.

Tisha gasped for breath, sobbing quietly. She was back in the woods, back in the clearing she had walked to so willingly. She was on the forest floor, groping, stomach down, through the wet leaves like a salamander.

And there was Jerome, walking slowly towards her, wand out, until he was directly over her, so close he could've put his boot down on the back of her head.

"You've just embarrassed yourself again, Tisha." He shook his head. "Take June and get out of here."

He walked off into the night.

*****

Tisha struggled up the hill towards the bus, half-walking, half-crawling, her eyes still sunken from what had happened. Outside the bus Lester stood like a general, surrounded by an army of floating spirits, immaterial clouds of mist, with sunken, lifeless faces.

"There you are!" he called to her.

She approached him slowly.

"What happened to you?"

"Jerome happened," she said weakly.

"You found him?"

"Yeah, I found him, alright."

"Well, that's great! I was just getting ready for our next attack!"

"No."

June, hiding in the shadows a little ways off, smiled to herself.

"Your services are no longer required, Mr. Topshun." Tisha stood up as tall as she could.

"What?" he spat.

"You'll leave in the morning."

She was too worn out for talking now. She limped towards the door of the bus to go lay down.

"Just because you lost a fight?" Lester called after her. "You weren't ready! You still have— I've still gotta teach you more!"

Tisha turned on the steps to face him. "I am not a magician, Mr. Topshun, and I have never wished to become one. Paying you does not bring me personal strength. It only allows me to feel—"

"I don't want to listen to a fucking inspirational speech," he growled. "If you don't want me protecting you anymore, then fine. Have it your way. But the contract you signed doesn't allow for refunds."

Tisha turned to go inside. "I'm going to bed, Lester. In my own bed. I hope you'll be gone by the time I wake up."

*****

Tisha was laying on the old mattress, still awake, when June came in and hugged her.

"That was really brave, Mom. I'm proud of you."

"I love you, sweetie," Tisha said with a smile. She closed her eyes peacefully.

Chapter 41

June tiptoed into an old barn near the bus. There among the splintering wood and sunken walls, set off aways in the shadows, the strange man from the lake lay asleep in the straw.

Malrose, he'd told them his name was. Hayman Malrose.

She reached out to him and patted his shoulder, only what she touched wasn't human.

"Do you want something?" he asked, standing behind her.

In her hands were only his coat and some old pants, stuffed with straw. She looked at him, a little confused.

"I like to see who comes after me in my sleep."

She stood up.

"I don't actually sleep," he told her. She kept staring at him. "Anyway, what do you want?"

She took a moment to collect her words. "Do you still want to go to New York?"

"I have to go to New York, if that's what you mean."

"Then you have to learn to drive tonight. The car won't be here in the morning."

*****

June held up a key, a spare she'd swiped from Lester's stuff when he was asleep.

The inside of the truck was surprisingly clean. Immaculate drink holders and recently shampooed seats. The truck sat high off the ground, and from the passenger's seat, June could see clearly through the dark windows of the bus.

"Okay, so..." she studied the slip of paper in her hand. "There're two pedals down there, you feel them?"

"Yes…."

"Right side goes faster, left side, slower."

Malrose practiced pushing on the pedals without the engine running.

"What about the third pedal?" he asked.

"The third pedal?"

*****

The truck moved choppily out onto the open road, sometimes going too fast, more often going too slow. Malrose's whole body was tense and focused.

"You've got to go faster, I think." June said. "Like riding a bike."

"Faster?"

June nodded, unsure of herself.

Malrose mashed the gas pedal and the truck jolted forwards.

He smiled.

"Feel, don't think!" June shouted.

"Feel, don't think!" he repeated back to her.

The truck went faster and faster, flying around turns. Suddenly a tractor trailer appeared in the other lane and Malrose swerved. The 18 wheeler sounded its horn. Surprised by the loud sound, and the sheer size of the other vehicle, Malrose swerved again, this time off the road.

In a shower of broken glass and snapping metal, Lester's truck collided into a group of pine trees.

*****

Malrose came to. There was an eerie stillness over everything. June was still in the passenger's seat, not moving. There was blood on her forehead.

He got out of the truck and went to the other side to try and open the passenger's side door. It was stuck, but he managed to force it open.

Malrose got the little girl out of the truck, lay her out on the grass and prepared to check her pulse. That was when they appeared. All around him, floating like clouds of mist, wafting in and out of recognizable forms.

Slowly, Malrose took out his wand.

Chapter 42

Tisha walked slowly up to the dark place in the forest where Jerome was once again perched up in a tree. He closed his eyes, not wanting to see her.

"Please don't make us do this again," he said.

She stopped walking and just looked up at him.

"No more magic," she said. "No more war. After this I'll leave and never look back."

Jerome studied her cautiously.

"What're you here about?"

"You were worse to me than anyone else."

He waited for her to say more.

"Is that all you came to say?"

"Better, also." She clinched her lips to keep from crying. "Better to me than anyone, at one point. But these past few years… you've been a monster. You made me who I am, but you also destroyed me." She couldn't hold it in anymore. She was crying now. "You destroyed me!" she said again. She was angry now and she opened her mouth to go on, but before she could, the Scream returned. That rolling, ambient and otherworldly scream that would haunt her dreams and keep her up nights. That scream that echoed from the very shadows of the night.

"Odium?" Jerome whispered.

Then the voice, sharp and harsh, fast, loud, slow and aggressive. "She loves me more now! *Odium, odium, odium.*" The darkest part of the night was speaking to them. "Woman, you have given me your heart, and I have a gift in return."

Tisha shivered.

"Reach into your back pocket, woman," the strange voice growled.

She reached into her pocket and felt something long and hard in it. She pulled it forth and found it to be a dark, craggily, wicked looking wand.

"The strongest you have touched. *Odium, odium, odium….* He destroyed you, now you can destroy him. *Odium, odium, odium….* You know what to do."

For the first time that night, Jerome looked truly afraid.

Suddenly, from the night emerged a figure, a sort of skeleton, dark and cracked, moving in an almost effervescent sort of way. He stood beside Tisha, gently stroking her shoulder. He was there with her, holding her, kissing her on the mouth.

"All this time, I thought you were my enemy," Tisha said, mesmerized by the figure's kiss. "When really you were coming to help me!"

"That's right. *Odium, odium, odium….* I have my price, like the fat man, but I am far more powerful. Would you like to kiss me again, or are you ready to kill him?"

"I'm ready. It's time I got this over with."

She turned to face Jerome.

Chapter 43

Malrose lay unconscious in the grass beside the road. The demons were all over him now, like a mass of smoke and gelatin surrounding him, consuming his flesh and being.

June lay a little ways off, discarded. A pool of blood forming around her head.

(Chapter 44)

All living men since baby's breath,
Know one thing: to fear death.
Till Beelzebub comes to suck you dry,
To take you for a walk through the wild rye,
Keep your breath as long as you can,
Keep on moving like an attic fan,
Sooner or later your flesh will rot,
And you'll be buried in the ground like rifle shot.

Chapter 45

Tisha raised her wand, pointing it carefully towards Jerome's forehead. It is a strange thing killing the man you once loved, she thought. In doing so, you must inevitably kill a little bit of yourself at the same time, a person that you once where, a viewpoint and a value scale you once inhabited.

"I am in your veins now," the beautiful skeleton whispered to her. "In your brain and in your heart. I will give you the strength you've always wanted. *Odium, odium, odium*.... All it takes now is one flick of your wrist!"

"Mrs. Lacon! Mrs. Lacon!" It was Tim calling from somewhere close, obviously upset.

Tisha and Jerome kept staring at each other.

"Mrs. Lacon! It's about June!"

They didn't move.

Her hand shook slightly. She stared into the eyes of the man who had stolen her heart when she was just a child, and taken her from her family, had dominated every aspect of her life, had terrorized and tormented her for any question of his authority.

All her life she had been weak, and now she could finally do it. Now she could finally be the one in control.

"Mrs. Lacon! June's in trouble!"

She could hear Tim crashing around in the brush, looking for them. She hesitated, still clinching the wand as tight as she could.

"I'm over here!" Tisha called finally. None of the others could see the skeleton anymore, but it was still there, still inside her, still whispering to her sweetly.

Tim burst into the clearing. "My dad got a call. She's in the hospital!"

Tisha and Jerome both gaped, but she did not lower her wand.

Tim noticed it, and understood what was happening.

"Mrs. Lacon?"

"It's time," the being whispered. "*Odium, odium, odium.*"

Tisha turned her focus back to Jerome, gripping the wand with new found strength.

"Mrs. Lacon! She's in trouble! You should go to her!"

"Jerome, you have been cruel to me and cruel to my daughter, which is why—"

"Our daughter."

She flinched. "What?"

"I'm sorry I haven't been perfect, Tisha. I admit Odium came to my heart first. But, she is my daughter, and I do love her, just as I love you...."

The whisper in her head melted away. She raised an eyebrow. "We have a lot to talk about," she said.

"Yes, but maybe not just yet," Tim said, grabbing her by the shirt sleeve and leading them out of the clearing. "I'll explain on the way."

Chapter 46

Jerome and Tisha burst into the hospital waiting room, trailed closely by Tim.

"Can I help you?" a young man in scrubs asked them.

"My daughter came in—" Jerome said. "Was brought in by an ambulance. June Lacon. Little twelve year old girl—"

"Oh yes, she came in with the man we couldn't identify."

Jerome and Tisha glanced at each other. Jerome raised an eyebrow.

"Is she okay?" Tisha asked.

"Yes," the nurse said. "She's still unconscious from the shock, but there were no serious injuries. She should wake up very soon with no more than a bad headache."

"Can we see her?"

"Sure. We just need you to sign some paperwork."

The nurse offered them a clipboard. Tisha signed it quickly without bothering to read it. Jerome glanced at it and signed as well.

"Jerome Lacon, right?"

He nodded.

"I've always wanted your autograph."

Jerome gave him a weird look.

"She's right this way." He led them to a small two bed room near the end of the hall. June and Malrose lay in standard issue exam beds just a few feet from each other. Every inch of Malrose's skin was covered in strange blue scarring, like hard ridges rising up from his flesh.

"I'll be back in a moment," the nurse said, leaving the five of them alone.

They surrounded June, holding her hands and stroking her hair. Whispering things to her sweetly, in case she could hear them.

Another nurse came in and began examining Malrose.

"Do you have any idea what happened to him?" she asked them.

Jerome shook his head.

"They were in a car accident, but we've never seen lacerations like these before. Like some strange acid burn. We don't know how to treat it."

She shrugged and left.

The others turned their attention back to June, who was now slowly waking up. Her demeanor was weak, but she smiled when she saw them.

"You're okay!" Tisha squeezed her hand.

"I'm glad you came." June looked at Tim. "All three of you."

Jerome smiled at her, a tired look in his eyes.

"I think I'm gonna sleep a little longer."

"Yes, that's good, dear," her Father told her.

She locked eyes with Tim once, for just a moment. She smiled, then closed her eyes and drifted off back to sleep.

The door swung open and the male nurse entered, this time carrying a briefcase.

"She woke up!" Tisha said with a smile.

The nurse looked at Tim. "Sorry, son, only immediate family allowed in this time of night. You'll have to leave."

Tim looked a little hurt, but he did as he was told. The nurse closed the door and blinds behind him, then turned to face Tisha and Jerome. He wore a strange expression now, a dead, soulless, absent sort of look. Then, slowly but surely, his face began to melt away, leaving in its place that of Lester Topshun.

He smiled seeing their crestfallen faces.

"Sorry to interupt your grieving, but I'm afraid I have contracts on both your souls. Two for you, Mrs. Lacon." He held up the contracts for them to see. "I'm here to collect."

In a flash they were both gone, and in their place were two small figurines, just like the others from the briefcase.

Lester scooped them up as though they were easter eggs, and left the room with a smile on his face.

Chapter 47

Tim peered around the door into the hospital room. He'd seen Lester leaving and knew it was a bad sign. The two patients were both still asleep.

"June?" he said sweetly, nervously.

She opened an eye.

"Topshun took your parents."

She was fully awake now. "What do you mean? Took them where?"

"I dunno, but they're gone."

She tried to get out of bed, but her weak legs collapsed under the weight of her body.

"I don't think—don't think I can go anywhere right now. I—" Her heart beat fast in her chest. She was shaking slightly. She couldn't think clearly.

Tim helped her up back to the bed.

She noticed the man beside her for the first time.

"Malrose?" She edged her way towards his bed. "Did you check the hall? They're no where around?"

Tim checked the hall once more to be sure.

"They're gone."

Her ears were ringing. Everything felt far away. Her mind itself ached.

"Malrose?" She noticed she was still connected to the bed. "Tim, can you help me get these tubes out?"

Tim rolled the machine so she had room to move.

"Better," she said sadly, letting herself fall back against the pillow, exhausted. She pursed her lips. She was trying not to cry. "What's the game plan, Tim?"

"I got nothing."

They stared off into space, trying desperately to think.

"I might be able to help," a man's voice said. "Ever been to New York?"

Malrose flashed a crooked smile.

Chapter 48

June opened the door of the school bus carrying an old vintage suitcase in one hand, and in the other, the biggest bottle of deep earth water she could carry. She began down the steps towards Tim.

"Hey June," he said somberly.

"Hey Tim."

"How do you feel?"

"Okay, I guess, considering."

They turned and began to walk away from the bus.

"Is that going to be enough water?" Tim asked.

"Malrose says he knows a place we can get more once we're in New York. This just has to last 'till we get there."

She listened to the sound of birds singing, to the hum of southern summer.

"Tim, I'm sorry that I've been hard to get along with these past few weeks."

"It's okay, you've been under a lot of stress, I—"

She stopped walking and turned to face him.

"No really, Tim. You've been so sweet to me and I've just been a jerk."

He nodded.

"You're going to make some girl really happy some day."

He frowned. "You've got bigger things to worry about right now, June."

Tim began walking again and she followed.

"Like getting my parents back?"

"Right. That'd probably make the list." He turned to look at her again. "I wish I could go with you."

"Me too," she said.

"Good luck, old girl." He took hold of her hand and held it as tight as he could one last time before she walked off into the trees.

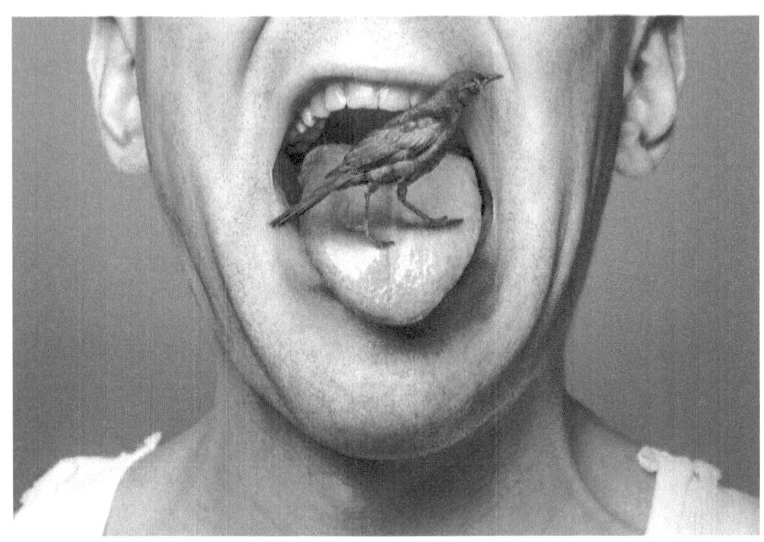

POSTFACE

I don't know if I'll ever be able to retell the stories I heard that day quite the way they were told to me. It was more than just a history of what had happened, and what had been seen. I felt as though I knew each of them. From Parishey, to Rob, to little June. I knew them, and in a strange way, they were also me.

After I said goodbye to the three eyed man and walked slowly back to my house, I began to feel as though he had been a dream, a creation of my wandering mind. Yet, the people he had told me about stuck with me.

As I sat at my desk typing feverishly for the next several days, trying to get it all down before it drifted away like unpinnable clouds, I increasingly felt a tremendous responsibility to the people whose stories I had heard that day.

You will find none of them in the history books. None of them immortalized in the halls of glory. The only one who bore witness to their lonely lives was the three eyed man, and for whatever reason he chose me to communicate them to you.

The entirety of their legacy became dependent on how my fingers would glide and fall over my keyboard.

I have done the best I can. And now their legacy is up to you.

Owen Essen is an American designer and author. He is known for highly stylized 'poetic prose,' and story projects that transcend individual mediums. He lives with his family in central North Carolina.

www.OwenEssen.com

www.ingramcontent.com/pod-product-compliance
Lightning Source LLC
Chambersburg PA
CBHW020551310726
48979CB00008B/1171/J

* 9 7 8 0 9 9 8 2 4 5 5 2 2 *